American Revolution 2056

A Novel by Fred Snyder

First Amazon Book edition, October 2020.

Cover design by Trish Gieseke
Author Photo by Ava Hahn

Manufactured in the United States of America

ISBN 978-1-7358960-0-7 (e-book)
ISBN 978-1-7358960-1-4 (paperback)

Acknowledgments

It would be impossible to say thank you adequately to those who helped make this book possible, so this will have to do.

Heather Condon, LaVonne Smasel, Alan Meier Ruth Koestler and Jennifer Valley- thanks for all of your support and wisdom.

Jeff Snyder- thanks for your insight into the makings of a revolution. Any errors are mine, not yours.

My family and friends- thanks for always supporting me and supplying me with an incredible array of ideas.

"Revolution is not a one time thing."

Audre Lord

Chapter One

How in the world had she become number one on the FBI's Most Wanted List? That thought overwhelmed Jenn's brain as she pushed through the screen door onto the back porch. She stumbled across the short distance to the rickety rocking chair and flung herself down. Her breath came in short gasps, her mouth dry from the effort. In through the nose, out through the mouth. It was all she could manage.

A long week ago she had been a 45-year old, mini-van driving mother of two and now she was a wanted fugitive. Now she was leading a revolt against her own government. She slipped off her glasses and set them on a small table, allowing her hands to press into her eye sockets in a feeble attempt to block it all out.

A noise made her look up and find her glasses. Across the farm, an old man drove a tractor out of the barn, letting several others close the door behind him. Watching the scene unfold did not help her blood pressure. These people were putting their lives in her hands. People whose names she might or might not remember were counting on her.

What on Earth was she doing? It had been so easy to talk about revolution, but now she and her family were changed forever. Their home was gone, burned by the government. One daughter now carried a gun like she used to carry her dolls and the other had made blowing things up her new hobby. She gulped hard trying not to think about her husband Tom's situation, but she couldn't get the image of his smile as he waved goodbye out of her head. The man she loved had put himself in a situation that might well result in his death. He might be dead already for all she knew.

Her own situation was hardly better. There were people now living and dying on her command. Two more of her patients had died from their injuries, including one she thought was out of the woods. Now even her medical skills weren't enough and that was something she was good at! How could she keep people alive on a battlefield? Her head swirled in a mosaic of colors. Her hubris was catching up with them and it was only a matter of time until someone close to her died. It was all too much.

From inside the house, the sound of her daughters fighting reached her ears. They were the reason she had started this whole thing. What had she done? What was going to happen to them? What had happened to her country to bring it to this madness? One breath at a time.

Within a minute or two, her focus had returned. Her heart was back to normal and she was able to think more clearly. She reached deep into the recesses of her mind. How had her government come to be the enemy? And more importantly, how had she, Jenn Erickson come to be contemplating such a thing?

She closed her brown eyes and thought hard. Her latte colored face betrayed none of the confusion and anger she felt. The changes had been so slow that nobody noticed the foundation of their country eroding away. She thought of a video clip she had seen of a frog in a pot of boiling water. The water had heated up so slowly around the poor thing that it never realized its situation and never even tried to escape the pot. Americans had become frogs in a giant pot of slowly warming water that was now boiling.

How had it gotten this far? What had started to heat the water around her? Jenn continued to breathe with a purpose, letting her keen mind work. If it were only one thing, it would be easy. If it was just one person, it would be easy. If it were only one thing, they'd have fixed it by now and she could be enjoying herself at home instead of hiding out on a near stranger's farm.

A phrase crept into her mind: "The contempt of the governed." To paraphrase the Declaration of Independence's "Consent of the governed," the state of the country had changed over the last 75 years or so, the people of the United States had lost faith in their country. Or more accurately, those governing their country. And equally as problematic, the government had lost faith in its own citizens. The idea that the government's moral right and legitimate power came from the people was now seemingly banished to history books.

Jenn no longer knew who lost it first. Only recently had she come to care about the answer. At the moment, all she knew was that she, her family, her closest friends and now a number of strangers were all in mortal peril thanks to her.

Her head began to swirl again. One breath at a time. High overhead, the sound of two passing Air Force jets roared past bringing her back to the real world. Only the contrails stretching out behind them revealed their location and flight path.

How had she gotten to this point? A woman wanted for treason? She thought hard. Almost imperceptibly the answers began to float back into her head. For her, it all started on a "routine" day at work. She couldn't remember the exact date, but the incident was so clear she could taste the bile in her throat. That day played like a movie in her head.

Chapter Two

A late-season snowstorm was dropping wet, heavy snow across Des Moines and a large swath of the upper Midwest. Tom was at his wretched job but school had been canceled due to the weather, so her girls were on their own for the day. Her first patient after her lunch break started it all.

The receptionist told her she had a patient rolling into bay one and handed her a clipboard. Technically, a "Customer Records Access Portal," but in reality, a fancy clipboard flashing red around the edges. The information it contained from the paramedics was not what she wanted to see, it never was. It was yet another patient with no apparent means of paying for their medical care, which simply meant she couldn't treat them. That her patient was a kid with a head injury had made things even worse.

She loved the challenge that her work as a physician assistant brought, but now there were so few rewards compared to the frustrations. She had taken the Hippocratic Oath to help people, but now the law and her employer said she didn't have to if they couldn't pay. Over her twenty-some years in medicine, things had changed, and not for the better.

Flashing lights filled the ambulance entrance alerting Jenn to her duty. It made no sound, of course, they wouldn't be running with sirens with a patient like this. Jenn put her black hair back into its ponytail before hurrying through the sliding door.

She watched, her foot tapping the hempcrete below as the paramedics rolled out their patient, a small boy she could already hear whimpering in pain. "What's the latest?" she asked as soon as she could. She had read the chart, but she preferred information straight from the ambulance team. The good ones were more concerned about the patient than the administration.

The paramedic looked up from the boy. "White male, eight years old. We found him unconscious by the park, head trauma." His eyes shifted, unable to look into Jenn's. "I don't think you need to hurry. We ran his fingerprints and his mom doesn't have insurance." Jenn's head dropped; this was not why she went into medicine.

She looked into the boy's glazed eyes, hoping he didn't mistake her frustration with anything he had done. "Hey, buddy. How are you feeling?" she asked gently. "What happened?"

The boy was trying to fight back the tears welling up in his eyes. "I fell on some ice and hit my head. It hurts." She slipped her hand around the back of the boy's head, wincing at the egg-sized lump.

"Alright, buddy, you're going to be OK. Can you tell me your name? Your parent's names?" The computer scan had already given her this information, but it always helped to have a relationship with the patient.

"My name's Marshall," the boy said. "My mom's name is Jamie, Jamie Page."

"Take him inside and find him a chair," Jenn ordered the paramedics. She spoke into the omniphone computer on her wrist and began to read about the boy's home as she followed them inside. By the time she stood behind the reception desk, her hopes were dimming. She knew from the address that it was unlikely to be a productive conversation.

After three rings, the hologram of a woman rubbing her eyes rose from the monitor. It looked to Jenn like she had woken the woman up from a deep sleep. She answered with a tentative "Hello?"

"Miss Page? This is Jenn Erickson at the West Side Clinic. We have your son, Marshall, here, he's had an accident."

"Oh no!" the woman shrieked, now wide awake. "What happened? Is he OK? Yes, that's my son."

The taste of acid filled the back of Jenn's throat. She would have reacted the same way if it was one of her daughters. Her experience kicked in allowing her to reply with her professional voice. He says he slipped on some ice and hit his head. He has a large bump back there and is in a lot of pain." Jenn braced herself before asking the next question. "Ma'am, do you have any means of paying for his treatment?"

"No, I don't," replied the boy's mother. "My work doesn't offer insurance and who can afford it on their own? And I don't have that kind of money laying around."

"OK, ma'am. We've got him resting in a chair, but you'll have to come pick him up as soon as possible."

"I understand. "I'll get there as soon as I can." Painful resignation resonated in her voice. Like too many people there was nothing she could do to change her situation.

As the hologram faded away, Jenn surveyed the patients across the room. The boy was slouched over in a chair, his eyes closed. Next to him was an older, Hispanic man wheezing desperately and beyond him a black woman wrapping a scarf around her daughter's neck. Jenn had seen this girl, too, she had cut her hand. Slumped in the corner was yet another overdose victim; she seemed to see more of them every day if that was possible.

She had not been allowed to treat any of them. They had no means of paying for the clinic's services and their policy was to get them out the door as fast as possible to make room for paying customers. "Jenn?" the receptionist said. "Another overdose is rolling up in bay four."

"It's 2056 for God's sake, the kid deserves better than this" she whispered to herself. The boy's whimpers hung in the air as she headed off to her next patient.

Chapter Three

A smile crossed Bob Wright's face as he walked onto his factory floor. The installers were finally done placing the company motto, "The Safety of America is in Our Hands," on the wall across from the main doors where everyone could see it. The two-foot-high script sprang out from the wall and lit up in the company's patented color, "Wright Red." His head cocked to the side when the up-tempo song blaring from the overhead speakers changed. His head bobbed to the beat for just a moment before he recognized it from his teenage years. While it wasn't his taste, he gave his workers what they wanted and this was it. He smiled again, resting his beefy arms on the guardrail.

Across the massive space, employees seemed happy to be at work. The warmth from the machines was an added benefit to working for him on a day like this. Being able to give them some extra comfort added to the paternal feelings he felt towards his workers. The workers here in Des Moines actually worked, which coupled with the lower costs, made it a fine place to do business. However, no matter how much he tried to give back and nurture the community, he spent as much time as he could at his residence outside of Chicago. The social opportunities here were so painful.

Bob's thoughts were interrupted by the arrival of his two most trusted, senior staff members, Kristen and Mollie. "Good afternoon, ladies," he said, "how are your days going?"

Kristen's half-moon glasses were halfway down her sharp nose. She looked over them and smiled politely. "Fine, sir, and yours?"

Mollie's broad face lit up as she blurted out "My youngest son got admitted to Harvard this morning!"

"Oh, that's great," Bob replied, "really great," feigning interest. She sulked if he didn't and became miserable to work with. However, she was a wizard with supply chain management and was worthy of his attention.

Kristen held out a small computer with some documents displayed. "Here are the figures from last quarter you asked for." Her expertise in budget management made her invaluable. Kristen had no children and had never been married. For her, life was all about work and always had been. It was the feature he liked best about her.

Bob held the computer at arm's length and looked over the figures, his white eyebrows rising in surprise. "Excellent, even better than I'd hoped." His company was now the largest manufacturer of home and business security equipment in America and the third largest in the world.

"The new computer system really helped us be more efficient," said Kristen. "We were able to generate another quarter million units without hiring a single worker. Once we get it fully implemented in our plants in Taiwan and Munich it will really be a game changer."

"If this keeps up, our profits will grow another six percent this year" Mollie added.

Bob pressed his thumb to the keypad and let the computer read his DNA, verifying his identity. Once it was satisfied, the computer signed the document and he returned it to Kristen. "This should mean some great bonuses this year."

Kristen and Mollie nodded in silent agreement, their eyes shining in anticipation. They knew what the company's growth meant for them. Nearly thirty years previous, Bob had recognized their loyalty and had advanced their careers accordingly. In return for their service, Mollie's kids were educated in exclusive private schools and they each lived in gated, protected communities away from the troubles around the city.

"Remember," Mollie said, "you have the dedication of Wright Fields this afternoon."

"That's right, thank you."

"Thank you, sir," Kristen said as they turned to leave. "We'll see you tomorrow."

The two women exited and returned to their offices through a brightly lit, glass walkway which led to the towering office building across the compound. They finished their chat about vacation plans as the executive elevator delivered them to the 15th floor of the Wright Building. They paid no attention to their staff as they breezed past into the conference room.

Both walls were made entirely of glass, which provided them an excellent view of the lake outside, especially at sunset. Today it made it seem like they were living inside an old-fashioned snow globe. The expanse of the room allowed them to spread out and stretch their legs if they needed. They knew its function was to allow them to work more productively, but its high-tech tools and creature comforts were fun nonetheless.

Kristen set her computer down on the conference table before submitting to the computer's security scan. At the counter, Mollie drummed her fingers on the counter, the gold rings clanking on the manufactured marble. While she waited for her cup of green tea to brew, she studied the painting of their company founder, Robert Wright Sr. looking benignly over the room. "Would you like anything?" she asked. After so much time together, she knew what Kristen wanted, but always asked anyway.

"Yes, a Colombian coffee, cream and two sugars, please and thank you," Kristen replied without looking up. She was focused on the documents for tomorrow's board meeting. Their job was to demonstrate and document all of the great things they were doing to generate revenue and save costs. The computer system made it easy to put together presentations and skew things their way.

A muffled knock at the door was followed by the entrance of three of their assistants. Mollie didn't offer them a beverage or even greet them as she placed the gold rimmed cup in front of Kristen. These people were helpful enough, but they had no great love for the company, despite what Bob thought. Still, they were useful functionaries, so she tolerated them as much as she did any of the company's workers.

Kristen looked up from her computer. "OK," she said, "time to put it all together. Hugh, make sure the long-term projections show the Congressman how much his work has done for us. Leigh, you make sure they're media friendly and demonstrate what we've done to help the community. Penny, are all of the on-site preparations ready?"

A middle-aged black woman looked up from her notebook, her face an impassive mask. Penelope Stevens had been doing this, and many other tasks, for years. She hated that Kristen and Mollie called her "Penny," that was reserved for people she was close to, but Kristen was the boss. She held her tongue and said, "Yes, ma'am." The others nodded and mumbled they'd be ready.

"Let's keep our eyes on the prize, people," Kristen replied, dismissing the group. She and Mollie alone could be trusted to do the real work of making the presentation to the board to their own standards.

Penny left, along with Hugh and Leigh. She'd worked with the pair for long enough to know they shared similar frustrations. They all knew corporate profits were at an all-time high and yet none of that money made its way down to the workers. That part was infuriating. The whole situation was but at least it was steady, simple work that had always allowed her to spend time with her kids.

The thought of her three kids brought a smile to her face. They weren't kids any more, only one was even still at home, but they were the brightest part of her life. So far, she and her husband, Scott, had managed to keep the kids on the right track in life, but it was becoming harder and harder.

The three split up and went to their cubicles to focus on their work. Penny could soon hear Hugh and Leigh speaking with hushed voices as they utilized the new software, which actually read their thoughts and anticipated their needs. The computer's artificial intelligence then applied that knowledge the next time the user needed it, making it even faster. It seemed the machines did more and more these days. Penny often wondered how long it would be until even she was rendered obsolete. "Oh well", she thought with another smile, "it's Thursday and soon enough it'll be the weekend." A few final details would take care of her prep work and then it was off to run some errands for Kristen and Mollie.

After making her calls, Penny put on her coat and headed for the elevator. An animated conversation from the last cubicle caught her attention. None of her peers ever got that excited about work and she had seen more than one co-worker fired for being too chatty about personal matters. She poked her head around the cubicle wall to find two communications clerks huddled over a computer screen, their eyes glued to what looked like a news station. Penny spoke, her voice scarcely above a whisper, "What's the excitement?"

One of the clerks, Nancy, flinched like she'd been hit by a whip. The other, Lori, turned around and looked relieved to see Penny's face. "Thank goodness it's you," she said, "It's some crazy footage about a riot out in Arizona."

"What?" Penny asked, stepping closer to get a better look at the screen. The video was of some angry looking men and women gathered at a dried-up reservoir facing off with dozens of police officers.

The riot scene shifted to a small corner of the screen as the face of a blonde, female reporter took over. "Authorities tell us that the gathered mob is here claiming that they are not getting their fair share of water from the Colorado River. With the worsening drought, water has been severely rationed in this part of the state by the government. The mob, many of whom claim to be farmers and ranchers who have lived here for years, are frustrated by both the lack of water and lack of concern from the Water Control Board. We spoke earlier to a spokesman for that group."

The image shifted again to a middle-aged man with a turquoise bolo tie, identified as Kyl Reese, Chairman of the Water Control Board. "We, the county, are merely enforcing the state and federal agreements about water rights in this state. Those agreements clearly state that the larger corporations get their share of the water first. As much as we sympathize, there's simply nothing we can do about it. We're just doing our jobs."

A voice behind them snapped them all back to attention. "What are you three looking at?!" Kristen's face was flushed, her nostrils flared in anger. It was a look they all knew too well.

Penny was the first to react. "Oh, I'm glad you're here. You have to see this report. I'm afraid we may have trouble with one of our suppliers out in Arizona." Once again she silently gave thanks to her inherent gift for thinking quickly.

Kristen looked in, her bloodless lips turned down. On the screen, the reporter continued to talk about how local companies were managing to withstand the drought, even mentioning their supplier by name. "OK," Kristen grumbled, "you did the right thing by paying attention to it. Let me know if there is anything we should be aware of." She spun away and headed towards Hugh's cube.

Lori waited until the clicking of Kristen's heels faded before letting out a sigh of relief. Nancy smiled and whispered, "Thanks, that was awesome."

Penny smiled back, her brown eyes twinkling; it was always good to put one over on the boss, no matter how small. "Alright ladies, I'm outta here," she said as she left for the elevator and ultimately the dry-cleaner. "Have a good night. I'll see you tomorrow."

"Hm," she thought as she entered the elevator and told it to take her to the parking level. "Maybe 'dry' cleaning is the way we'll all be going in the future." Here in Iowa, nobody much worried about water, it was still plentiful without flooding like the coasts or limited like in the desert

Southwest. It had never occurred to her that people might not have something as basic as water. Apparently, every different part of the country had its own concerns. Nor had it occurred to her that the police might be needed to keep the peace over something like that. She left the elevator shaking her head at the thought of that whole mess.

Chapter Four

Jenn trudged through the inch or so of snow trying to forget her day. She couldn't shake the image of the boy with the lump on his head. Those were the ones that still got to her, the kids. "Man," she thought, "too many of them never have a chance."

She finally reached her mini-van and brushed the snow off while it warmed up. It was the infamous "heart attack" snow that had killed her father. Jenn shook her head and tried to force her thoughts to a happier subject. She kicked the slush built up behind her tire, chuckling as it fell to the parking lot. It was the kind of thing her husband, Tom, loved to do for some reason she'd never understood. She was smiling at last as she climbed in. Tom was a like a favorite book to her. She loved to hold it in her hands and always found something new inside.

She flashed her ID badge to the security guard at the gate, who barely glanced up from his monitor before waving her through. She'd been at the clinic so long that she was sure they knew her ancient vehicle by the sounds it made. In a few minutes was on the freeway headed east back into the city, the memories of her day mostly drifting into oblivion. At her command, the radio began to channel surf through the local stations as she preferred. It worked its way past several ads, two annoying disc jockeys and a pop song that made Jenn's head ache before landing on a news station.

"And in Chicago today, President Little's campaign visit was marred by violent clashes between local police and angry residents of the south side. National Guard units assisted the police in suppressing the rioters, an unknown number of whom were injured during the incident. The President's Press Secretary later made a statement, saying 'We are grateful for the work of our brave police officers and military members. Their work in keeping order in our streets is symbolic of what our administration stands for. Violence and dissent have no place in our society. Two officers were slightly injured and taken to a local hospital."

The computer switched to an oldies station as the news faded into another ad. As she weaved through traffic, Jenn wondered if she'd be allowed to treat injured protesters. She knew everything possible would be done for the police, but the protesters might well not get treated at all. She laughed out loud as she thought "Gee, maybe that's what they're protesting."

Ten minutes later, Jenn was approaching home. She honked and waved as she passed her older daughter,

Stephanie, out running with her best friend, Anne. The two girls were matching each other's pace, their hair bouncing with every step. The girls were both juniors in high school and members of their school's cross-country team.

She pulled into the garage attached to their turn of the century, split-level home. Even now she laughed at the realtor's description of it as "almond, not like the more common cream or linen colors of their neighbors." She stepped out of the mini-van just as the girls reached the driveway. Neither girl was even breathing heavily Jenn noticed as the girls walked the last few steps and began stretching their leg muscles. They were already training for the upcoming season despite the slush on the ground. "Hi girls," Jenn greeted them.

The girls' response was a blend of their voices speaking as one. "Hi, Mama Jenn, Hi, Mom."

"Anne, are you staying for dinner?"

"Sorry, I can't. I told mom I'd be home right after our run." She looked at Steph, "I'll see you later."

"Yeah, see ya," Steph replied. Anne left, leaving Steph alone with her mother. "How was work?"

"Oh, the usual. Helped a few, couldn't help a few...you know."

"I think that sucks that you can't like treat people," Steph said, the frustration clear in her voice. "I mean, like maybe not a heart transplant, but colds and overdoses and stuff like that."

"Yeah," Jenn said, "you're right. I don't even know where to start." Her face tightened with pain as she thought about all the people she couldn't help that day. Steph stepped close and hugged her mother. "Thanks, sweetie."

Steph pulled away. "I just wanted to see how much taller I am than you now." She winked at her mother. At 5' 7" she'd been taller for a couple years and it was a running joke.

Jenn shook her head and sighed. "I'd say two inches. And if you keep growing you may catch your father." She wrapped her arm around her daughter and they entered the house together, stopping abruptly at the overwhelming aroma of garlic coming from the kitchen. Jenn's younger daughter, Ellen, was at the stove. She was 15 and a sophomore in high school.

She turned when she heard them enter. "Hi Mom, hey Steph," she said, "Dinner's almost ready. The spaghetti needs eight more minutes." She paused to wipe some steam off her glasses.

Jenn coughed and dabbed at her eye. "It smells great dear. I doubt we'll have any vampires around here anytime soon."

"Yeah," Steph added, "and no boys, either. I'm going upstairs to take a shower." She walked past her sister and up the narrow staircase to her bedroom.

Jenn hugged Ellen, too, her hands meeting behind Ellen's ponytail. The long, black hair was about all she had in common with her sister. Where Steph ran, Ellen built robots. Where Steph sought popularity in school, Ellen sought friends through her computer. Where Steph had no big plans in life, Ellen wanted to change the world. They were both great kids and Jenn couldn't imagine her life without them. "Thanks for making dinner, sweetie," she whispered in her ear.

"No problem, Mom," Ellen replied, pulling away and returning her attention to the stove to give her sauce a quick stir. "Since we didn't have school today, it's not a big deal." She was brilliantly smart and reminded Jenn of herself as a teenager. She even looked like Jenn, down to high cheekbones and perky nose.

Jenn escaped the garlic by going upstairs to her bedroom, where a pair of faded pants and a sweatshirt that read "Runner Mom" from the kids' school quickly replaced her work scrubs. She returned downstairs, surprised to find her husband home already, standing by the stove with a beer in his hand. The tension radiating from his every pore told her that he was not a happy man.

He looked up and managed a smile. "Hey babe," he said as she came over and kissed him. He held her in his arms for what seemed like a long time before separating. "I got a little suspension at work today" he said, anger and hatred rising in his voice. "That prick, Lester Hatch, didn't think I was welding the way I should and when I tried to enlighten him, he got pissy and I get tomorrow off."

"Oh honey, that's awful," Jenn said. She knew his frustration was high, it had been growing for years. He had always been a great welder, that wasn't the issue. His problem was that he got angry when people tried to tell him how to do his job and he couldn't control his tongue.

Tom finished his beer with a long pull. "I'd like to tell that little," he paused when he noticed Ellen watching, "that little jerk where to go." He set the empty bottle on the counter and opened the refrigerator for another one.

"Honey, you know you can't do that." She brushed her fingers across the tattoo of their daughters' footprints on his bicep. "We have a mortgage to pay, remember?" He'd said the same exact thing to her more times than she could remember.

"I know, I know. 'It's just business,' he likes to say. He's such a pompous little ass. I hate him."

"It'll be OK, honey, you're better and stronger than he is," Jenn reminded him. "How about I call Penny and have them come over tonight?"

Tom ran his hand over the gray-brown stubble that was the remainder of his hair and nodded his approval. "Thanks, that's always a good idea."

He loved their neighbors, Scott and Penny. The day they had moved in, a little girl named Anne had come across the street and knocked on their door while her parents watched through the window. "Can your daughters come out and play?" was how it had all started. They were the first black family he had ever really known, but after he had gotten past his initial reservations, they had become fast friends. He and Scott had bonded over technology and beers and their wives had bonded over the kids. They had now been friends so long their wives couldn't remember which one was the bad influence.

Over dinner, Tom was finally able to relax and enjoy his family. Jenn insisted they eat together at the table whenever they could, but the age-old challenge of their busy lives made that difficult. This was the first time in weeks both girls had been home at the same time, so their parents made the most of it.

After dinner, the girls went to their rooms to study, while Tom and Jenn cleared the dishes and straightened up the kitchen before their guests arrived. They were pushing the chairs under the table when the door swung open and their friends walked in. "Scotty!" Tom proclaimed.

"Tommy!" Scott replied as he stuck his large hand out. Tom shook it, followed by a hug for Penny. More hugs were exchanged, followed by a fresh round of drinks.

The two couples sat around the cozy living room as they often did. Jenn and Penny on one couch, Scott and Tom on the longer one, with a mix of private and group conversations. In the summer, they sat out on the porch or driveway of one of their houses and enjoyed talking to people walking by.

The door swung open again, followed by Anne carrying her laptop computer. "Hi all," she said, walking past them and up the stairs. "We've got a big project to finish." Of course the girls were working together, they did everything together.

Penny watched her daughter disappear and smiled wistfully. Her youngest was soon going to be out of the house, too, then she'd have nothing really to keep her excited at home. Scott was a good and faithful husband, but their marriage was pretty stale now. They'd stayed together nearly 30 years and the magic had been gone for quite a while.

Jenn noticed the look, but didn't say anything. Her heart ached knowing she couldn't help her friends, but that was a battle they alone could fight. She was blessed with Tom and often wondered what she had done to deserve him. "Crazy stuff in Chicago today, huh?" she offered, drawing Penny away from her thoughts.

Scott spoke first, "Yeah, I seen that. That's some crazy shit."

"Yeah, and did you see the water thing out in Arizona?" Penny added. None of them had, so she explained briefly what she had seen. They were more interested in her fast thinking than in the water riot. They had all heard enough stories about Kristen to know she was mentally disturbed.

Tom shared his work story with his friends, who both shook their heads in shared disgust. Since Lester was Bob Wright's assistant, Penny knew him well and was in full agreement about Tom's assessment of his personality. "So, what are you going to do with your day off?" she asked.

"I have some work I want to do on the wind turbine and I have a side job to finish up," he replied. "Neither one pays cash, but my boss is a whole lot better," he added with a wry smile.

The small wind turbine was a joint project he and Scott had put together. Scott's work as an electrician at the university had made the project almost too easy. Now they were refining their work to make it more efficient and maybe even a money-maker.

As the population had exploded and more people had moved to cities, power usage had become a major challenge across the country. Everyone needed electricity, but nobody wanted to pay for the infrastructure to provide it to everyone. The turbine had been a lifesaver during the previous summer's rolling brown-outs, especially when the temperatures had pushed past 100 for four straight weeks.

"Is that the Kaplans' fence?" Scott asked.

"Yeah, it'll be nice to finally get that finished," Tom answered. It was his end of a trade with some friends who had helped them get a vegetable garden started two years earlier. Neither he nor Jenn had been born with a green thumb, but with some guidance, the garden had flourished and now helped put fresh vegetables on the table. This fall they were hoping to have enough produce to learn how to can things.

"It sure took you long enough, man" Scott teased him. Scott had wired the Kaplans' patio in return for their own garden.

"Well, not everything is as easy as what you do," Tom teased back. The men both laughed and raised their drinks in a toast.

The women laughed, too. It felt good to have friends like this. "Any chance the election will do us any good?" Jenn asked.

Tom threw up his hands, "I doubt it."

"Yeah," Penny added, "they're all bought and paid for. Our congressman, too. Shit, telling him how to vote is even part of our board meeting tomorrow."

The other three looked at her with a combination of amazement and horror. She looked back at each of them and added, "It's true. I help make the agenda and that's part of it."

Tom finally spoke up. "I'm glad we work for such a stand-up guy."

"How is it you've never told us this before?" Jenn asked.

"I don't know," Penny answered. "Maybe I was trying to repress those thoughts?" They all laughed at the look on her face. They certainly understood her feelings.

Scott had another drink and burped loudly before he spoke. "Excuse me," he said to appease Penny. "It's really no better at the university. Education ain't the main deal, it's all about the money and looking good for the public."

"It's daunting, that's for sure," Jenn said. "I'm nervous as Hell about the future our kids will have."

"Or not have," Penny added. "With the way things are going, God only knows what kind of country they'll live in."

The guys nodded in agreement, quietly finishing their beers, deep in their own thoughts and fears that the 'American Dream' was dead. They had both grown up in working class homes with some hope for the future, but now that hope was fading. They shared the same commitment to giving their kids a better life but were doubting their ability to deliver.

"On that cheery note, I think it's time we head home," Penny said, standing up.

"Yeah," Scott added with a wink at Tom, "some of us have to work in the morning." With that, the evening broke up. Most of them did have to work in and mornings seemed to come earlier and earlier as they got older.

Chapter Five

Jenn's eyes fluttered open to the aroma of freshly brewed coffee under her nose and the sight of her husband's unshaven face gazing down at her. Once more she marveled at how he could get up and be so chipper after drinking that much, but she didn't ask, she sat up slowly and accepted the coffee. Tom knew not to speak yet. He kissed her on the forehead and went back down to the kitchen. It was one of their little rituals and one of the things she adored.

Downstairs, Steph and Ellen were standing at the kitchen island, each with their own cup of coffee in front of them. Ellen's attention was already on her digipad, but Steph glanced up at him through half-closed eyes before returning her focus to peeling her banana. Tom gave each girl's back a quick scratch before asking Steph, "Did you get your project finished?"

"We did," she answered.

"And what was it about?"

"The Hungarian Revolt of 1956." More details would not be given up easily.

"And...?"

She sighed. "We're studying world history from a hundred years ago. In 1956, the people of Hungary rose up against the Russian occupiers and their Hungarian stooges and tried to gain freedom from the oppression of communism. It was wild! They, like, had teenagers attacking tanks with Molotov cocktails!"

"Well, nobody can ever say those kids didn't try to go change their own future now, can they?"

Ellen looked up from her computer, her face a giant question mark. "Teenagers? How'd that work for 'em?"

"Not so well in the end," Steph admitted. "The whole thing involved, like, students and factory workers and pretty much all of the regular people, but in the end, the Russians came in and crushed them. Lots of people were killed or became refugees." She shook her head and finished her coffee.

"Wow," Ellen said, "they must have been pretty desperate." She closed her computer and thought about what her sister had said. She didn't always give her older sister much credit for her school work, or much of anything for that matter, but this time it sounded like she had uncovered something unique. Elvis or something else from pop history maybe, but revolution? Maybe it was Anne's idea?

She grabbed Steph's cup and plate and put them in the dishwasher along with her own. They were headed towards the door, but stopped when their mother came down the stairs, already dressed for work, knowing she wanted a hug before they left. While they were growing into adulthood, she still hugged them when she could get away with it.

The girls left and Jenn finally spoke to her husband. "Good morning," she said, her voice still clinging to a deep, sleepy tone.

"Morning, babe," he replied as he made her another cup of coffee. He loved her voice like that. "Want some eggs?"

"Sure, two scrambled, please."

Tom pulled out the necessary ingredients, which caused the refrigerator to flash a notice to him, "More eggs needed." He knew they could use synthetic "food," but Jenn insisted they use real food at all costs. "It's the most affordable health care I know," she had said repeatedly. He smiled to himself as he broke the eggs into a bowl. Cooking was one of the only positive memories of his grandfather and their rituals as he had grown up.

Jenn was slowly waking up as she sat at the island. She touched a button on the wall and a view screen on the counter sprang to life with the news. She skipped over the celebrity news, that didn't count in her world. She was a news junkie, always trying to keep up with current events. None of it was good, but it gave her things to talk about with her patients. She looked up from the screen and finally spoke for real. "Did Steph tell you that she and Anne want to visit the university soon?"

Tom turned away from the stove with a bewildered look on his face. "Really? Our Stephanie?"

"Yes, our Stephanie." Steph had never really talked about college before.

"Hm, OK. Can you go with her? You know a lot more about that stuff than I do."

Jenn nodded her assent. School had been her thing from an early age. Steph not only looked like her father, she had always been more like him, barely getting by in all of her classes. "I'll try to set something up soon before she changes her mind."

"She could always go to trade school," Tom said with a grin. Once he had found his niche, he discovered brains he hadn't known he had. Today almost no kids went to trade school. It gave him job security, but he wasn't convinced that was a good thing.

Jenn shook her head and returned to her monitor. She thought the kids should go to college and find themselves there. They had finally agreed not to push the girls, but to support them in finding their own path.

Silence returned as both parents tried to visualize a future for their kids. These days, kids without opportunities had few options. It broke both of their hearts to think of what their kids faced. The lack of hope made it difficult to believe in the future.

There was even a worst case scenario in their minds. With the decimation of the world's bee population, crops had struggled to keep up with the surge in population. That had filtered down to starving populations across the country and around the world. Throughout America's agricultural industry, millions of meaningful jobs had been lost. Kids without opportunities mostly ended up working in one of the synthetic food manufacturing plants or as pollinators in the massive industrial farm fields. The labor in the fields was back breaking with few rewards, which had further fueled the ongoing drug crisis. Others toiled for long hours to manufacture nutrition supplements that passed for food and their lives were no better. The only positive aspect was that the lack of food had all but eliminated America's obesity epidemic from the start of the century.

"Voilá" Tom said as he delivered a plate of eggs and sausage to his wife. He also slid the fruit bowl in front of her since he knew she'd have something from there, too.

The fruit was expensive, but it was an investment they were willing to make. He sat down across from her with his own plate and buttered his toast. She closed her screen and they ate together, simply enjoying one another's presence.

When they were done eating, Jenn kissed Tom goodbye and departed for the clinic. Tom was anxious to get started on his projects, but first he checked around the kitchen to see if it met Jenn's standards. After wiping off some spattered spaghetti sauce, he deemed it clean enough. He knew well that his definition of clean was different than hers and he tried to live up to her standards. It worked most of the time.

He donned a stained work jacket and his customary Minnesota Twins hat and went out to the garage, part of which served as his workshop and sanctuary. He spent many an evening out here tinkering with stuff and supplementing their income. With changes in the tax structure over the past thirty years, it was much more manageable to exchange services rather than pay the regressive taxes.

Jenn refused to barter with her medical knowledge, though. She helped anyone who stopped, asking for nothing in return. While her skills could have been valuable in that market, he respected her decision. She was the kindest person he knew and he could never fault her for that. He was not as generous, however, and had turned his abilities into quite a side business, bartering for things with a wide array of people they knew.

At Tom's command, the overhead door opened and the radio came to life. Within minutes, he was working on the last piece of the trellis, lost in his own world.

It seemed to Tom that only minutes had passed, but the clock told him that hours had disappeared when he removed his protective face shield. He stretched his back before admiring his work. It wasn't overly ornate, but it was one of his best pieces of work to date if he did say so himself. With great care, he turned off his equipment and set the trellis on the ground before heading inside. While his plate of leftover spaghetti warmed up, he spoke to the computer "Call Joseph Kaplan." A moment later, a hologram of a gray haired, bearded older man appeared.

"Kaplan's Market" the man answered.

"Hi Joseph," Tom said, "It's Tom Erickson." He knew the phone system had already identified him to Joseph, but it was still polite.

"Hi Tom, how's it going?"

"Can't complain. I have the day off, so I finished your trellis. Want me to bring it over?"

"Oh, that's great! Rebecca is home today, so any time you want to stop by would be fine."

"OK," Tom said, "say about half an hour?"

"That would be fine. I'll let her know you're coming." The men said good-bye and ended their conversation, allowing Tom to wolf down his lunch over the sink. He finished and added his plate and fork to the dishwasher, which sensed it was full and began to clean accordingly.

With a grunt, he loaded the trellis into the back of his vintage pick-up truck and secured it with some well-used straps. The price of gas always made him question the use of the truck, but the piece was too awkward and heavy to carry the three blocks to the Kaplans' house and it wouldn't fit into his small sedan. He checked one more time to make sure his equipment was turned off and waited to see the garage door close completely before leaving. While he didn't expect to be gone long, his tools were a big investment and a tempting target for thieves. His neighborhood wasn't the worst in town, but he took no chances.

Tom eased the truck into gear and lifted a hand politely to his neighbor across the cul-de-sac, who waved back. He and Jenn didn't socialize with the Spencers, but they were the neighbors. Dylan and Bella and their twins, Sam and Colt, were a little too much on the hillbilly side of things for his liking. Was it too much to ask that they mow their lawn a few more times each summer?

It took less than five minutes to reach the Kaplans' house. Jenn loved shopping in their family-run market a few blocks further north. That was how they had first met the Kaplans, in fact. The market had been in their family for nearly 90 years, going back to when it had been in a good neighborhood. A petite older woman wearing overalls and dirt-covered gardening gloves came out of her greenhouse when he pulled up. "Hello Tom," she greeted him warmly as she came over to give him a hug.

"Hi Rebecca, I finally have your trellis finished," he replied with a smile. Rebecca Kaplan was the definition of dignity. Tim often dreamed of his daughters growing to be like her. They walked to the back of the truck and he showed her his work.

She inspected it from top to bottom and proclaimed, "It's beautiful!" She reached out a dainty hand, touching the cold steel gently. "It's even better than I'd hoped for."

Tom blushed and unloaded his creation, careful not to scratch it on the truck. He carried it over to the greenhouse and leaned it up against the side of the structure. "You call me when you're ready to install it and I'll come help."

"Thank you," Rebecca said, "would you like to come inside for a cup of tea?"

Tom shook his head. "No thanks, I have some other work I need to get back to."

"I understand, but you and Jenn will have to come over soon." She hugged him again before he got back in his truck. As always, she refused to turn her back on him as he departed, watching until he turned the corner before returning to her plants. Tom's return trip was quick and he was soon happily lost in the work on his wind turbine.

———

Across town, Penny was struggling to stay focused as the board meeting neared its end. "Thank God," she was all she could think. While the computers recorded the meeting and generated the minutes, she was there to take special notes for Kristen and Mollie. On a regular basis throughout the meeting, one or the other would look at her and whisper "Write that down" or "Make a note to follow-up on that." They were at the far end of the conference table, with the board members between them and Bob Wright.

Lester was seated next to Bob, his lazy left eye keeping constant vigilance over Penny while he took his own notes. On the other was a middle-aged man in a black silk suit with an artificial tan, Congressman Casey Frost. The Congressman had been attending their board meetings for over a year, ever since Bob's patronage had gotten him elected to Congress.

"Any final questions?" Bob asked. He looked around the room and smiled. They were making piles of money and that was their only real concern. "Hearing none, I declare this meeting over." He then spoke to the computer, "Stop recording."

Penny looked up in surprise. Never in all of her years had he done such a thing. She leaned closer, and along with everyone else in the room, began to listen more attentively.

"Ladies and gentlemen, I have some growing concerns about our future." Penny squinted her eyes in surprise and concern. Everything she had heard and seen indicated that the business was on firm financial footing and was growing by leaps and bounds.

"I'm sure that you know there is growing unrest around the country. Yesterday, some people out in Arizona staged a riot and it negatively impacted one of our suppliers there. And my sources inside the plant suggest that some people are not happy with our idea to streamline our leave policy. I am worried that these people will become a distraction to the rest, ultimately hurting our bottom line."

The board members whispered among themselves for a moment before one of them spoke up. "Do you really think they would disrupt their own livelihood? It's not like they have a lot of choices."

The gin blossoms on Bob's face glowed even redder as he turned to face the man. "I wouldn't have brought it up if I wasn't concerned. I'm afraid that if we push them too far we might lose some people and you know how expensive training new workers is."

"Penny, what have you heard?" Mollie asked loud enough for all to hear.

Penny was caught off guard; she had never been asked to speak to the board. A deep breath and a pondering look bought her the moment she needed. "I've had many conversations around the plant, both with white and blue-collar workers and I haven't heard anything out of line. A little kvetching about missing stuff with their families, but nothing too serious." She knew she could have said "grumbling," but she enjoyed the look on Mollie's face when she used an unfamiliar, educated word, which she did often.

Another board member spoke up, "Congressman, what do you think?"

"I think it's time for some new legislation," the congressman said with a flash of his perfect smile. "Maybe something to guarantee that a business' rights come first."

"I like it," Bob said, a smile spreading across his face. "I'll work on that with you personally this weekend, then have our legal people write something up. In the meantime, let's keep this idea in mind. We need to be proactive in weeding out the bad apples. Now we're adjourned."

The board members filed out, congratulating themselves on their work, leaving Penny alone in the room with Lester. She made every effort to ignore him, but his presence was hard to miss. His close-set eyes stared as she cleaned up the room, paying special attention as she leaned over the table. Finally, he spoke. "So why did you lie to the board?"

Penny looked up from her stack of coffee cups, "Excuse me?"

"I have had lots of conversations around the plant, too, and there is a lot of discontent. Why did you lie and say there wasn't?"

Penny stared at him. He was so smug. He always was. "I don't know what you're talking about, Lester. The people I've talked to didn't seem that wound up. Sorry."

"Well, I think you're lying. Maybe you're one of the subversives? I know you live next to that Tom Erickson and I also know what a problem he is. We'll see what Bob thinks about all this." With that, he turned and left Penny to finish her work.

Lester was right, she had stretched the truth. People across the plant were upset, even angry, but Penny was not going to rat them out. They worked hard and well, but most of them barely made enough to get by. In truth, the people she had spoken to would all quit if they had other options, which they didn't have.

The Bob Wrights of the world knew this and took full advantage of the situation. Congressman Frost and his father before him had been influential in changing laws to benefit their wealthy sponsors and the large corporations who paid for their campaigns. Whether it was limiting environmental restraints or eliminating health insurance, politicians were willing to do whatever they were told. Penny tried to remember the last politician she believed in. She couldn't think of even one.

"I kinda miss the good old days when they at least tried to hide their corruption," she thought, lest the computers record her words. She sighed and pushed the last chairs under the conference table before returning to her cubicle. Overhead, she could hear Bob's helicopter departing for Chicago and the regional dog show where Bob would show his prized corgis.

Penny was startled when she turned the corner into her cube and saw an over-sized head of bleached blond hair protruding over her chair. Waiting for her at her desk with his back turned was Robert Wright III, the boss' oldest son and heir apparent to the company. He preferred to be called Robert to demonstrate that he was his own man, but most people privately laughed at that, Penny included. Robert was the son of privilege, who was quite used to having everything given to him. Penny was sure he had never even broken a nail in his thirty-some years on Earth. He was leaning back in her chair looking at the pictures of her kids, causing Penny to bite her tongue at the intrusion into her privacy. Robert turned when he heard her approach. "Hello, Penelope," he greeted her, not getting out of the chair.

"Hello, sir," she replied, "can I help you with anything?"

"Your son here, he's in the army?" Robert asked, holding out a picture.

Penny glanced at the picture of Andrew from his Army graduation. He was the spitting image of her husband at that age. Her daughters had much darker skin like herself. "Yes, he's a First Lieutenant. He commands a platoon of tanks," she answered, her voice brimming with pride. "They are preparing to deploy to the Middle East as we speak."

"Why would he join the army? I can't imagine that pays very well."

"Well, he seemed to think it was his best chance to get some experience and money for college. The plant wasn't hiring when he graduated high school, so he went that route," she explained.

"Hm. Does he like it?" Robert seemed to genuinely be curious, as if he'd never thought about the subject before.

"He says he does. It has its ups and downs, but for the most part I think he enjoys what he does. I know it's helped him grow quite a bit."

"Interesting. I don't know how that could be, but to each their own," Robert said as he set the picture down. His tone changed as he got to his real purpose. "I wanted to follow up on what you said in the meeting, the part about people complaining. If anything was wrong, you'd tell us, right?"

"Of course," Penny continued her charade. "This company means a lot to me."

The chair groaned in relief as the large, chunky man rose to his feet. "Good to know. We would certainly make it worth your while if you had information for us. And, you should know, the penalty for not coming forward would be severe. Do I make myself clear?"

A chill went down Penny's spine at the threat. "Crystal, sir. I'll let you know if I hear anything. You'll be the first to know."

"Good, good, good," Robert said, "Have a nice weekend."

"I'll try, sir. You have a good one, too," Penny said to the back of his head as he walked away. She looked at the picture of Andrew and smiled. He had already grown to be more of a man than Robert Wright would ever be, that was for sure.

She sat at her desk and proceeded to process all of the things from their meeting until it was time to go home. She sent the documents to their computers before closing her work station for the weekend. She knew Kristen and Mollie were long gone, it was rare to find them in the office after noon on Friday.

Penny left work, passing a number of the second shift workers on their way in. Along the way, she greeted some old high school friends and nodded to Ricky, Jenn's first husband. She knew those workers were even angrier than the ones she worked with more closely. Maybe these were the ones Lester talked with? Nobody she knew would tell him about their discontent, but who knew what happened on the late shift.

"Oh well," she thought as she stepped outside into the fading sunshine, "It's the weekend and I really am done caring for the week." The weather was shifting again and the previous day's snow was already gone. She was looking forward to a relaxing weekend with her kids and not even the memory of Lester's questioning could bring her down.

Chapter Six

The Wright mansion was bustling with activity that evening. Bob, along with his family and Congressman Frost had all left Des Moines in his private jet for his mansion overlooking Lake Michigan. The house was part of a small, extremely wealthy gated community protected by security equipment Bob's company had manufactured. He had, of course, made a tidy profit on it, but they understood; it was the cost of doing business.

In one of the rooms on the fourth floor, Bob gazed out the massive bay window at the boat lights twinkling across the choppy water and breathed a deep sigh of contentment. Watching the boats had always brought him great pleasure and tonight was no exception. He finished his gin and tonic and dreamed of being on the lake in his yacht, the "Minion," once it warmed up. From down the hall, he could hear his third wife, Marsha, barking orders to the servants, who were busy making sure everything was in order for the dog show.

"Quite the place you have here," said Casey Frost, breaking his solace. "I've always enjoyed it." He had a scotch and soda in his hand and was admiring a Renoir on the wall. From the marble columns in the massive entryway to the collection of masterpieces that adorned the walls to the servant's wing, the house was an epic display of his wealth.

"So have I," Bob replied. He was slightly annoyed by the interruption, but knew they had work to do tonight. The problems they had discussed around the conference table earlier had him on edge. He had worked too long and too hard to have anything interfere with his life. "Let's get this out of the way so we can enjoy ourselves." Bob poured himself another large drink and the two men walked to the nearby study.

Bob motioned Casey to one leather chair and eased himself down into one facing it. "We have to stop this nonsense before it really starts. I have too much at stake."

"I agree," the congressman said, "your work can't be interrupted by a few malcontents."

Bob took a long drink before continuing. "Got any ideas?"

Casey flashed his smile out of habit. "I do," he said. "What if we make it harder for employees to publicly protest their workplace? Obviously, we can't really stop them from griping at home, but publicly, including at work, would be grounds for firing them."

Bob scowled at him and shook his head slightly. "Damn it, that doesn't go far enough! I've worked hard to create jobs for these people, they owe me their loyalty!" He finished his drink and set the heavy crystal glass down hard on the mahogany table next to his chair.

"OK," Casey replied, a little shaken by the intensity of Bob's response. "How about we make dissent like that a crime? Something along the lines of inciting a riot?"

Bob closed his eyes and thought for a moment before speaking. "That has potential, but what about those 'free speech' people?"

Casey's teeth flashed again as he answered. "The Supreme Court has held for a long time that there are limits to free speech when the public good is at stake. Like yelling 'fire' in a crowded theater. We can argue that dissension in the workplace is similar in that it can cause an undo disruption to the economy and is therefore a threat to the public good. The courts are much more sympathetic now and will find in our favor."

Now Bob was smiling, too. "I think that has potential," he said with a nod. "I can then create an incentive plan for workers to turn each other in. I'm sure that will root out those people. And I'm sure I can rally support from the business sector to get you the votes." He grunted as he got out of his chair. "Meeting adjourned."

The two men returned to the living room's bar for fresh drinks, when the sound of voices made them turn. It was Marsha and their teenage twins, Mallory and Vanessa, dressed to go out shopping. Shopping was one of Marsha's favorite pastimes and she was raising the girls to enjoy it, too. She breezed up to Bob and kissed him on the cheek. "We won't be too late, we do have to get up early for the show tomorrow." Bob nodded and kissed her cheek as well. The girls looked bored as their parents went through their routine. "Congressman Frost," she added with a nod. Casey lifted his drink in acknowledgment.

The women left, closing the heavy door behind them. Bob knew they were off to their favorite sushi restaurant, followed by some high-end shops with personal shoppers. He himself couldn't stand being out among anonymous people that much, but the girls seemed to enjoy it, especially with his money. He much preferred his privacy and comfort of his own home.

He tried to connect with his daughters, more than his own father had ever done with him. His father had always been work, work, work. And while he worked hard, Bob tried to balance providing for his family with staying close emotionally. Bob watched the door for a moment after they left, assuring himself that he was a better father than his had been. Tonight he'd let them have their alone time, allowing him to enjoy the leisure time he had worked so hard for. He turned to Casey, "Let's get some food and watch a movie down in the theater. I just had some Cuban cigars brought in that I think you'll enjoy." Congressman Frost, as always, agreed without hesitation.

———

The Friday night vibe at the Stevens house was vastly different. The small house was full both with people and the feelings of love and happiness. Abigail had come home for dinner, which had allowed Scott and Penny a rare meal with both their daughters. Their group of friends would arrive shortly and they would share some good laughs. They never knew exactly who would come over, but that wasn't the point; it was always entertaining, which made it a frequent way they spent their Friday nights. The combination of laughs and talking smart was what they all wanted. And needed.

Soon, Tom and Jenn appeared, accompanied by her brother, Lane. Scott greeted them at the door. "How's the hemp business, man?"

Lane's face lit up at the offer. "Growing like a weed!" It was one of his favorite old jokes and he was always more than happy to tell it. He was a hard man to read. Still a single man, Lane's job as a security director at a hemp farm outside of the city gave him lots of time to contemplate the world. He didn't socialize with a lot of people, but those he did get to know found him to be a fun addition to any gathering.

Abigail decided she didn't need to get back to campus quite so soon, so she stuck around, too. An hour into the festivities, a knock at the door was followed by the arrival of new guests, Brett Kaplan and his girlfriend, Robyn Miller. Even though they had all eaten, Robyn brought snacks to go along with those already on the counter.

Brett was the only son of Joseph and Rebecca Kaplan and still lived at home with them. He and Robyn had been a couple for over a year, although no one could really understand why they were together. They were a little younger than the others, but they brought an energy level that was always welcome. Brett finished chewing a chip dripping with Jenn's homemade salsa and smacked his lips in appreciation. "Dang that was good!" He said the words loudly as he often did.

"Thanks," she replied, "The recipe is from my abuela, Elena. I made it with vegetables your mom taught me to grow. She's right, it is that much better with fresh ingredients." Food was one way Jenn honored her mixed heritage. Her father was Hispanic and her mother was of German descent, which had made for some wide variety of meals over the years.

"I'll have to tell her that you're learning quickly," Brett said as he grabbed another chip. Jenn welcomed the compliment. She hadn't really known much about gardening until Rebecca came along, but as with things she put her mind to, she was a quick learner.

"I have to agree with him," Abigail added. "The food on campus isn't nearly this good." She looked at Penny and quickly added, "Or yours, Mom."

Penny tried to make an angry face before laughing with her daughter. "Thanks, dear, I know she beats me in the kitchen." She, too, had learned from Rebecca, but wasn't as committed as Jenn was to healthy eating. Scott kept his head down and his mouth shut.

The pounding of footsteps up the stairs announced Anne's arrival from her bedroom. It was easy to see she was going somewhere there would be boys. She had spent extra time on her hair and make-up and looked much older than her 17 years. "Bye Mom, bye Dad, bye everyone. I'm going out with Steph." She turned and headed for the door.

"Wait, please," Jenn stopped her. Anne turned and faced her, one hand on the doorknob. "I set up a campus tour for you two. It's Wednesday, about three weeks from now."

"Oh, thanks!" Anne replied. "I can't wait. Can you have Mom put that on the calendar?"

"Already done," Jenn said with a laugh. "Go have fun!"

"Not too much fun," Scott and Tom said together, sending everyone into gales of laughter.

Anne rolled her eyes as only a teenage girl can, but her eyes were twinkling as her face contorted in an attempt not to laugh. "Got it, Dads." With that, she headed out the door.

Jenn and Tom exchanged glances. They knew the girls were good kids and made reasonably good decisions, but it was an ever-crazier world out there. She was less worried tonight about Ellen, because she was safely at home on her computer, probably talking to people she'd never meet in person. While that was its own issue, that daughter was unlikely to get into much trouble tonight.

"Do they have an idea of what they want to study?" Robyn asked. She had gone to college for a while, but had dropped out. Now she worked as a care giver at a senior living center. As with so many of her friends, it wasn't an exciting job, but there were millions of elderly people and that gave her job security.

Scott answered this one, "Oh God no. I'm not even sure if she'll get in, much less what she wants to study."

Penny scowled at her husband. "She is plenty smart enough to get in." She sometimes wondered what her husband was thinking.

"That's not..." Scott started, then stopped. "I mean..." He looked away and returned his focus to his beer, which he finished in one large swallow before retreating to the kitchen for another one.

"I'm sure she's fine," Tom tried to play peacemaker. He exchanged another look with Jenn and followed Scott into the kitchen. The rest of the group got quiet and fidgeted uncomfortably.

Tom arrived in the kitchen to find Scott with his head in his hands. Tom slapped him gently on the shoulder, "Hey."

Scott looked up, his eyes on the brink of tears. "Hey, sorry about that. I messed up again."

"Yeah," Tom replied, "but it's not the end of the world."

"I know, but I feel like shit. I do love her, you know. I just don't know how to show it."

"I know, I know," Tom said awkwardly.

"How the Hell do you two do it?"

"I don't know, man." Tom paused to drink his own beer. "It's work, I guess. It's working on it 24/7. I don't know what Jenn sees in me, never have, so I know I have to work on it. Maybe try paying attention to things she says and try doing some of the little things." She was an old pair of jeans in her world. Comfortable and reassuring, yet always something that he enjoyed.

"I'll try," Scott said. He didn't look convinced, but Tom didn't want to push the issue any further. The two men grabbed fresh beers and returned to the living room.

They walked in to find the atmosphere changed and the group returned to their general feeling of bonhomie. Lane telling a story from his lifetime in the Army. When in doubt, sharing them was his way of staying part of a conversation. "So Private Kelly opens the door and there's these two kids, the girl's ten toes to the sun, if you know what I mean." The door crashing open stopped him abruptly. Ellen followed, her face pale and her cheeks flushed. Jenn sensed something wrong and stood up. "What's wrong, honey?"

"Mom, it's horrible," Ellen said, her voice shaking. "Remember that thing in Chicago? The shooting thing?"

"Yes, honey."

"The news people lied. I was talking to a friend in Chicago and it wasn't really what they said. Some people died and a lot more were hurt. And they weren't 'rioting' like the news said, they were only demonstrating peacefully."

"What?" Tom said as he also stood up. "How did that get past the government's security programs?" For years, the government had been using "the threat of radical terrorism" to censor and control all forms of communication. Normally, key words and phrases triggered an artificial intelligence program that delayed or prevented messages from being transmitted. Oftentimes, the participants in any given message were soon visited by the police or Federal authorities in the name of national security.

A sheepish look took over Ellen's face and she looked away from her father. "I, ah, was kinda in a part of the internet you might not approve of, Pops. Part that is a little beyond where their security programs go."

"I think we'll save that discussion for another time. Tell us more about what you saw."

"They were standing up for their rights," Ellen replied, "Like the constitution says they could!"

"What the Hell! What else happened?" Brett asked.

"From what she said, they were demonstrating about affordable housing and stuff near the President's speech and the police opened fire on them. They weren't throwing rocks or bricks or anything like the news reports said! She even had some video!"

The adults were left silent with shock. They knew the media fed them lies every day, but this was crazy. And crazier still was the idea that police would shoot at protesters. Was it a hoax? A homemade video to make the police look bad?

Lane finally broke the silence. "Hey, kiddo, have you ever actually met this girl?" He was usually one to believe the official police reports.

Ellen looked perplexed at the question. "Of course, Uncle Lane. She's a good girl."

"I mean, have you ever actually met her? Like, in person?"

"Oh, right." Ellen finally understood his question. "Not in person, but we've been friends for years on-line."

"OK," Lane replied. "You truly believe you can trust what she's telling you about the thing in Chicago? I mean, those are pretty serious accusations." In his world, outside of the police and military, he felt it hard to trust someone he had never met face to face.

Ellen stood as tall and straight as she could and looked her uncle in the eye, "I really do." She turned to her father, "I do believe her, Pops." Her face and tone of voice reminded Tom of Jenn. He also knew that they meant her daughter fully believed what she was telling them.

Brett broke the silence. "They've gone too far! 'We the people' is dead! What happened to people's rights? And government responsibility?" No one spoke, because no one really knew what to say.

Brett continued his ranting. "Those lapdogs at the capitol and in Washington really don't give a shit about us anymore. They are simply controlled by their wealthy masters. And those bastards will do anything they can to make a buck, even if it kills people! America was supposed to be a place where the people ruled and had rights, and any kid off the street had a chance to go do great things, but now if you're not one of the chosen few, you're screwed or dead."

The group looked at him with no real reaction. He often talked about state of the country and how horrible things were. Generally, though, they'd always brushed him off as a loudmouth. While their own lives weren't amazing, they had food and their kids had clothes. Things weren't that bad, were they?

Brett took a drink before he continued, this time in a quieter voice. "Did you know I lost relatives in the holocaust? I did. Not often, you know, but my parents and grandparents talked about it. The Nazis took over and things went downhill fast. They started doing things "for the good of the people," too and good people let it happen. First it was laws and then violence and then the camps and ovens. I'm not sure we're on that track, but we're sure as Hell not on one George Washington would have approved of."

Finally, Abigail was able to get a word in, "He's kinda right. I've been studying some of this and we are really off track. Whatever happened to 'promote the general welfare' or 'secure the blessings of liberty?' Years ago, the people fought for what they believed in, like when black people were slaves or women couldn't vote or gay people couldn't get married! Now we take it like ignorant subjects, not the citizens we are." Her voice trembled with a combination of fear and anger.

Penny's face froze. She had never seen her daughter this way. Abigail had been a timid, quiet girl, who was evidently growing into her own skin. On one hand, her daughter's words unnerved her, but on the other hand, she was proud to hear them coming out of her mouth.

Brett nodded in agreement. He didn't know Abigail well, but she seemed a kindred spirit. "That's right! People were willing to sacrifice everything for a better life!"

"Are you willing to do that?" Jenn asked, "Sacrifice everything?"

Now it was Brett's turn to be taken aback. No one had ever challenged his bluster before.
"I'd like to think I am" he finally answered.

Jenn had to push him. She had heard Brett says lots of things and was growing tired of his railing against the establishment. "Everything? As in your family store? Your home? Your own life? Are things really that bad?"

Brett fumbled for an answer, but Abigail saved him. "Mama Jenn, I love my country, but something needs to change. When I'm your age, I can't even imagine what it'll be like. I'm not sure I'm willing to die quite yet, but we have to start speaking out. The idea of America is great, but we have to change some things."

"It's like Aunt Michelle, Mom," Ellen blurted out. "If you could have stopped her from taking drugs before it was a really big problem, she might be around today."

That left Jenn speechless; they didn't talk about her sister much. Years ago, Michelle, like so many others, had started taking drugs and disappeared into that dark underworld. She missed her sister but hadn't spoken to her in years. The mere thought of her made Jenn want to cry. Heck, she didn't even know where she was at this point. Fighting over how to deal with her had caused a rift in her relationship with Lane for many years that had only recently been reconciled.

Tom sensed her pain and took over. "Sweetie," he said looking at his daughter, "that's a pretty big jump."

"But Pops, it's true! Mom talks about how much easier it is to treat diseases early and this is the same thing. Our country is sick and we need to make it better before it dies."

The adults all looked at her in surprise. It was clear from the look on their faces that they had never imagined hearing such words come from her. Finally, Jenn rallied and looked up at her daughter. "Wow, that's brilliant." Ellen's face turned red and she looked away.

"Good thing she's got her mom's brains," Lane said. Everyone laughed, Tom included.

"I just think it's not too late and it's not going to get any easier," Ellen said.

"I have hope for the future," Brett chimed in. "We need to start taking action now!"

Tom sensed that Brett was about to get started again, so he stood up. "I've had enough fun for tonight," he said, "it's time we headed home."

Jenn was relieved and stood up as well. "You're right, sweetie, time to go." It was a little earlier than usual, but it beat listening to more preaching.

Robyn was also relieved. She also got fed up with Brett's tirades. "Yeah, you guys are right. I have to work tomorrow anyway."

Hugs and handshakes were exchanged all around and the group broke up, leaving Scott and Penny alone with

Abigail. "Those are big words you spoke earlier. I want you to be careful, those ideas can get you in trouble," Scott said.

Abigail looked back at her father and for the first time realized that he looked much older than she knew he was. Gray hairs poked through the few remaining black ones and worry lines crossed his face. "Don't worry, Dad, I'll be careful. But I want to do what's right, too."

Penny smiled proudly and hugged her daughter. "Your room is ready if you want to stay for breakfast, too."

Chapter Seven

A clattering along the edge of the porch interrupted her memories. A fat, gray squirrel ran along the top of the rail, stopping abruptly to stare at her. Without her glasses, the squirrel was a gray blob, but she could make out enough to smile. "It's OK little one," she said, "I'm not gonna hurt you."

Without bothering to put her glasses back on, she watched the squirrel. Any sudden movement might scare it away and she needed a moment of normalcy in her life after the last month.

It was crazy to think now of what was her routine a short month prior. A month ago? That was it? She had lived a lifetime since then. And to think that her world really began to change when she was enjoying a little bit of nature. She continued to sit motionless, trying to focus on her visitor until thoughts of the past month came back to life in her head.

———

Several weeks had passed since that first fateful day and spring had arrived to stay. The rains had come and washed away the dingy gray of winter, replacing them with an overnight explosion of color. The daffodils and tulips were in bloom and buds were popping out of the tree branches. Throughout the neighborhood, people had come alive, too, and were at last able to work and play outside.

Around the Erickson house, the only change was the constant talk of Steph's upcoming college visit. She had spent a good portion of her time this weekend looking for the right outfit and talking with her mother about what kind of things to ask. Frankly, Jenn was relieved to get out of the house on Sunday afternoon and go grocery shopping with Ellen.

They had, as they always did, planned the menu for the coming week before walking to Kaplan's Market. Planning things was embedded deep in Jenn's heart and soul. In the case of food, it helped keep their costs in check and limited their waste, both of which were important to Jenn and now the girls. The closer they got to the market, the more people Jenn saw whose hollow cheeks and empty eyes told her they didn't get enough to eat. On a global scale, the population of over 10 billion had collided with a volatile combination of droughts and floods around the world and resulted in massive famine and violent conflicts over natural resources.

One downside to the warmer weather was that it brought a lot of rough characters out as well. As they approached the market, many of the streets and doorways filled with addicts, dealers, prostitutes and the always growing number of homeless people. Jenn kept a wary eye on a wild looking man raving in the street about how the government was controlling the weather.

Kaplan's Market stood between one of the many pawn shops and one of the even more common liquor stores. Across the street was one of the city's biggest gun stores. Sadly, the market had become the kind of place that Jenn only wanted to visit during the day time. The police had mostly given up on this area, even removing the cameras that documented the goings-on in the wealthier areas they protected.

Joseph Kaplan greeted them with a wave and a smile as they entered. Jenn had never been to the store when he wasn't working. She and Tom worked hard, but he was in a league of his own. "Hi, Joseph," she said, "how are you this glorious day?"

Joseph came around the counter, "I am still on the right side of the ground, so I can't complain. You ladies look well."

Ellen answered for her mother. "We are, thanks. At least now that we're out of the house."

Joseph chuckled. He had heard all about Steph's college visit from his son. "Well, nobody ever said parenting was for the weak. Did you hear Brett's news?" When Jenn and Ellen shook their heads, he went on. "Robyn left him the other night."

While Jenn wasn't the least surprised, it was still a shock to hear that Robyn had finally gone through with it. "What happened?" Ellen asked. "They, I mean, he, didn't come over last night." She was not quite as in tune with the inner workings of close relationships.

"I think she wanted him to talk about her a little more and about revolution a little less" Joseph answered. A customer at the register saved him from having to explain further. Jenn was not so blessed.

"What does he mean by that?" Ellen asked, her voice barely audible over the shuffling of her feet as they proceeded down the produce aisle.

"Oh honey, I don't know. My guess is that she wanted him to focus more on their relationship, not some pie in the sky dream about changing the world. He's always been a lot of talk and not much action. And don't shuffle your feet, please."

They stopped at the first fresh lettuce of the season and looked over the display before picking a good-looking bunch. Jenn knew it was from the Kaplans own greenhouse, not the nearby hydroponic plant. Ellen had visited that operation on a school field trip and while it was amazing, the plants were better tasting if they were grown in real soil.

She put the lettuce in their cart as Ellen went on, "I think I understand. Eventually he has to actually do something. I think she can do better than him."

"Keep that thought in mind, sweetie. When your time comes, don't settle for someone who doesn't deserve you." The words were easy for Jenn to say, but she wasn't so old that she couldn't remember when that idea was hard. She had married her first husband, Ricky, because she was afraid of being alone. It had taken a few years of discontent for her to divorce him and quite a few more for her to feel confident in marrying Tom. She still wasn't sure if he didn't think he'd settled sometimes. He was the best guy she'd ever met, even her parents had loved him. She smiled, remembering how Tom had always volunteered to mow the lawn or shovel the snow after her father had passed away.

Their last stop in the market was at the meat counter, where Brett was slicing some corned beef. He wiped off his hands and came over to see them. "What's on the menu this time, Jenn?" he greeted them.

Jenn was silently happy that he didn't bring up Robyn. "Looks like Tom's grilled chicken tonight. Two, please. We're going to be sitting in the driveway afterwards if you want to swing by. We missed you the other night."

Brett packed up their chickens. "Thanks, I'll take you up on that. It's been a long week."

"Til then," Jenn said with a smile. The two women took their package and proceeded to Joseph at the checkout, where Jenn also invited him and Rebecca to the house. They were a great couple and she hoped they'd come over. She also hoped the presence of his parents would keep Brett's rhetoric to a minimum.

They made their way around a one-armed man in an army jacket raving about how aliens controlled the military and began discussing Ellen's latest school project when a woman carrying a coughing boy in her arms interrupted them. "Perdona me," she said, "pero mi hijo esta enfermo. Ayudame, por favor?"

Jenn set her bag on the ground and touched the woman's arm. "Si, señora." Her hand moved up to the boy's back, "Como te sientes, buddy?"

As she had many times, Ellen could only stand back and admire as her mother comforted the woman while simultaneously interacting with the boy. It was moments like this that reinforced her plans to go into medicine when she grew up. It didn't take Jenn long to reassure the woman and suggest some home treatments. As they left, the boy even gave them a shy wave before burrowing back into his mother's shoulder.

Eventually they arrived home, where Tom was in the driveway cleaning off the picnic table for its first use of the season. He couldn't hide his enthusiasm when he checked inside Jenn's bag. "This is gonna be good," he said.

"Ellen, tell your father about your project," Jenn replied and headed inside to put her groceries away.

"It's pretty cool, Pops," Ellen started, her voice growing more high pitched as she got excited. "We're learning about unoccupied aerial vehicles and what they can do."

"Unoccupied aerial vehicles? You mean drones?"

"Yes, Pops, only now UAVs are so much more than drones. We're making our own and are trying to make the fastest non-military one ever built!"

"I was a kid when they became big," Tom said. They couldn't do all the things they do now, but they had to start somewhere. Actually, they gave us some amazing shots of southern California when the earthquake hit and it slid into the ocean. And of the East coast as it got covered by the ocean. Miami was quite a city once."

Ellen grinned. "Did you use them to chase dinosaurs, too?"

Tom had to laugh with her and grinned back. "No! But they did give us some cool footage of elephants and polar bears before they became extinct, though."

"Wow, really? I was kidding about the dinosaurs, but you got to see those things when they were alive?"

"Yeah. It's been sad seeing so many animals die off. When the world's population exploded, a lot of animals went extinct, not all of them lizards in the rain forest, either."

Tom left his daughter with that thought and started the charcoal. His grandfather had gotten him hooked on old-fashioned cooking and technology couldn't quite replicate the taste of meat on a grill. And luckily, pigs and chickens were not extinct.

"That must have been something to see," Ellen said mostly to herself. She brought her bags inside and returned a moment later with a fresh bottle of beer for her father. "Here Pops, it looks like you could use this."

"Thanks, I was about to go inside to grab one and get the chicken ready." Tom headed towards the house.

"OK, I'm just gonna hang out here."

In the kitchen, Tom began coating the chickens with his secret homemade rub that turned them a deep burgundy color, barely noticing Jenn and Steph working around him. Steph let him finish the chickens in silence before she spoke up, "Hey, Pops, do you want to see my outfit for Tuesday? It has real cotton in it."

Tom looked at his platter of chicken and then at his daughter. "I, uh...I think I..."

Jenn cut him off. "He'd love to. I'll take the chicken outside and get the grill ready while you two go upstairs," she said as she took the platter gently from his hands.

"Yes, that's what I meant. I'd love to see it." Tom knew when he was defeated. He washed his hands in the sink and followed Steph up the stairs to her bedroom.

Jenn shook her head and chuckled at her husband. There were still times that he was so lost as to what was important to his daughters. She continued to chuckle as she proceeded out the door and through the garage to the picnic table, where she set down the chickens and a tablecloth. The coals were burning a bright red as she spread them out before opening the vents and putting the lid back on the grill.

The call of a cardinal high up in their aspen tree commanded her attention, filling both her ears and her heart. Jenn could barely see through the branches, but at last she could make out the red speck at the top. She closed her eyes and inhaled the bouquet of recently thawed ground mixed with charcoal smoke on the gentle breeze. The simple joys of spring made the world right, if only for the time being. Behind her, the shuffling of feet broke her reverie. "Ellen! I thought we talked about this," she said without even opening her eyes.

A bolt of shock went through her when someone grabbed her wrist and spun her around. It was not Ellen, but an emaciated, dirty, strung-out looking man. His bloodshot eyes looked at her and he said "I know you're a doctor. I seen you at the clinic. You gotta get me some stuff." His breath caused her eyes to water.

Jenn was choked with fear. This man was at her home! He wanted her to get him drugs! She had never imagined someone would come to her home and try to force her to help him with something like this. A small squeal came out of her mouth as she twisted and struggled to break out of his grasp. However strung-out he was, though, the man kept a vice-like grip on her wrist. "Don't fight me, doc. I need some stuff!"

Finally Jenn's voice returned and she stopped struggling. "Look, I'm not a doctor. I can't get you anything." She hoped against hope that reason would make him leave.

"Damn it, don't mess with me! I seen you at the clinic!" His eyes were getting wilder with each passing second.

"Mom, what's going on?" It was Ellen, coming around the corner of the garage.

Before Jenn could get out a word of warning, the man released her and quickly leaped over to grab Ellen by the ponytail. "Now, let's you and me figure out how you're gonna help me before I have to hurt your little girl here." He pulled Ellen's head to one side and glared at Jenn.

Ellen screamed in pain and shock. "No!" Jenn shouted at him. "Don't hurt her. I can help you. Don't hurt her."

"That's real good. I don't wanna hurt nobody but I will if I have to."

Jenn knew there were opium-based painkillers at work, but she had never really thought about how to get them for a drug addict. There were so many safeguards in place now that she wasn't sure it was possible, but he had her daughter. "Look, we can all get in my car and head to the clinic. I don't have any of that stuff here."

The man seemed to relax a little and stepped towards Jenn, his hand still full of Ellen's hair. "That's a good-" A spray of crimson exploded in the air as two shots boomed and the man crumbled to the ground grasping at his chest. Ellen was dragged down screaming, but quickly broke free and rolled away into the grass.

Jenn whirled around to see Dylan Spencer with a large handgun aimed at the man on the ground, smoke still rising from the barrel. "Oh my God!" she screamed and ran to Ellen, who was covered in blood. "Are you OK? Are you OK?" For all her years of training and experience, the thought of her daughter being hurt like this made her panic.

Ellen was in a daze as she looked from the man to her mother. Jenn knelt down next to her and touched her tenderly on the arm. She was quickly regaining her composure and began looking over her daughter. "Honey? Are you OK?" She began feeling her daughter's shaking arms and legs looking for an injury.

"I'm fine, Mom. I'm, I'm, I'm not hurt. It's, it's his blood. Just scared." Ellen words came out in gasps, barely escaping through her chattering teeth. Jenn grabbed the tablecloth off the picnic table and was wrapping it around her daughter when Tom and Steph came bursting out of the house.

"What the Hell is going on out here?" Tom shouted.

Steph stared. "Smellen!" she said before she ran over and cradled Ellen's head in her arms.

Dylan was the first one to speak. He had left his sidewalk and was now standing in their driveway, his eyes and gun still on the man he had shot. "This guy was attacking your girl and I shot him." His voice gave no sign of remorse.

Jenn switched gears and knelt next to the man. She felt for a pulse in his neck and couldn't find one. She looked up at Dylan. "He's dead."

Dylan finally took his eyes off the man to look over at Ellen and Steph, who were now sobbing together. "I guess I'm a pretty good shot, huh? I couldn't let him hurt your little girl."

Tom looked up at the sound of sirens approaching. He walked over to the neighbor he had resented so many times. "Thank you" he said as he stuck his hand out. Dylan flicked the safety on his gun and set it carefully on the ground at his feet before shaking his hand. The men looked at each other in silence and waited for the police.

Two police cars passed a growing number of gawkers before pulling up in front of the house. A male officer got out of one car and a female officer out of the other. Both officers had their guns drawn as they surveyed the situation. "What's going on here?" the male officer demanded. They both could see the gun on the ground, a girl spattered with blood wrapped in a red checked tablecloth and a man who looked to be dead lying beneath a smoking hot barbecue grill. It wasn't the strangest scene either one had ever encountered, but it certainly wasn't something they saw every day.

"Everybody keep your hands where we can see them!" the male officer ordered.

"I live here," Jenn said. Her hands were carefully out in front of her body. "This man attacked us," she said pointing at the man on the ground. "And this man saved us," she said gesturing towards Dylan. "The man on the ground is dead."

"Don't I know you?" asked the female officer. "You work at the West Side Clinic."

"That's right," Jenn replied. "I'm a physician assistant there."

"Yeah. You helped treat a car accident patient I brought in there a couple months ago. A drunk driver? Smashed his car into a stop light?"

"I'm sorry, I don't really remember. I treat too many of those types of patients."

The officer lowered her gun a fraction. "I'm Cruz, that's Walker," she tilted her head at the other officer. "It's OK. You were pretty focused on him once we got him inside. It makes sense you wouldn't remember me."

She looked over at Officer Walker, who had picked up Dylan's gun and was ejecting the magazine. "She's alright. I think we have a clean shoot." Officer Cruz returned her gun to its holster and kneeled by the dead man. She, too, felt for a pulse and found none. She spoke into her radio, "One twenty-six to central. On scene. It looks like self-defense here. Weapon is secure. Perp is DOA. Ambulance can roll quietly. Over"

A voice on the radio squawked back "One twenty-six, acknowledged. Ambulance and additional units in route."

Officer Walker was taking a statement from Dylan when a third police car pulled up. A female sergeant got out and assumed command. After conferring with her two officers she proceeded to direct the investigators and ambulance personnel as they arrived. Pictures were taken of the scene and statements were taken from Dylan, Jenn and Ellen. They even took a statement from Bella Spencer, who had been inside and called the police even before the shooting started, explaining the fast response time.

Before the coals on the grill got cold, the ambulance crew removed the body, the police left and the crowd of onlookers returned to their own homes. Steph and Anne had taken Ellen inside, leaving Tom and Jenn sitting at the picnic table looking around numbly. This had been such a quiet street when they moved in.

Scott and Penny took control of the situation like family does. Penny took the food back inside, no one really had an appetite anyway, and Scott got out a hose to wash the blood off the driveway. Finally, they took Jenn and Tom over to sit on their porch. They were all still tense, but at least things were settling down and Jenn could start to describe what happened.

Penny saw Dylan and Bella reemerge from their house and waved them over. She and Scott didn't socialize with the Spencers either, but tonight was clearly different. She stood and gave them both hugs, while Scott offered them a beer, which both gladly accepted. "This is some night, huh?" Dylan said.

"That's the understatement of the year. Thanks again for saving my family," Tom said softly. He was now regretting any bad thoughts he'd had towards his neighbors.

"Ain't no thing, man," Dylan responded. "I got kids, too. Ours are off at her folks today."

"Yeah, but you were there and I..." Tom choked up on his words and couldn't speak.

"Shit, I got lucky. You woulda done the same for us I expect. Hell, I damn near pissed myself."

They all laughed at that. It felt good to release some of the pressure from their systems. "Anyway," Tom tried again, "thanks."

"That was crazy, wasn't it?" Bella said. "I never thought we'd have something like that happen here."

A voice called from the sidewalk, "Are you still receiving guests?" It was Joseph Kaplan, leading Rebecca and Brett through the hedge.

"Come on in!" Scott called back. He and Tom went into the garage to get more chairs as the Kaplans were introduced to the Spencers and brought up to speed on the recent happenings. They agreed it was a crazy series of events.

"My goodness, Jenn" Rebecca said, "I'm glad you're all OK."

"Thank you, so am I. I feel awful for that poor man, being so sick to think he had to hunt me down. And then to end up dead."

Dylan was puzzled. "You feel bad for him?"

"Yeah. Don't get me wrong, he scared me and I'm glad we're safe, but I still feel sorry for him. I see patients like him every day at work and the stories are all the same. They give up hope and turn to drugs to numb their pain. Sometimes they get this desperate, I guess. And I have this sister, Michelle..." For a rare moment, no one interrupted her as she detailed how her sister had gotten hooked."

When she was finished, Jenn looked around at the group. They all shared the same grim, hopeless look. While Jenn's work at the clinic and at an opioid orphanage during college gave her the most clinical experience, they all knew someone who had fallen victim to the drug epidemic of the last half century. Traditional narcotics and some synthetic drugs were now truly everywhere. They were so invasive the overstretched police simply tried to keep the users from committing violent crimes in "good" neighborhoods. Tonight had demonstrated that their plan wasn't always perfect.

Brett's loud voice broke the silence. "It's another way the man is trying to keep us down. They keep people hooked so they have bodies to put in their prisons and people can't think for themselves anymore!"

Dylan and Bella hadn't heard his routine before, so they looked on with interest as Brett continued. "If people could think for themselves, they'd be really pissed. They don't know how much the rich guys have and how much power we should have."

"That's right," Dylan finally spoke. "I been saying that for a long time. America is screwed up and screwed over."

"I concur." They were bewildered when they realized it was Joseph Kaplan agreeing with his son. He had never shared his opinion before. "There was a time when the government actually tried to work to help people. And there was a time when folks like all of us got along a whole lot better, too. We didn't agree on everything, no sir, but we listened to each other more and we found ways to compromise and live together."

"I miss those days," his wife added, touching his arm. "People realized that they had to live together and so they worked at being civil towards one another."

"What do you think it would it take to get back to those days?" Jenn asked her.

"I don't know, dear. Things are pretty divided right now and have been for some time. The only thing that has brought people together in my lifetime has been a national tragedy or something similar. People don't really 'need' each other anymore and so many people live in their own little worlds thinking it's all about them."

"You know," Brett continued, "the Declaration of Independence and the Constitution had a lot of compromise in them. We need to get back to our fundamentals."

Scott squinted his eyes at him, his head tilted. "Man, how do you think we're gonna get back to those? Hell, until tonight, I hadn't said ten words to these guys" he said gesturing to Dylan and Bella with his beer. "No offense," he offered up as an apology.

"None taken," Bella said, "I was thinking the same thing about you."

"Hell, if all it takes is shooting some drug addict to bring the country together, I think I can help." Dylan had another beer in his hand and a smile on his face.

"I don't think you can go around shooting people on the street," Bella replied to her husband, but she was smiling, too.

"Maybe not," Brett interrupted, "but something's got to make people come together before it's too late. Maybe we can start a revolution right here on our street."

His mother looked over at him. "Son, I thought you were going to leave the revolution talk at home tonight?"

"Sorry, Mom, I get so upset when I think of how messed up things are and how nobody's doing anything about it."

"Don't you be sorry, man," Dylan spoke up. "I agree with you, so does Bella. I still have hope that we can fix things, I just ain't smart enough to know how. I know how to protect my family, but I can't fix the world." The group grew quiet again.

Penny spoke for the first time in a while. "Maybe tonight is a good start. We all have our differences, but here we are all agreeing that we have problems and we need to work together on them. Maybe not a revolution, but we can make our neighborhood better and safer."

Brett couldn't let it go. "That's where revolutions always start!"

Jenn was once again done with his big talk. "On that note, we should probably get home and see how Ellen is doing. I don't think she'll be going to school tomorrow and the other girls are iffy at best." Tom helped her out of her chair and the other guests took that as their cue to leave, too. Friends new and old exchanged their farewells and headed back to their homes.

"I'll be damned," Tom thought as he held hands with Jenn and walked across the lawn. "That was a perfectly crazy ending to a perfectly crazy day."

Chapter Eight

Congressman Casey Frost inspected his flawlessly manicured nails as he stood outside the congressional meeting room. The leadership team was inside and he was waiting along with a dozen other congressmen and women to discuss the issues of the day. They had all heard about the shooting in his district the night before and he knew that would be on the docket along with the unrest around the country. The red-eye flight to get here after being briefed on the incident had left him exhausted, but there was work to do. They would have to do something soon if they wanted to keep the peace and keep commerce flowing. His meeting with Bob Wright had only served to reinforce his belief that most citizens didn't know what was good for them.

The door to the meeting room swung open and the group went inside. Over-sized leather chairs surrounded the conference table in the center of the room. Paintings of former congressional leaders kept an eye on the proceedings from the walls, while computer monitors graced every spot. House Speaker Eli Gregorian of

Massachusetts sat at the head of the table reviewing notes on his computer. From his jet black hair to his trim physique to his spit shined shoes, he epitomized his position. Years of political favors and backroom deals had paid off handsomely with his rise to power. Everyone took the seat they always took and made themselves comfortable. Uniformed servers refilled coffee cups as needed and brought beverages and pastries to others before departing.

"Ladies and gentlemen," the Speaker began, "welcome back. We'll get down to business." As he spoke, an aide pushed a button, transmitting the agenda to each of their screens. Congressman Frost was correct in his belief that the shooting would be on the agenda, right behind the unrest. The Speaker continued, "As you can see, we now have protests and outright riots in nine states. That poses a threat to us and to the American way of life."

A congresswoman from Pennsylvania spoke first. "I had a protest turn violent in my district last week. The local police were happy to get it under control without military help."

"So did I," a congressman from Oklahoma added. "Reports are it got pretty awful."

The Speaker let two others add their stories before he cut them off. "Yes, yes, the stories are pretty much the same. Now, what are we going to do about it?"

The group was quiet. They hadn't had to think for themselves in quite some time. Finally, a congresswoman from what was left of California spoke, "We need to make sure the local police have the equipment they need to suppress riots. I mean, if people turn violent, they're going to need armored vehicles." The others looked relieved that someone else had spoken.

"That would have been helpful," the woman from Pennsylvania agreed. "I wish we'd had those last week."

"And we need to increase the penalty for violent protests," a congressman from Maryland added. "Lock 'em up and throw away the key."

"And we need to make sure those people can't sue the state if the police have to use force," added a woman from Michigan who was a long-time prosecutor. "I suspect the police will have to take more aggressive action to keep control and showing our support for law enforcement will look good."

"You know," Casey added, "I was talking about this with one of my constituents the other night and we may also want to consider infiltrating some of those groups. Maybe the FBI or Homeland Security?"

"Now we're thinking," the Speaker said. He was nodding his head in agreement with the ideas. "If we can come down hard, we can stop this before it becomes a major problem. And if we can jail the troublemakers, we might be able to make a real difference here. People must be kept safe from protests."

The aides made some notes and were already formulating the wording of their legislation as the discussion continued for over an hour. They all hoped someday to fill one of the leather chairs themselves and knew the best way to do that was to go along with what was being said. If they could improve on some of the ideas, it would be even better for their careers.

"OK," the Speaker announced, "we will now switch topics and talk about the shooting in Des Moines last night. Obviously, we are not cracking down hard enough on these drug abusers."

Casey relayed the details of the event to his peers. He had spent some time talking with Des Moines' Chief of Police about the shooting and had some insight to share. "Fortunately," he concluded, "the neighbor had a gun and was able to take care of it. If he keeps it up, we might not need so many police officers." He chuckled at the implication, as did most of his peers. None of them had much time for drug addicts.

The congressman from Oklahoma spoke again. "It's gotten so bad in my district, that it's hard to find workers who aren't addicted." That was met by a series of nods and dour smiles. They had all spoken with the business interests in their districts and knew the situation. Not enough workers was bad for business.

A congressman from Virginia, one of the more liberal members of the group finally spoke. "What if we could keep kids from taking the drugs? Wouldn't that help solve the problem?"

"That might help in ten years, but we need to do something now!" Casey shot back. "I have people hunting down medical professionals in my district and that's a big problem."

"He's right," said the woman from Michigan. "And we should also consider how many jobs a prison creates, it's a lot."

"She's right. It's short term construction jobs and long-term prison jobs, not to mention the support industries like restaurants and liquor stores." This was Oklahoma again, Casey knew he had a number of state and federal prisons in his district.

Speaker Gregorian glanced around the room. "OK then," he said, I'll have my staff draw up the legislation we have discussed and we'll start moving on it shortly. We need to make this happen in time for the election. Thank you all for your dedication to our cause." With that, the meeting broke up and the representatives went back to their respective offices.

Casey had barely sat down at his oak desk, when a knock at his door signaled a visitor. It was Speaker Gregorian himself, who walked in before Casey could respond. Casey rose and shook his hand, "Mr. Speaker."

"Congressman Frost," the Speaker replied, "I need to have some more discussion with you."

The two men sat down in guest chairs facing one another. "Casey, tell me more about the incident in Des Moines."

"What else would you like to know? I covered everything important in our meeting."

"Tell me more about the doctor involved. What kind of family does she represent? Is she someone who could be a spokesperson for us?"

Casey paused as he grasped what the Speaker was asking. He rose and went to his desk where he opened a computer file and read for a moment. "She is a physician assistant, actually, not a real doctor. She might be perfect for us, actually. She's been married to the same man for twenty years and is the mother of two girls. Parents deceased, one brother, one sister...she's not close to either one of them. She's been in healthcare for a long time, her record is excellent. Her husband works at a local production plant. No criminal record, no indications of any real political leanings, either." He read a little further before looking back up. "This might be helpful, her sister is an addict." He sat back down and looked inquisitively at the Speaker.

Speaker Gregorian smiled his own perfect smile. "She sounds like we might be able to use her. Can you do a little more vetting of her and her family? Maybe meet them and break the ice?"

Casey smiled back and nodded. "Absolutely. I'll get my people right on it and meet with her ASAP."

The Speaker rose and extended his hand. "I think she may prove quite useful to us."

Casey also stood and took his hand again. "I think you're right."

Casey ushered Speaker Gregorian out of his private office and watched silently as he left. He then turned towards the cubicles of his aides. "All right people, listen up. I want to meet in the conference room in ten minutes. We have a lot of work to do."

Chapter Nine

As expected, Ellen was not able to go to school in the morning. She had not slept well the night before, nor had she had much of an appetite. Between that and the shock of the shooting, it was decided that she could stay home. She was a little dismayed, since she hadn't missed a day of school in years, but was buoyed by the fact that she could stay caught up via her computer.

Steph and Anne decided to go, however. They had their first cross country meet later in the week and they knew that missing school might put that in jeopardy. Jenn longed to stay home with Ellen but was already taking a day off for the campus visit, so she headed off to the clinic and crossed her fingers for an easy day. Tom also went to work, triple checking that the garage and house were locked behind him.

By the reception she received at the clinic, Jenn knew the story was out. The guard took an extra-long look at her as she came in, but he also smiled and nodded his support. When she got inside, she repeated her story to what seemed like every one of her co-workers. They were all as shocked as she was and realized that it could easily have been any of them that was assaulted. On the upside, they were all incredibly supportive, giving her frequent hugs and there was a veritable buffet in the break room. Jenn was uncomfortable talking about herself this much and was oddly thankful to get called to treat a patient. She was privately relieved to find it was a garden variety sprained ankle, rather than an overdose patient; she wasn't sure how she'd react to that today.

Five minutes before noon, her omniphone vibrated. As she looked at the caller ID, she blinked in surprise as her Congressman's name came up on the screen. She answered with her usual greeting, "Hi, this is Jenn."

The Congressman's hologram sprang out of the phone. "Hello, this is Congressman Casey Frost," he said, "let me tell you how happy I am to hear you're alright after last night's affair."

Jenn was taken aback. She had never imagined speaking with her congressman. She hadn't voted for him and in fact, hadn't voted at all in quite a few years. It all seemed so pointless to her. "Thank you, Congressman. We're happy to be alive today."

"I bet you are," he replied. "And how is your daughter, Ellen?"

"She is physically OK, but she's pretty traumatized emotionally." Jenn responded reflexively to the medical question.

"Good, good. I'm happy to hear that. I hope the rest of the family and your neighbors are able to return to normal soon."

"As do I, sir. As do I."

"Say," the Congressman continued, "if it's alright with you, I'd like to stop out and visit with you and your family. I'd like to get your opinions on the drug crisis and see if we can't start trying to figure out how to deal with it. Any night this week would work great."

Jenn was again caught off guard. She hoped her own hologram didn't give away her feelings. "Wow, OK. Let's see, tonight is too soon. How about Tuesday night?"

"That will work fine."

"If you'd like, sir, I can also invite some of our neighbors who were involved. They might have some great insight." While Jenn believed what she was saying, she was also silently hoping to have extra people there to help keep her nerves in check.

"Thank you, but I'd rather have the time dedicated exclusively to your family."

Jenn gulped before continuing. "OK, the family it is, then. Say about 6:30? We can have you for dinner."

"That would be super. I'll be bringing a couple of aides with me, too," the Congressman said. "I'll see you then. Have a good day."

"Thank you. Good-bye." Jenn shook her head in disbelief once the hologram disappeared. As if her week hadn't already been adequately crazy. She looked at her omniphone and said, "Call Ellen."

After a moment, Ellen's hologram appeared. She was still in her pajamas, but Jenn didn't mind today. "Hi, Mom," she answered.

"Hi sweetie, how are you doing?"

"OK, I guess. I'm having trouble focusing on stuff. I keep flashing back to last night." While she didn't cry, Jenn could hear a tremor in her voice.

"I know, so do I, but we'll be OK." Much like with Congressman Frost, Jenn hoped her own emotions didn't show through too much.

"I was just so scared! It..." Crying now cut off Ellen's words.

"Oh baby, I know. I wish I could be home with you right now." Like all mothers, it ripped Jenn apart when her daughter was suffering. That pain made her own pale in comparison. "I wish I could give you a hug right now. When are they going to make a phone that lets me do that?"

Ellen's crying was now interrupted by her own laughter. "Maybe I'll make that my science fair project, the hug-o-phone."

Jenn laughed so loud that the receptionist down the hall looked over at her. "Ellen, that sounds like a winner. And I wouldn't bet against you, that's for sure." She could see her daughter was now smiling and blowing her nose. It made her heart feel better, if only temporarily.

"OK, Mom, I have to try and get back to my schoolwork."

"Wait, I have one more thing to tell you," Jenn said before her daughter could end the call. "Believe it or not, our congressman wants to come to our house and talk with us about the, well, you can guess and the drug situation Tuesday night."

"What?" Jenn could see the surprise on her daughter's face. "Casey Frost is coming here? That's weird, why would he want to talk to us? We don't have any money." While she believed in the concept of America's government, she had well founded misgivings of how it actually worked.

"I can't argue with you, but he's coming Tuesday night, so if you need a distraction from studying, you could feel free to do some cleaning around the house."

"Yeah, I can do that. With my attention span today, that might be about what I can handle."

"Thanks, sweetie, I appreciate it. I'll see you when I get home. Love you!"

"Love you, too, Mom." Their call ended and they both went about their day as best they could.

———

Penny's return to work had also attracted more than a few strange looks. People knew the shooting had happened in her neighborhood and were naturally curious. Most were shocked to learn it had been next door to her house. But, as with Jenn's co-workers, they too knew someone who was lost to the epidemic and shared some understanding of the man's motives.

Except for Kristen and Mollie, who chastised Penny for talking too much during work hours. "I'm only letting you talk about this so much because I'm so understanding, you know," Mollie had had the gall to say to her. Another meeting called Mollie away before Penny could say anything back to her boss.

Penny was still seething when her day got worse. Lester was now leering over the edge of her cube before he spoke. "So, I hear you had some excitement last night."

Through clenched teeth, Penny was able to answer, "Yes, right next door."

"Oh, I know where you live. Too bad it's not enough to make Erickson up and leave. Or is it?"

Penny looked up at him in scarcely hidden disgust. "I'm fine, thanks for asking. As are all the Ericksons. I suspect they'll be around here for a long, long time."

"Well, nothing I can do about that...yet. Maybe you all need to look at moving to a safer neighborhood. Or maybe we can cut you a deal on some new security equipment?" He was always excited about high profile crimes; they helped the company sell more product.

Penny continued to gaze at Lester with as blank of a look as she could manage. She knew that he was aware that moving wasn't an option for them. They couldn't afford that, nor could they afford her own company's products. They were as trapped in their current home as she was in her cubicle, but she'd be damned if she'd break down in front of him.

Finally, the silence got to Lester. "OK," he said, "maybe moving isn't something you can do, but you be careful how close you get to Erickson. I told you he was trouble."

With that and a smirk, he turned and left her alone with her thoughts.

With her eyes closed and her head in her hands, Penny's thoughts drifted away. She hadn't given the vile little man the satisfaction of making her cry, even though it all felt so hopeless. Her job sucked, her husband had issues, and her kids were leaving the nest; what was going to help her keep going? Fate smiled as no one interrupted her escape and after a few minutes of deep breathing, she regained her composure enough to get back to her work.

Chapter Ten

Tom returned home from work the next afternoon and blinked hard as he looked around the house. The entire Erickson family had spent the previous night cleaning the house inside and out, making it cleaner than it had been since they moved in. Tom's feelings had boiled over in the form of short comments and even yelling at the hedge trimmer when it wouldn't work. Ellen had stayed home again and had used her time wisely, Tom noted as he pulled a beer from the refrigerator. A fresh green salad and some vegetables were waiting to be grilled along with the unused chicken from the other night.

Ellen came bouncing down the stairs and hugged her father. "Notice anything different?"

Tom stepped back, feeling fortunate to see it was something obvious. "You cut off your hair!"

"Do you like it? It's called a pixie cut."

"You look beautiful, sweetie. The important thing is, though, is if you like it."

"I do like it, thanks. I had to get rid of my long hair after the other night."

Tom didn't know what to say, so he hugged her again, hard. His feelings of guilt would not go away. His main job on Earth was to protect his daughters and somebody else had been there, not him. Finally, he was able to speak and let her go. "The house looks and smells great, thank you."

"And look at this," Ellen said. She produced a chocolate cake from the counter for his approval.

"Wow, that looks like it should be in the movies." Ellen giggled as he sampled the frosting and dreamily gave his approval. "I'm going to get started on the grill before I eat this whole thing."

By 6:00 PM, Jenn proclaimed everything ready to her satisfaction and they tried to relax before their guests arrived. While they were ready physically, emotionally was another story. They were all still shaken from Sunday's shooting and now they had a Congressman nobody really trusted coming into their home. None of them knew exactly what to expect and that made them nervous.

"Congressman Frost, welcome to our home," Tom greeted their guests when they arrived promptly at 6:30. He extended his hand. "I'm Tom Erickson."

"It's a pleasure to meet you," the Congressman replied, cupping Tom's hand in both of his. Over his shoulder, Tom could see the Spencers watching the scene carefully from their window. He imagined he could feel every eye on the street watching them as Jenn and the girls came out of the house to welcome their visitors.

"And you must be Jenn," the Congressman said with his trademark smile.

"It's a pleasure to meet you," Jenn said as he gently shook her hand as well. "These are our girls, Stephanie and Ellen."

"Good evening, girls," he greeted Steph and Ellen. The girls shook his hand, surprising him when they both looked him in the eye and gave him the firm handshake their mother had insisted they develop. He smiled at them. "With a handshake like that, maybe you should run for office someday."

Ellen was the first to respond. "I don't think so. I want to go into medicine like my mom."

"Good for you. I hope you're recovering after that ugliness?"

"I'll be OK. I just need some time. I've been talking to lots of people and they've all been so supportive it's overwhelming."

"That's good to hear." He turned to Steph, "And what's in your future?"

"I'm not a hundred percent sure," Steph replied. "I think I want to go to college, but, I don't know what I want to study."

"Well, I'm sure you'll figure it out. Let me introduce my staff. This is Lance, my assistant and Zoey, my driver. She doubles as my protective detail," he added with a wink. "You can never be too careful in this neighborhood."

More handshakes were exchanged and Lance produced two pies from the back of the car. "I couldn't come empty handed, you know," said the Congressman, again with a wink.

"Of course, thank you," Jenn said. "Girls, can you take these inside, please?" The girls did as they were asked and left their parents in the driveway. Jenn tried to keep a straight face as she imagined the thoughts going through Ellen's head as she carried in the store-bought pie.

"Would you like a seat?" Jenn asked gesturing to the lawn chairs set up in a circle upwind of the grill's smoke. "Tom is making his world-famous chicken on the grill. It should be ready soon." She looked over at her husband, who nodded.

"That would be great, thank you," the Congressman answered. He brushed off the bottom of his chair and took a seat. Lance chose a seat two spaces away while Zoey seated herself where she could watch the street. "Please," he said to Jenn, "sit here next to me."

Jenn accepted his offer and sat down. The whole situation seemed unbelievable to her, but her experience with arrogant doctors allowed her to keep her composure. Tom, who was not as accustomed to people like this, watched and listened from the safety of the grill. The girls returned, carrying a tray of glasses filled with ice and a pitcher of tea, which they distributed to all before joining their father at the grill.

By the time the chicken was done, Jenn, the Congressman and his staff had discussed the weather, the baseball season, Jenn's job and their yard. It took all of Tom's self-restraint not to laugh as his girls exchanged looks of amusement at the conversation.

Jenn led the group inside, where everything was as ready as humanly possible. Jenn had fretted that their dishes weren't fancy enough, but Tom had talked her out of buying a new set they'd never use again. "Make sure your mother and I get the ones with the chips, please," he had told Steph when she set the table. Seats were taken and food passed around, but the mood was much more tense than usual with the addition of their special guests. Jenn noticed that the Congressman let his aide try the chicken first and didn't touch his until Lance had made sure it was safe. "I wonder what they would have done if it was under cooked?" she thought to herself.

The dinner conversation continued with all the depth of a shallow grave, talking about almost everything but 'the incident.' After the pie was consumed, the group adjourned to the living room, where Tom served a bottle of wine from a local vineyard.

"Well," Congressman Frost started, "is there anything about the shooting that I didn't get from the police and the media?"

Jenn was relieved to finally get to the point of his visit. "No, they got all of the details right. We were getting set to cook dinner, the chicken we had tonight, in fact, when all Hell broke loose."

"Yeah, it was pretty terrifying," Ellen added.

"I bet," Lance said looking up from his computer notepad.

Casey continued, "What do you think we should do about the drug situation?"

Jenn answered first, "From a medical perspective, we need the funding resources to treat overdoses. At my work, we deny treatment every day to people we could save." Casey nodded and Lance continued his note taking.

"I've talked to a lot of my friends," Steph started, "and they've given up hope on a future. Some of them are already hooked. They've simply lost hope."

"Me, too," Ellen said, "a lot of kids at my school don't have meaningful things in their lives and are finding ways to pass the time and eliminate their pain, if only for a little while. They need positive things to do."

Even Tom chimed in, "At the plant we have workers who are hooked and would like to quit, but it's expensive and they can't afford it. It puts them in a really bad situation and it's dangerous for all of us."

"That's interesting," Casey said, "very interesting." He sipped his wine before continuing. "I'll take all of those ideas back with me to Washington. But, I'm wondering if you would be interested in speaking on behalf of some of our drug interdiction efforts? You know, to try and show people that it's quit or die or go to jail?"

Lance spoke up again, "We could film something right here on your street."

Jenn looked at her kids and then at her husband before speaking. "I don't know. I'm not sure if we want to get involved or even if that's the message we'd promote." Tom, Steph and Ellen all silently nodded their heads.

"I see," said the Congressman. "Why don't you take some time to discuss it in private and we can talk later this week.

I'm sure we can even arrange for some financial compensation for your efforts."

"Boy, it's really not my thing," Tom said. "And I have doubts about putting my girls in that situation."

The Congressman finished his wine and set the glass down. "Like I said, take some time. We'll be in touch." His aides took his cue and stood up to leave. "Thank you all for a lovely evening." Tom and Jenn ushered their guests out to their car and watched them depart.

When the car had turned the corner, Jenn continued to stare down the street. "He didn't hear a single word we said."

Tom wrapped his arm around his wife and they headed back into the house. "Nope. But at least we have cake for tomorrow."

Chapter Eleven

The clattering was back, louder than before. Jenn squinted again at the railing, now able to see two gray blurs chasing each other around and ultimately off the porch. One side of her mouth turned upward. How nice it was to have even a moment of levity.

High above, the sun broke past another cloud, spreading its light and warmth on everything below. Her mouth turned back down. It struck her as odd that sunshine could change her mood for the worse, but for her, the memory of a similar day was all it took. She pressed her eyes closed again. One breath at a time. The sunlight overwhelmed the darkening power of her eyelids, filling her with a translucent glow. And one of her worst memories.

———

The bright sunlight shining through the windows gave Jenn an optimistic start for the day's adventure. Today was Steph and Anne's campus visit and she was up early. Not as early as Tom, who had already gone to work, but earlier than the girls, whom she could now hear stirring upstairs. She took a seat in the sun and opened the admissions materials for one last look. They had all been on the campus for games or to see theater productions, but this was different. Now Steph was going to college. How was that possible? For as much as Jenn thought she was prepared for her girls to grow up, she realized it was nerve-wracking, too.

Jenn closed her eyes as she sipped her coffee and mulled over how she and the world had changed since she had gone to college. Part of it seemed so long ago, while part of it seemed like yesterday. She had been so optimistic. She had started college with a plan to change the world of medicine, but now she felt her world spinning more and more out of control every day.

A creak behind her brought Jenn back and she turned to see Ellen coming down the stairs, dressed for school. Jenn stood and looked at her with concern. "Think you're ready to go back?"

"I think I am," Ellen replied, "at least it will be a change of scenery. And at least I finally slept OK."

Jenn tried to smile as she hugged her daughter. "I understand. Be strong and if it gets to be too much, you can come home. I should be back early with your sister."

"Thanks, Mom, good luck." Ellen grabbed an apple and headed for the door. Jenn watched her depart proudly; the girl was wishing her good luck today!

Steph was next down the stairs. She paused at the bottom and twirled around to show off her new outfit. "Mornin', Mom."

"Good morning, Steph, you look great. Ready for the big day?"

"I'm as ready as I'll ever be." Jenn could tell by the tremble in her voice how nervous she really was.

"You're going to do great. Try and relax and be yourself." Jenn hoped her confidence would transfer to her daughter.

Before Steph could respond, Anne walked through the door. She, too, was wearing a new outfit for the occasion. "Would you like something to eat?" Jenn offered.

"No thanks. But do you have any orange juice?"

"No problem, sweetie, I'll get it." Jenn turned and got a carton of orange juice from the refrigerator, while Anne got glasses from the cabinet. Jenn knew that real juice was something the Stevens' house didn't have often enough, so she was glad to be able to help. She poured the juice and slid the glasses to the girls. They made small talk while Jenn made some toast that she forced upon them. "Trust me," she told them, "you'll need something in your system today."

Finally, after one last look in the mirror and a reminder to stand up straight, they headed across town to the university. Traffic was flowing smoothly for a change, which gave a good start to their journey. Jenn had debated having Abigail give them a tour, but then decided they needed a neutral guide.

————

Abigail's day had also started early. Months of talking with her friends and other students had brought them all to the conclusion that they needed to make their voices heard about their future and the future of their country. A few them had read old history stories about student protests of the last century and how that had changed the course of the country; now it was their turn. More careful study had convinced them that non-violent demonstrations, like Gandhi and King had staged, would be their most effective strategy. The students had spent the last several nights making signs and banners at the cost of their academic work. One of her friends, Darby, had even offered up a sound system so they could speak to the group.

She had heard that there could be dozens of students at the demonstration. Some students, like Abigail and her roommate, Hannah, were involved to change the world. Some, she knew, would be there mainly there to get out of class.

University policy had required them to inform the administration of their plan to hold the demonstration on campus grounds, which they had grudgingly done. The administration had given their permission with equal reluctance. But, regardless of those outside factors, today was the day and nothing could stop them now.

Abigail was sitting cross-legged on the floor of her apartment looking at her notes again. Even though she had developed them, written them down and toyed with them for days, her pulse still pounded at the thought of speaking to a large group. They would meet up at 11:00 AM, march to the administration building and be done by 1:00 PM, she hoped. She looked up as Hannah came out of the restroom dabbing at her mouth. "Yeah, I just threw up," her friend blurted out.

Abigail looked at her and laughed. "I've had that feeling all morning." Hannah breathed deeply and got herself a glass of water from the kitchen.

After a few moments of silence, Hannah came back and stretched her hand down to Abigail. "Let's go," she said. "We got this."

Abigail smiled even more broadly than before and reached up to take her hand. "Let's do it!"

It took twenty minutes for the women to meet up with their comrades and to walk the short distance to the student union as planned. Some were carrying armloads of signs while others struggled to manage the banners. As they walked, the excitement of the moment overtook Abigail's fear and by the time they reached their destination, she felt ready for anything.

They joined Darby in assembling the sound system and began passing out signs to new people who came to join them. To their surprise, they ran out almost immediately however, as "dozens" of students turned into hundreds, most of whom Abigail did not know. She and her friends worked hard to spread the word that they were to remain peaceful and non-violent. Abigail was worried that somebody would be stupid and start breaking windows or lighting something on fire. She remembered what Ellen had told them about Chicago and was going to give the police no reason to turn violent.

As 11:00 AM approached, the mood of the crowd changed. Nobody in the crowd had been a part of anything like this in their lifetime and now a murmur of excitement filled the air. Abigail was dumbstruck as she took stock of the scene in front of her. Never had she imagined a crowd like this. Was it possible that this many people really believed in her cause? The presence of a dozen campus security personnel and police officers around the edges of the crowd only added to her apprehension, but she tried to block them out and stay focused on her work.

Abigail looked at Hannah and mouthed "Wow." Hannah threw her hands up in agreement, then patted her heart in solidarity. Abigail returned the gesture and climbed up on a small ladder with her headset microphone turned on. From her new perch, Abigail could see the crowd was even bigger than she first thought. She really couldn't tell, but it had to be 1,000 students or more. All she knew was that it was far beyond her wildest expectations. She swallowed hard, waved her hands over her head and took a deep breath. "Ladies and gentlemen, welcome to the future!" she said slowly. The crowd grew quiet before erupting into wild applause and cheering. Abigail had to wait over a minute while the crowd applauded and roared their approval.

"We are here to let the politicians across town and across the country know that we want a future! We want them to know that 'we the people' is not merely an idea, but that we are the people and they will hear our words!" More applause filled the air.

———

President Mariah Bailey looked down out of her fourth-floor office window at the throng of students gathered on the university square and felt her stomach turn. Nothing in her experience had prepared her for something like this. Between some distant buildings, the flashing lights of two police vans caught her eye and made her even more uneasy.

A uniformed police sergeant, whose name tag said "Rodney" and her Director of Campus Safety stood next to her in silence. They had been aware for days that the demonstration was happening but had expected it to be significantly smaller than this. A planned event of a few dozen was now a massive group of students with signs and banners that covered the entire square. President Bailey turned to the men, "Jacob, what can we do about this?"

Jacob Hunter looked back at her and shrugged. "They have a permit and aren't being violent. There's not much we can do at this point. It's a lot bigger than we were told to expect, but our best option is to let it burn itself out."

Sergeant Rodney remained stone-faced. "I've got more units coming. If this gets out of hand at all, we will take care of it. We have instructions from on-high to put down any mass demonstrations that begin to threaten the public safety."

Hunter felt a tingle shoot up the back of his neck. "What exactly do you mean by 'put down' the demonstration?" His stare told the officer that he already knew the answer.

Rodney stared back at him. "If we deem force necessary, we'll use force. It's out of your hands now."

"President Bailey," Jacob began, "this is not right. These are our students and what he's implying alarms me. We can't assault them and call ourselves educators."

Sergeant Rodney cut her off. "Look here, the police are not educators. We have an obligation to the public and the taxpayers who fund this university to keep the peace. And we will do what we need to do to keep that peace."

President Bailey looked back and forth between the two men. "Gentlemen, surely there's a way to manage this without anyone getting hurt."

Sergeant Rodney shook his head. "Maybe, but we'll do what we have to do."

———

Jenn and the girls met up with their tour guide, an energetic young man named Ahmad, and five other prospective students with assorted parents. Ahmad was busy showing off the campus and his knowledge of its history. "This was the first university in the Midwest to get rid of its library, since all of its publications can be accessed on-line," he told them.

The girls were impressed with the athletic facilities, since both had hopes of continuing their running careers in college. They were less impressed with the classrooms they saw. They were nondescript rooms, whose only bright spot was the technology that Ahmad was eager to explain to them all. "Many of our faculty teach from off-site locations, which allows us access to the best educators in the nation. We simply project them into the classroom."

After stops at three different housing units, Ahmad led the group towards the student union. He paused at a crosswalk to allow three police cars to pass. "I'm sure that's part of our outstanding law enforcement training program," he told the group.

––––––

Directly below President Bailey's office, Sergeant Rodney and Director Hunter stepped out of the Administration Building and took up position along the edge of the demonstration. Their vantage point allowed them to hear the words coming from the speakers without being among the crowd. She could see that Sergeant Rodney had donned a tactical headset on over his crew cut hair and that he was watching the video feed from a surveillance UAV circling the demonstration on his omniphone. The headset allowed him to switch back and forth between communications with his officers now surrounding the scene and his superiors back at the station.

Sergeant Rodney stepped away from Hunter and tilted his head to hear the message coming through more clearly. Hunter could see him speaking into his microphone but couldn't hear the words over the crowd. All of his experience told him that something was wrong. He couldn't put his finger on it, but it felt wrong.

The students would say their piece and then go about their business. In a few days, things would be forgotten if this gung-ho bastard would let it. He glanced up at the President's Office and shook his head. Even through the window's tinted glass, President Bailey could feel the growing tension in the air from blocks away.

———

Abigail looked to her right to see Darby giving her the "wrap it up" signal. She nodded and turned back to the crowd. "OK people, it's time to march to the administration building. Remember, this is a peaceful demonstration! No matter what you think or feel, use your words to express yourself! Keep it safe and peaceful!" With that, she took off her headset and jumped to the ground. She looked at Hannah and shook her head. "Holy crap, this is crazy!"

Hannah shook her head, too. "Man, this is wild." Hannah was carrying a bullhorn and was ready to lead the march. She switched it on and took a deep breath. "OK people, here we go. Follow me!" Hannah and Abigail began to walk across the open space to their left, towards the administration building. They were flanked by students carrying a large banner saying, "Democracy Lives!" and another saying, "We Want a Voice." They were followed first by their core group of followers with signs and then a sea of students that went back as far as they could see.

———

As they cross the street on to the block leading to the student union, Jenn could begin to hear a buzz in the air. She couldn't identify words, but she could see some of the other parents exchanging confused glances. The girls looked at each other and then at Jenn, they couldn't identify it either. Only Ahmad seemed unfazed by the sound as he continued his tour. "Up ahead, you'll see the student union. It has over 200,000 square feet of space, containing meeting rooms, a food court, a performance space with all the latest theater technology, a convenience store and a lot more. Really, almost everything you need outside of class is in here. On the far side of the union is the university square, which is where we'll end our tour. It was designed as a central place on campus where students could gather outside and enjoy some fresh air. It is, as is our entire campus, fully covered by our central computer network." The group continued walking towards the glass-fronted building.

The closer they got to the building, the more Jenn was able to understand some of the words. "What do we want?" seemed to be amplified electronically and "A future" seemed to be coming from a mass of people shouting.

"Maybe I'm jumpy from the other night?" she thought to herself.

———

The crowd of students approached the administration building and surrounded its base, the students filling in over half of the university square. Abigail and Hannah looked up at the top floor at the President's Office but couldn't see through the sunlight reflecting off the glass. In her mind, Abigail imagined she could see President Bailey looking down on them and wondered what she was thinking. "If only she would come down and listen to us," Abigail thought. She wasn't sure what she'd say to the President, but she wanted the opportunity.

Hannah looked down from the building and out at the students crowded behind her. She put the microphone to her mouth. "We're here! Let's make sure the university hears us!" The loudest cheer yet rose from the crowd.

———

Ahmad strode around the corner of the student union and collided with a police officer looking at the wall of students in front of his group. He stood and stared, unable to speak for the first time that day. The officer stumbled and turned angrily at the young man. "You watch where you're going!" he screamed.

Jenn, the girls and all of the tour group stared, too. None of them had ever seen a demonstration in action, much less one that had dozens of police officers in riot gear around it.

———

Director Hunter stood on his tip-toes to see the leaders at the front of the demonstration. It looked like a couple of generic female students with a bullhorn and some signs. His eyes darted back to Sergeant Rodney, who was again tilting his head. Hunter saw his face go from blank to angry and this time he could read the sergeant's lips: "Get ready. Engage!"

Chapter Twelve

"Attention students!" blared from a loudspeaker on top of one of the police vans. "You are hereby ordered to disperse! Return to your classrooms or your dorm rooms, but you must disperse! You must leave this area at once!" Jenn watched in astonishment as police officers pulled nightsticks out of their belts and lowered the visors on their helmets. A dozen officers loaded tear gas canisters into their weapons and fired towards the far edge of the crowd before the announcement had even faded away. Before most of the students even realized what was happening, the officers reloaded and fired again at different spots in the crowd

After their third round, the helmeted officers began moving directly into the crowd, shoving students from behind and knocking them to the ground. Instinctively Jenn pushed her two girls behind her and they backed away a few steps, seeking shelter on the side of the building. While Jenn couldn't believe her eyes, she couldn't make them look elsewhere.

Ahead of her, chaos was erupting as the officers began to push their way through the crowd. About half of the officers simply used their nightsticks to push students, but the rest were actively swinging their weapons at students who got in their way. Many of the students still had no idea what was really happening, all they knew is they were beginning to choke on the tear gas and be pushed out of the area by the police.

Screams soon erupted as students began to run from the scene, knocking over those too dazed to move. Jenn's shock turned to dismay as, right in front of her, two students were trampled by the crowd. The police continued their push towards the front where Abigail and Hannah were only now realizing the situation. Hannah returned to her bullhorn. "Stay calm! Please, stay calm! Don't fight back! Violence is not the answer! Stay calm!" Next to her, another woman tried to film Hannah while keeping the camera hidden from the police.

The tear gas filling the air made it hard to see more than about 50 feet, but Jenn could make out dozens of bodies already on the ground close to her. The police van continued to order students away from the scene as the officers on foot pushed deeper into the crowd. The crush of bodies made their progress slow and Jenn could only watch as more officers began actively swinging at any student who didn't move fast enough or raised a hand in defense. She lost count as more and more students fell to the ground clutching their injuries. Through it all, the distant voice continued to plead with the students to remain calm and peaceful. Her words went mostly unheard by the students and a full-fledged panic ensued.

Jenn turned to Steph and Anne and grabbed each of them by the hand. She struggled to keep control of her voice as she spoke. "Girls, you have to get out of here. I have to stay and help, but you girls have to get to safety."

"No!" the girls said in such unison that Jenn was forced to smile.

"Girls, you have to go and go now.

Steph looked at her mother with tears welling up in her eyes. "Mom, we're not leaving you." Anne nodded her agreement.

"Girls, listen. I have to stay, but I won't be of any help if I'm worried about you two. You've got to get to safety."

Steph looked at her mother, her eyes as wide as they could possibly be. "Mom?"

Jenn looked back and forth between the girls. "Look," she said, "you two stay together. Get back to the car and then get home. I'll call you when I can, but I have to help, there are people hurt here." To emphasize her point, she fished a pair of protective gloves out of her purse before handing it to Steph. She hugged both girls. "Now, run."

Much to her surprise, the girls did exactly as she asked. "Be careful, Mom," Steph yelled as she grabbed Anne's hand and they turned to leave. In a flash, the girls were lost in the crowd fleeing the scene.

Jenn breathed a deep sigh of relief as she turned back to the spectacle on the university square. The crowd of students had grown considerably smaller as they fled the police. She could begin to see individuals through the haze of the tear gas dissipating in the breeze, including a few students were now actively trying to defend themselves with their bare hands or bricks from a nearby construction project. Jenn saw an officer take a brick to the helmet and get knocked down. Before the officer could rise, a swarm of officers reached that student, who went down under their clubs and was dragged back to the police van.

Again she could hear the voice on the bullhorn, "Stay calm! Don't trample each other!" The crowd had thinned to the point where she could see a young woman holding a bullhorn in one arm and the microphone in the other. Directly in front of the speaker, Jenn watched another officer get tangled up with a pair of fleeing students and go down in a heap. The students scrambled up and ran off before the officer could get to his feet. The officer rose and shook his head before turning to the student with the bullhorn.

Time stopped. Jenn watched horrified as the helmeted figure drew his gun and took aim at the speaker. Two shots rang out and the speaker fell to the ground, her bullhorn clattering to the cement next to her head.

Jenn closed her eyes and shook her head wake herself from the nightmare. When she opened her eyes, time returned to normal and she knew it wasn't a dream. She was able to see that most of the students had escaped, leaving only the wounded behind. The police van kept up its announcements as the police began to pull back from the demonstration. Jenn knew this was a good sign, but nothing good was really in her head. First things first, she thought as she ordered her omniphone to call for help. A moment later, a woman's head rose from the phone, "911, what is the nature of your emergency?"

Her years in medicine allowed her to speak in a slow, calm manner. "My name is Jennifer Erickson, I'm a physician assistant. We have a mass casualty incident at Des Moines University. We have at least one victim with a gunshot wound and dozens of others injured. We're going to need lots of help here."

"Ma'am, we are aware of the situation and we have been ordered not to respond."

Jenn stared, open mouthed. "I'm sorry? We have critically wounded people here!"

"I'm sorry ma'am, no help will be coming. If you get them to a hospital, maybe they can treat them," the woman said as she ended the call.

The call left Jenn numb. What in the world!? She walked towards where the young woman had been shot, the smell of gunpowder and tear gas still heavy in the air. While she passed dozens of students on the ground with cuts and bruises, she knew she had to get to this woman. Within moments, she reached her and was stunned to find Abigail, covered in blood, cradling Hannah's unmoving body.

"Oh my God, Abigail! Are you OK?" The words were all too familiar to Jenn. Visions of Ellen the other evening filled her head. She knelt by Abigail and grabbed her hands. "Honey, are you OK?"

Tears were flowing down Abigail's face when she finally looked up. "She's dead, isn't she?"

Jenn reached over to Hannah's neck and felt for a pulse. "I'm sorry, she's gone," she whispered hoarsely. She grabbed Abigail in a fierce hug and began to cry herself. "There's nothing we can do for her."

For how long she held Abigail, Jenn didn't know. She knew that Abigail was shaking uncontrollably and that for now, a hug was the only medicine she had to offer. Jenn did, however, loosen her grip enough to look around the scene. The police were mainly milling about the perimeter of the square congratulating themselves. She could see students still on the ground, their moans reaching her ears, calling her to service.

Jenn let go of Abigail and looked into her still teary eyes. "Honey, I have to go help some of the others. There's nothing I can do to help your friend."

Silently, Abigail nodded and loosened her own grip on Jenn, who moved off to the nearest student she could find. Her first patient was a young man sitting with his back to a lamp post clutching a gash on his head that was dripping blood. A young woman with a "Des Moines University" sweatshirt tied around her waist was crouched next to him looking frantic. Jenn leaned over, "I'm Jenn, I can help."

"Please help him!" the woman shouted. "I don't know what to do!"

"OK, I can help." Jenn looked at the woman. "First, I need you to calm down and take a couple of deep breaths. If you want to help him, you have to get yourself under control." The woman nodded and sat down hard. "Good," Jenn said, putting on her gloves, "just breathe for a minute."

Jenn swiveled on her knee to face her new patient, but before she could speak, a hand grabbed her shoulder. Her muscles tensed as she again flashed back to the assault in her driveway. She turned to see an angry police officer glaring down at her. "Who are you?" the officer demanded.

Jenn was shocked. As a medical professional, she wasn't used to being questioned like this. "I'm Jennifer Erickson, I'm a physician assistant. I'm going to help this boy."

"Don't bother," the officer said. "He earned what he got."

Now Jenn was angry. She wasn't sure if it was the officer's callous attitude or the whole situation, but she was angrier than she could ever recall being. Jenn stood up, her eyes locking with those of the officer, who suddenly felt the urge to step back. "This boy is hurt and I am going to help him. You will not get in my way" she said in her best medical voice. The officer wasn't prepared to be confronted like this, but recognized a command voice when he heard one. He backed away and began speaking into his radio.

Jenn crouched down next to the young man. "How you doing?"

He looked up at her as best he could. His left eye was swollen shut already and coated with blood. "It hurts."

"I can help you," Jenn offered, "just take a deep breath." She probed gently at his eye socket. He winced but didn't pull away. "Can you follow my finger?" she asked as she held up her index finger and moved it slowly from side to side." She watched his right eye struggle to follow her movements.

She turned back to the young woman. "I need you and your sweatshirt." The woman got on her knees and handed Jenn her sweatshirt, confused when Jenn tore off the left sleeve at the seam. Jenn folded the sleeve in two and pressed it on the wound. "I need you to stay with him and hold this in place. Keep a little pressure on it until more help arrives. When they come or you get him to help, tell them you think he has a concussion. Can you do that?" The woman nodded. Jenn took her hand and guided it to the bandage before leaving for another patient. "Keep pressure on it. Keep him and yourself calm."

Jenn proceeded to help students as best she was able. While her supply of patients seemed to have no end, she had no actual medical supplies. She made do with whatever she could scavenge, even making her appreciate the limited resources the clinic had to offer.

Jenn had lost count of how many patients she'd helped, when she paused to wipe the sweat out of her eyes and look around the square. As promised, no ambulances appeared, leaving her as the only medical professional on the scene. The police did not offer to help the wounded either and went as far as to drive off most of the others who tried to help them. A smile crossed her parched lips when she saw Abigail helping a couple of the less severely wounded students a few yards away.

Jenn knelt down to help another bleeding man when someone touched her shoulder more gently than earlier. She turned her head to see Scott standing over her. "My God," he said, "what's happening here? Where are the girls?" Are you OK? Are they OK?" His words came out in one long, jumbled sentence, but Jenn got the gist of it.

She stood and hugged him. "I'm OK and the girls are safe at home. Abigail is right over there being a champ."

Scott's head whipped around and he bolted to hug his daughter. Jenn gave them their privacy and returned to her patient. Before she was finished, Scott and Abigail rejoined her. "What can we do to help?" Abigail asked.

Jenn stood and surveyed the scene again. "We need to get a few of these kids to the hospital. They're hurt worse than we can treat here. Can you work on that?"

Abigail looked up at her father, who nodded. "Yeah, I can do that. Honey, you stay here with Jenn. I'll be back fast."

"OK, Dad," Abigail said. "Hurry." Scott touched her arm and nodded before trotting off without another word.

Jenn continued her work with Abigail's assistance, helping four more students before Scott returned in a university van, followed by three more. He jumped out and ran to Jenn. "I got the guys from the shop and their vehicles. Now what?

"Nice work," Jenn replied. "Abigail, you go with your father and take care of Hannah. I'll take care of the others." Within minutes, she was directing Scott's co-workers on how to safely move the more critical patients into their vans. From there, they went to local hospitals and where Jenn could only hope they'd receive the care they needed.

As dusk approached, Jenn her final patient limp away. Dust stuck to the sweat covering her face and glasses rendering her almost unrecognizable. Her clothes were thoroughly soaked in blood. Finally out of adrenaline, she sat down on a low rock wall and surveyed the situation. An eerie calm had settled over the area now that the police had departed, leaving the square virtually deserted. Signs and other debris littered the ground, the only evidence of the demonstration other than one horrible stain on the concrete. Abigail collapsed next to her and offered her a bottle of water, which Jenn was delighted to accept.

Abigail let Jenn down half the bottle before speaking. "You were incredible today."

Jenn wiped her lips and smiled. "Thanks. You were pretty awesome, too. I thought you'd go with Hannah?"

"I thought about it, but then I thought about what Hannah would want. She would have wanted me to stay and help more people. That's the kind of woman she was."

Abigail hung her head at her words. "None of this was supposed to happen. We were having a peaceful demonstration and..." Her sobs cut off her words.

Jenn wrapped an arm around her and could feel her shaking again. Jenn remained silent and let the young woman process her own feelings. Abigail looked up and wiped the tears out of her eyes. "What happened here? We were only trying to show we want a future. It got way bigger than we'd ever imagined, but this is crazy!"

"Wait, you were in charge here?" Jenn looked at Abigail with amazement and a new-found respect.

Abigail smiled. "Yeah, Hannah and I and a few others. We thought it would be maybe fifty of us, but then it kept growing. And I never imagined there would be violence. Oh, Hannah..." She began to weep again.

"Honey, you did great. Nobody could have guessed the police would go crazy and shoot people. You did what you thought was right and it looks like you did a great job of it. It had a terrible outcome, but that's not your fault. And then you bounced back and helped people, which says a lot about you."

The sound of footsteps drew Jenn's attention to a man and a woman approaching them. The woman spoke first, "I'm Mariah Bailey, President of the university. This is Jacob Hunter, Director of Campus Safety."

Jenn stood and offered her hand, "I'm Jenn Erickson, I was here on a tour today."

President Bailey and Director Hunter both shook her hand. Jacob looked from Jenn to Abigail and said, "This didn't have to happen. If the police had listened to us, this would never have happened." His voice was a combination of exhaustion, frustration and anger with a large dose of sadness in it.

"He's right," President Bailey added, "it didn't need to come to this." Her voice mirrored his, but with greater sadness.

Abigail finally stood and introduced herself. Director Hunter looked at her, his eyebrows raised. "You were in charge here, weren't you? I recognize your name from the permit."

"Yes," Abigail said, "I'm the one responsible. I'm the one who..."

President Bailey cut her off. "Young lady, you may have organized the demonstration, but you are in no way responsible for this," she waved her hands around the square, "this disaster. The police did this. You and your friends were doing an excellent job from what we could tell. And trust me, we were paying close attention."

That made Abigail smile. "Thanks, I guess. We wanted to have a voice."

"We know," the President replied, "and we at the university heard your voice. And frankly, it makes me proud to say you are one of our students. Contrary to what you might hear, there are still those of us who believe in education and putting that into practice."

Abigail blushed at the praise. Jenn smiled and said, "Wow, I thought I was the only one proud of you today." Jenn had known Abigail since she was a baby and loved her like a daughter, but this all made her see her in a new light.

President Bailey smiled, too. "The university is going to be closed for the foreseeable future. I can't imagine classes being productive after this."

"OK," Abigail said, "but where do we go from here? This can't be the end of things. Hannah can't have died for nothing!"

President Bailey and Director Hunter looked at one another, unable to hide their discomfort. Finally, Hunter spoke. "We're not sure. We've already been asked to expel you and the other student leaders. There are people who say you're a danger to the university."

Abigail stared at him. It took all her self-control not to scream.

The dirt and sweat couldn't hide the rage that overcame Jenn's face. "I have known this young lady forever and the only thing she's a danger to is the status quo." Director Hunter decided now was a good time to look down at his shoes.

President Bailey continued, "We're already getting pressure from powerful people, including the Board of Regents and the Governor's Office. Right now, the best we can do is to guarantee you a hearing before the Student Conduct Board."

Abigail broke her silence. "Fine, tell me when and where."

The President looked Abigail in the eye. "We'll let you know as soon as we can get that set up. I'm afraid, though, that that group can't meet as long as classes are canceled, which may be a while. A long, long while."

Jenn thought she detected a slight smile on the President's face as she turned to depart. "Thank you!" she said as the two administrators walked away.

Chapter Thirteen

It had taken quite some effort to get there, but at last Jenn was able to relax in the security of her own home. First, she and Abigail had to walk over a mile from the campus to get to where vehicle traffic was allowed. Along the way, they had been questioned and searched for weapons twice by police and stared at by countless strangers.

Finally, they reached the point where Tom had parked the mini-van. All three girls had insisted on coming along and their hugs nearly knocked her over. The love she felt refilled what the day's anguish had taken from her heart.

Jenn had never felt as appreciative for self-driving cars as she had during this trip. She and Abigail spent the entire drive telling them about their experience. From the passenger seat, Jenn could see Tom's hands clenched white on the steering wheel and lost track of how many times he had stared in disbelief. Tom took rare advantage of the car's auto-drive system, letting it get them all home safely. Abigail gave her one last hug before heading to her house to get cleaned up, but the others all followed Jenn inside.

Much to her surprise, she walked in to find her living room full of people. Penny and Scott were there, as were the Kaplans, the Spencers, her brother and even three people from Tom's work she didn't recognize. It was all a little overwhelming for her on top of the chaos of her day already. She made them wait, though, while she took a quick shower and donned some clean clothes; she had had quite enough of the blood for one day. She even drank a beer in that short time, which drew a snort of laughter from her husband.

Jenn returned from her shower and sat next to the Kaplans on her familiar couch. Rebecca touched her knee, "If you're ready, go ahead and tell us what happened." The group quieted down and gave her their undivided attention.

It took her ten minutes of uninterrupted talking to tell them all the details. She even remembered some things she had forgotten in the car. "It's funny," she thought to herself, "but now I can remember that Hannah's shirt was Kelly green under the blood." When she finished, the shocked crowd sat in silence for what felt like forever.

Finally, Rebecca broke the silence. "My goodness, dear, you're a hero."

Jenn smiled and felt uncomfortable. "No, I'm not a hero, I happened to be in the right place to help some people. It felt good to practice medicine without all of the restrictions."

"She's right, you saved a lot of lives today," Scott added. "I'm real glad you didn't have to work on Abigail, though." He was sitting on the other couch holding his daughter's hand.

Jenn looked at him. "Your daughter was amazing. She went from leading a wild demonstration to holding her roommate's dead body in her lap to helping me with dozens of patients. You raised a heck of a kid there."

Penny's face glowed with pride. "Thank you. Honestly, I knew she was growing up, but I never imagined a day like this. I mean, she talked about trying to change things, but this..." Scott nodded, he couldn't imagine his daughter doing anything of this sort either. Abigail sat quietly, uncomfortable with being the center of attention.

"Maybe this will be what really changes things," Brett said in his standard loud voice. "Revolutions always start with bloodshed like this."

"What do you mean?" Ellen asked. "The news is making it sound like the students attacked the police, who only defended themselves after telling the students to leave!"

Jenn looked at her daughter incredulously. "Honey, that's not even close to what happened. I-"

"Mom, I know! But I've been listening to the news and that's what they're saying. And they're reporting that five students were killed, Hannah was shot and four that were trampled in the stampede."

"Those sons of bitches." It was Lane who said what they were all thinking. "Those sons of bitches shot and killed kids because they were afraid of their ideas. That's not the America I swore to protect."

Again, the group fell silent. Jenn could tell from their expressions that some were afraid, some were bewildered and some were angry. Dylan Spencer brought them back when he asked Lane, "What do you mean by that?"

"I mean that I swore to defend the Constitution of the United States from all enemies foreign and domestic and this has gone too far. I had my doubts about what Ellen said about Chicago, but now I realize that I was wrong about a lot of things." He turned and looked at his niece, "I'm sorry. I hope you can forgive me?" Ellen smiled shyly and nodded.

The new guy with the armful of tattoos, Zach, added to Lane's thoughts. "We're with you. Too much of what's happened over the last few years shows me that the people with money and power control the government or are the government and that's not right. The government doesn't care about us and have let things go to Hell in our country and we're about fed up with 'em." His face was flush with anger. The other newcomer, the one with the long, sandy hair, Collin, grabbed his hand and nodded his agreement.

Collin continued, "We were climate refugees. We used to live along the coast of North Carolina but had to relocate when it became too dangerous."

"So, what are you going to do about it?" the even voice of Joseph Kaplan asked.

"The time has come," Zach answered, "we need to take back our country! And I don't mean by running somebody for Congress, either. We need to take back what's been stolen from us and all of the American people."

Had he said he was an alien from Mars, the room could not have been more stunned. To add to their shock, the first one to speak was Jenn herself. "He's right," she said. "What I've seen over the last week has made me sick and it has to change. My daughters need a future." Ellen and Steph stared; so did everyone else in the room. Slowly, a few of them began to nod in approval of her words.

Years of frustration were clear in their faces. All of them had lost people to drugs or violence or prison. They had watched loved ones suffer and even die from lack of health care. Across the country and around the world, global climate change had caused crop failure and famine on a massive scale, trumped only by the wars that followed as countries fought over the limited resources. Too many jobs now were meaningless and left people in poverty or teetering on the brink of disaster.

Politicians had destroyed local institutions and leveraged existing divisions among people to benefit themselves. Their elected officials existed in a moral desert without any sort of social conscience. Business leaders had been consumed by greed. America had become a house divided and for many people, the feeling of helplessness was at a tipping point.

Jenn could feel Tom's eyes on her. Almost afraid to learn what he was feeling, she turned slowly. The look of admiration on his face said everything she needed to know. He mouthed the words, "I love you," to her and raised his beer. She smiled briefly, her eyes sparkling at him, before her face returned to the look of resolve he knew all too well.

Joseph spoke up again, his voice as calm as ever. "I say again, what are you going to do about it? Are you saying you're ready to throw the bums out and take over?" Rebecca slipped her hand into his and gave him a reassuring nod.

"Yes, that's what I'm saying," Jenn replied, every bit as calm as he was. "If we don't do something now, my girls may not see my age and that's unacceptable. Our government needs to be changed."

"Jenn," Lane broke in, "you're talking about treason. Do you know what that means? What kind of risk that poses to you and Tom and the girls and, well, all of us?"

"Probably not," Jenn admitted, which drew some laughs, "but in principle, I know that what we have as a government right now is broken and needs fixing. And like a cancerous tumor, sometimes the only solution is to cut out the bad cells and kill it off. Then we can start over. My girls will have a future."

"Holy shit," Brett said, "that's what I've been saying!"

Scott laughed at him. "Man, I've heard you say a lot of things, but this ain't been one of 'em."

Brett's face flushed hot at the rebuke, but he continued. "Yeah, maybe, but Jenn's right. Working folks like us don't have a chance anymore and I'm willing to start working on it, the revolution, right now."

"I'm with you," said Dylan and Bella together. Everyone else in the room echoed their words.

Jenn was awestruck by the fact that it was everyone. Every. Single. One. Old, young, men, women, different races, different jobs. Everyone. "Well," she said, "OK then. Does anyone know how to start a revolution?"

She hadn't meant for her words to be funny, but the room exploded in laughter. It was absurd. They, a bunch of working class people from Middle America had decided to overthrow their government.

Chapter Fourteen

And there it was, the moment at which she had decided to do everything in her power to change the world. To overthrow the government. To commit treason. Her living room seemed so far away now.

————

After a few minutes of spontaneous fits of laughter, Jenn was finally able to regain control of herself and the group. When she got their attention, they could tell she was dead serious.

"Ladies and gentlemen," she began, "what we're talking about here is, as my brother so eloquently put it, 'treason.' For right now, I have to ask a question to this group, and no offense," she looked at the people from Tom's work, "but I don't know you. How can I trust you?"

Tom let that sink in before answering for them. "That's a pretty good question. I see what you mean. He sighed before continuing, "I can vouch for these guys." He nodded towards his co-workers. "I have had some interesting conversations with each of them and trust them completely."

Jenn looked at her husband and then back to the newcomers. "OK, that's good enough for me. Now, does anyone have any concerns about anyone else in this room?" She looked around at the somber faces. "A betrayal of this group would have serious consequences."

Again, the group was silent until Bella spoke up. "I don't want to be rude either, but can we trust the girls? I mean, they're kids."

Jenn nodded. "That's a fair question," she said. Inside she wanted to scream at Bella, but she knew that she had to build trust in the group by letting questions like this be voiced. "How about it girls?"

Steph and Anne looked at each other for a moment before Anne said, "We're both with you. After what we saw today, we have nothing to lose."

"Mom," Ellen said, her voice full of determination, "I reached that conclusion a couple of days ago, so yeah, I'm in."

Jenn shared a look with Penny. Both mothers tried, and failed, to hide their pride in their daughters. She turned back to Bella, "Is that good enough?"

Bella nodded, "Yeah, that'll do."

"OK," Jenn said, "If this thing, this revolution, is going to have a chance, we're going to have to trust each other, agreed?" Again, she got unanimous consent.

"Alright, then," she continued, "we're going to take a ten-minute break and then we're going to start planning our next moves. Steph, Anne and Ellen, I need to see you, please." The other members of the group stood and left Jenn to her business. Some visited the restroom, some got new drinks, some got fresh air outside, but all seemed somberly committed to their new cause.

Tom joined the girls in a small circle around Jenn in the corner as she knew he would. He listened quietly as she spoke, curious to know what she was going to say and how he could support her.

Jenn looked into the eyes of her daughters and smiled knowingly. "OK, girls, it's time to go to work. From what I know about revolutions, young people have always played a key role and you three are going to get that chance as well. My first job is to keep you and all of our people safe, but honestly, I don't know what's going to happen to any of us. But if you ever thought I was hard on you before, you ain't seen nothing yet. From here on out, I'm not only your mother, but it appears I'm now your commander-in-chief, too. And as such, there are times I'm going to need you to treat me like that and I'll need to treat you like other...um...soldiers, conspirators, insurgents, revolutionaries, whatever the word is. Got it? We're good?"

The girls looked back at her and nodded. Tom nodded, too. "I'm with you, babe."

Jenn let out a deep breath. "OK, first, Anne, go talk with your actual parents, this is a big decision that you'll need to make together." Anne nodded and slipped away.

"Ellen, get your digiti-do-dad," Jenn continued. Ellen shook her head slightly at the joke. Her father had coined the pet name for her digipad and it had stuck. Her favorite device was her link to the world. It was cutting edge technology that surpassed anything her family used around the house. And her parents had to poke fun at it even now.

Tom grabbed Jenn and hugged her tight. "I'm scared babe. I'm scared, but I'm with you," he whispered.

"Sorry we didn't get to talk about this alone," she whispered back, "but I was kinda busy today."

Tom laughed and hugged her even tighter. "Wow, think of the stories I could tell! My life with the head of the revolutionary forces."

She pushed him away and playfully slapped him on the chest. "Oh my God, don't call me that!" They split apart, still laughing at their exchange and wondering if anyone else had heard. They held hands while they watched the girls return and the rest of the group assemble back in their living room.

"Alright people, settle down. First, let's make sure we know each other, please. Maybe tell us your name and a bit about how you came to be in this room tonight? I'll start, I'm Jennifer Erickson, but everyone calls me Jenn..." The introductions took a few minutes, but they were important minutes. One of the newcomers, a woman with dead eyes named Jamie, choked up when she shared that her son had died needlessly. The story was all too familiar to Jenn and sharing the woman's pain built an immediate connection.

No one stepped up to question Jenn's role as de facto leader, so she put her curiosity about Jamie aside and began to move things forward. Her first move was to yield the floor to her brother.

Lane wiggled his fingers for a moment and scratched his nose, then cleared his throat and took a deep breath. "I retired as an E-8, that's a sergeant for most of you, after 20 years in the army, and the main thing I know is no one can defeat the modern army in a stand-up fight. If you're looking for a quick way to die, go for a head-on attack on any army unit. They have too many tools, like exoskeleton body armor and they will dominate the sky." Around the room Jenn could see people looking intimidated for the first time tonight. Lane continued, "Above all, they have soldiers that have incredible training and motivation. Many of them have combat experience in the ongoing war on terror and in some of the brush fire wars in South America. These guys bought the book in blood. They're not going to give up easily."

Dylan interrupted him. "Great, so what you're saying is we're going to get slaughtered really fast."

Lane sipped his beer before continuing. "Not necessarily, I thought you'd want the bad news first is all. First and foremost of the things in our favor, is that most soldiers truly love their country and swore an oath to protect it. Our biggest asset, is that there are plenty of veterans like myself who still have plenty of fight left in them, as well as training and weapons. If we can tap into that and their sense of patriotism, we have something to work with.

Also on our side is the fact that their hands will be tied because they will be reluctant to wage war on their own friends and neighbors. I doubt that soldiers will want to fire on civilians and that might be an opportunity for us. What are they going to do, launch cruise missiles against Cleveland?" That drew some nervous laughter.

"Lastly for now, I'm also willing to bet that we can play off the fact that corporations won't like the disruption of infrastructure and destruction of assets. Money is what they love and they are not going to want to give up their toys and their homes and their businesses. Anything that hinders the military at all plays to our favor."

The more he spoke, the more Jenn was amazed by her brother. Not only was he smart, but his ideas were deep and well thought out. He was talking about revolution with all of the objectivity of deciding what car to buy. He was careful to separate and clarify facts from his own opinions, which helped build trust with their new group. All the years they didn't speak now gave her a sick feeling.

Now Jamie spoke up. "OK, so it won't be a slaughter, I hope. So, what do we do now?"

Lane glanced at Ellen, "Take good notes." She nodded, so he continued. "Our best hope is to fight what we call an "asymmetric war." You know why we're still in the Middle East? Or how we couldn't win in Vietnam? Because we fought the war on their terms, not ours. If we fight by their rules, we're done, but if we can make them fight by ours, we have a chance. We work to create a national network of loosely connected cells of revolt, whose biggest asset would be that they look like everybody else. I mean, we can't be the only ones in America having this discussion, can we?" Lane looked around the room to see a mixture of people agreeing with him and people looking at him blankly. His thoughts drifted as he saw Jenn deep in thought, listening intently to his every word. She had always been this quiet, nerdy girl who thought about stuff with such incredible depth and then made great things happen. He hoped that would again be the case.

He took another drink and continued, "In the army, we tried to give the enemy more problems than they could handle at once and the simple weight of numbers should be a Hell of an advantage. The masses of people can do amazing things if we can get them pointed in the right direction. The groups can use low tech, guerrilla style attacks across the country and there's no way the military can counter all of them. The cells can share information, but should stay independent to keep operational security tight. I'm not saying it's going to be an easy victory for us, but that's our best chance."

Jenn spoke up, "In my work, we call it multiple organ failure or the much more catchy, death by a thousand paper cuts."

Ellen looked up from her digipad. "I get it. In nature, the ants always win. There are too many of them to stop."

Tom laughed first. "In my work, we just call it everything went to shit." Then everyone joined him in laughing.

Jenn took that as her cue. She began to brainstorm with the group as to how they could proceed. Ellen continued to take notes, while Steph and Anne laid things out in categories on their idea board.

They talked and argued for about 90 minutes, each member bringing forth ideas they thought would be important. Dylan brought up security, which lead to their group being called "The Book Club" and if they were ever asked, they were reading Alice Walker's *The Color Purple*. Ellen talked about cyber-security and how the high-tech world they lived in was both an opportunity and a challenge. Rebecca brought up food and supplies, which would be a challenge for large army, but then this was not a traditional army. The list was long, Jenn thought, but seemed to cover their needs.

As it turned out, Jenn discovered, planning a revolution was, on paper anyway, pretty similar to planning any other event. Her experiences in medicine and motherhood helped her listen to the ideas of her group and to ask some questions to help make their ideas even better. Her head ached, but she was already beginning to formulate plans to put their ideas into motion. She was nothing if not a fast learner.

The group seemed ready to call it a night, when Penny brought forth perhaps the most startling thought of all. "I hate to say it," she began, "but for all intents and purposes the Bob Wrights of the world are the government. It's like a snake with a bunch of heads, you can't cut off one head, they all need to go." Her voice grew in confidence as she retold her story about Congressman Frost and the recent board meeting, to the distaste of those who hadn't yet heard it.

When she was finished, Jenn waited a minute to see if anyone had more thoughts before speaking. "Well, where do we start?"

Anne spoke without hesitation. "One of the things we learned about on our Hungary project was the strike. People stopped going to work and students stopped going to classes. Could we do something like that?"

"I like it," Tom said. "It kinda eases us into things. It's a non-violent start and it helps spread our message. I bet lots of folks will follow and a general strike will shut down the city. Today's disaster at the university outraged people whether they had kids there or not. Best of all, it hits Bob Wright where it hurts. I say we try it and see where it leads."

"Do you think Bob is going to sit back and let you do that? You know he's going to fight you on it." Penny said.

"Of course not," Tom answered, "but if we have to fight, we have to fight. And if we have to take Bob as a prisoner and use him as a heck of a bargaining chip, so be it."

"Or you may have to kill him. And maybe his family, too," Joseph argued. "You may need to wipe the slate clean of all of these people."

Jenn was taken aback. She hadn't really thought this far ahead yet. "Whoa, whoa, whoa. I'm not sure I'm ready to kill civilians and their families. I realize that he's part of the problem, but isn't there a better way?"

"That son of a bitch killed my little boy, he can die and rot in Hell for all I care." Jenn's head jerked back in surprise at Jamie's blood lust.

"Look," Jenn said, "I'm a medical professional, I'm in the saving people business, not the killing part."

Lane grinned at her. "Hey, listen to me, here's how it really works. Most of what generals do is strategic planning. If you want a tactical plan, you let the grunts do it. You get me some good objectives and we'll take the heavy lifting from there."

"Yeah," her husband added, "you have the ability to see the big picture and plan and all that. I know I can't do that."

Jenn returned her brother's grin, "You've got a deal." She turned back to Penny before continuing. "As for killing everyone, let's think about that one for the time being. And, I guess, not only Bob, but Bob's family, too. How about his lackeys? Kristen and Mollie? Or Lester? Are they part of the problem or are they victims like us?" She could again sense the discomfort around the room. It was far easier to talk about overthrowing the government than it was to talk about killing people they knew.

"All right," Tom agreed, "I think we're a long way from that point anyway. "But what about the strike? Is it a go?"

"I like it," Steph spoke for the first time. "It should be pretty easy to get students to join and like skip out of school." Anne smiled and nodded as she added, "Strike/Student Walk-Out" to the board.

"I'm in," said Zach, Collin and Jamie simultaneously. Penny and Scott nodded their heads in agreement.

"Well?" Jenn asked the group. Lacking a formal structure, she simply looked around the room and hearing no objections, agreed that a strike was a good first step. Her husband, along with Zach and Collin, volunteered to make that happen, starting in the morning. At Lane's urging, Penny agreed to stay inside and spy on the company's plans.

Penny closed her eyes and thought back to her own recent conversations. She knew there was discontent at the plant, but was there even more than she suspected? It was clear now that her position in the main office kept her from some of that information and people had been more willing to share with Tom. "Yikes," she thought, "if things go really crazy, I hope the strikers realize I'm one of them, not one of Bob's people."

Jenn looked around the room and knew that it was time to call it quits. Joseph was rubbing his temples and she knew that the strikers would all need some sleep. "Nice work, everyone. I declare the first meeting of the Book Club both a success and adjourned." Most members left quietly, but Tom and his new team stayed behind to wrap up some details. Ellen encrypted files for safety without hesitation. Penny, Scott and their girls were the last to leave, their farewells far more subdued than usual. All in all, Jenn thought, it's a pretty good start.

Chapter Fifteen

Tom didn't sleep much that night. He was far too wound up over their plan of action and how it would affect his family. Next to him, Jenn rolled onto her back and began to snore lightly. How she could sleep was beyond him, but she had always had that gift. He finally gave up and crawled out of bed so as not to disturb her.

At the counter, his joints creaked when he sat down to work out last minute plans for his day. He knew Zach and Collin had gone home and begun calling coworkers they thought they could trust about the proposed strike. His job was to spread the word to other businesses and at the moment, he was stuck. How could he reach people he didn't know?

The sound of someone trying to be quiet broke his concentration. It was Steph, sneaking down the stairs. "Good morning, sweetie," he greeted her more pleasantly than he felt.

"Hey, Pops. How can Mom and Ellen sleep right now?" She got her own coffee and sat down across from her father.

"I don't know. Your mother has always been that way and your sister shows every sign of taking after her. I'm a little jealous of them right now."

"Me, too, I didn't sleep much at all." Steph smiled at her father and blew on her coffee. She could see he was making notes about something. "What are you working on?"

"Trying to figure out how to expand the strike idea and it's not going well. I can't figure out a way to spread our message like we need to. The government's people in the media won't spread it and their "anti-terrorism" programs shut down those messages most other means I know of. Short of running down the street shouting my message, I can't figure out how to do it."

Steph could see the concern and frustration on his face. "Pops, I don't think you can run quite that far. Me, yeah, but you? No." Her father shook his head with a chuckle. "But maybe," she continued, "we can like beat the system. Last night, Anne and I used the Indigo social platform to get messages out to our friends then to their friends and from what I can tell now, school is going to be a pretty lonely place today."

Tom looked at his daughter without fully getting what she was saying. "Good work, sweetie, but how does that help solve my problem?"

She crinkled her nose at him. "Don't you see? Today's message is simple, we'll just like have our friends tell their parents not to go into work today. They can all like call in sick or something. That's believable enough, right?"

Now Tom got it. There was always some way that the kids had to communicate that their parents didn't understand. In his youth, he had used social media to plan parties or get into trouble, but now, his daughter was proposing to use it for something good. Times really had changed. "OK, but can't the government shut it down?"

Steph sipped at her still too hot coffee before speaking. "Of course, but it's really not like on the radar of most adults and so it's really not something they're onto. And as of late last night, our messages were working like they always do."

"OK, then. That's great thinking. Can you make that happen with your friends? Tell them to spread it far and wide? Just the strike, though, not the whole revolt?"

"You mean Book Club!" she said with a wink. "Yeah, I'm on it." She took another big sip of coffee so she wouldn't spill and slipped quietly back up the stairs.

Tom rubbed the stubble on his face and stared out the window at the sunrise. It was red, an ominous sign for old sailors, he remembered; he wondered what it meant for him and his family.

His mind drifted to his girls. They were normal, great kids, he thought, all he could ever want in life. Through genetic engineering, a number of diseases had been eliminated and modern science had made it routine to create designer children. He knew plenty of people who had picked out the physical traits of their kids although he and Jenn had decided against that route; it seemed unnatural to both of them. He had actually cried when both girls had been born, not something he did every day.

They had tried to raise the girls to be good people. Not that he and Jenn were in the running for parents of the year, but they tried their hardest. It was every bit as hard as when he was a kid and maybe more so with the way the world worked now. They were turning into reasonable young adults and they gave him hope for the future. "Damn," he thought, "I was hoping my biggest worry would be boys, now we have this."

Steph returned a moment later. "I'm not sure who's up and getting them yet, but the first messages are out."

Tom got up and hugged his daughter. "Thanks, honey, I appreciate it. For your hard work, you can take the day off from school."

"Gosh, thanks, Pops." She headed back towards the stairs. "And since I don't have to go to school, I think I'll go back to bed."

Tom watched until she was out of sight, sensing the grin on her face even without seeing it. With a sigh, he got down to business and packed a lunch before leaving Jenn a message on the house computer and heading off to the plant.

The drive to work seemed like any other day as he drove the old mini-van to the plant. He chose a parking space two blocks away, facing away from the plant for a quick getaway, just in case. And after today, he figured he'd never get it out of the company parking structure anyway. He chuckled to himself as he contemplated how his thinking was already changing.

Tom reached the plant to be greeted by Zach and Collin, already sitting on a bench with energy drinks in their hands. Several empty cans already littered the ground below them. Their bloodshot eyes and unkempt hair told him they hadn't slept much either. They took turns explaining what they had done overnight and let him know that things were progressing nicely. In the back of their vehicle, they had assembled dozens of signs for people to carry. Ten minutes later, Jamie arrived, bringing with her coolers of water and signs of her own. A few words later, they were approaching the gate ready to take the revolution's first step.

They knew most of the security personnel and hoped there wouldn't be too much trouble with their strike, but this was all new to them. The guards looked at them through the fence and Tom could see one speaking into a telephone. Overhead, Tom thought he saw the security camera move a bit in their direction, but he wasn't sure. The guards did not, however, even leave their shack to talk to them, which left him perplexed. He shrugged his shoulders; at the moment, he had other things on his mind.

A trickle of new protesters turned into a flood as people arrived at what would have been their usual work time. While most workers grabbed signs or had their own, a few people, mostly from the office side of the company, went into work. Tom had not expected 100% participation, but he figured they were running about 75% and he was overjoyed with that. Without production workers nothing would get made, including money for the Wright family. As Penny walked past chatting with a friend, Tom knelt and retied his boot, not trusting himself to even talk with her.

The number of strikers was boosted by a good portion of the night shift workers who joined in as soon as they exited the gates. By 9:00 AM, several hundred marching, chanting protesters surrounded the entryway.

Tom's omniphone vibrated and he was greeted by Steph's smiling face. "Pops! The word is spreading and the strike looks like it's on across the city! People are like really upset about the shooting yesterday. They closed our school since there were so few kids there. And even better, like almost no teachers showed up!"

Tom closed his eyes for a moment. It was working. Well, the first phase anyway. He was still not entirely sure how the strike and then the revolution would proceed, but for now it was working as planned. "Thanks, Steph. I appreciate the update and your work."

"You're welcome, Pops. I have to go, we're going for a run. Be careful out there!"

"Thanks. Love you!" Tom ended the call and returned to the picket line. The workers were in pretty good spirits for now, their mood buoyed by the bright sunshine. Every chance he got, he spoke to individuals or small groups and was gratified to learn there was support for a broader action. At first he was shocked, these were real people with jobs and families and things to risk. It didn't take long, however, to find that nearly everyone had the same frustrations and fears about the future that he did and wanted to change their country.

Noon brought a lull in their excitement. The sun had disappeared behind some thick clouds and most of the strikers had stopped for lunch. Nothing was organized, but like Tom, many of them had lunches from home and shared with those that didn't. Tom sat on the ground with his fellow Book Club members to hear that they, too, had found great support among other workers.

His attention was drawn to a group of people walking towards the gate with Robert Wright in the lead. He was closely followed by his Security Director, the Director of Human Assets and four armed security guards. He didn't know most of them, but still he knew this couldn't be good. As calmly as he could, he packed up his lunch box and forced himself to his feet. His back cracked as he stretched it and turned to face the boss. Jamie, Zach and Collin stood at his side with dozens of his fellow strikers in a semi-circle behind them.

Robert Wright reached the gate and looked through it at Tom. "I understand that you four are the leaders of this illegal work stoppage, is that correct?" His voice was full of anger and condescension.

"Yes, yes we are," Tom replied. "We are exercising our rights to non-violently protest yesterday's shooting at the university. Until this company uses its influence for good and makes some changes to treat workers better, work here will stop." Tom wasn't wearing a $15,000 suit, but he spoke with unmistakable conviction.

"Is that a fact? Well, let me tell you this. You four are hereby fired. As for the rest of you," his voice became a shout, "anyone not at their work station in one hour will also be fired. Anyone still outside these gates protesting may face worse consequences." He glanced up at the sky as a few fat drops of rain began to fall on him. He nodded curtly to Tom before turning on his heel and leading his crew back to the building.

Behind him, the crowd buzzed with nervous excitement as word of Wright's order spread. Tom wasn't entirely surprised by their firing, but hearing the words still came as a shock. He looked at Jamie, Zach and Collin, all of whom had a look of resolve on their faces. "And so it begins," he said.

Tom let the crowd discuss their options for ten minutes before he stood up on a bench to address them. He was again incredibly thankful for Jenn, who had coached him on answering some questions she knew would come. "Ladies and gentlemen, you have heard Bob Wright's threat. I know you're scared about losing your job and what that means, but we have to stand together. I have already been fired as have several other people here. I know it will be hard, but many of you have already said you want to do your part for a better future for yourselves and your children. We owe it to our kids to do whatever it takes to make things change!" Tom was shouting and he knew his words were being relayed to those in the back. He could see some animated gestures and hear angry conversations all around him.

Finally, a voice rose up with a question. "What if I want to go in and work? Are you going to stop me?"

Tom couldn't see who asked it, but he knew the question was on a lot of minds. "No," he shouted, "we're not going to stop you. Our problem is with the Bob Wrights of the world, not with you. If you think that going into work is a better choice than standing up for your family, we won't stop you."

"What are we going to do to eat? To live?" another voice asked.

"We will have to learn to share and to live with a little less. There has to be some sacrifice from all of us. Remember your history lessons! Whether it was Washington's army at Valley Forge or food rationing during World War II, people have always sacrificed. I know the future may be scary, but if we stick together, we can make it a better future for all of us!"

Tom looked down at the faces in the crowd. Some he knew, some he did not, but nearly all of them were turning to looks of determination. He made his final plea. "People, a lot of you know me. I've worked with some of you for a long time. I've sweated alongside you and bled and called Bob Wright every name in the book. I never thought I'd be doing this, not in a million years. But you all know what happened to my family the other night and some of you know that my wife was caught up in yesterday's shooting. Every one of you here has been screwed over by Bob Wright and by his kind and by a government that has simply given up and sold out. The time has come to change how things are done in our country. America is a big idea, big enough for all of us and whatever differences we may have, but we have to be willing to fight for it! Our little part starts right here, right now! We are going to hit Bob Wright where it hurts and make people listen!" With that, he jumped down and picked up a sign.

The crowd was silent for a moment before bursting into cheers and applause. Tom couldn't believe it. He had meant every word he had said, but he had never imagined a reaction like this. People shook his hand and clapped him on the back. The energy that had been lost over lunch had returned with a vengeance that even the light rain couldn't diminish.

At the stroke of 1:00, the company group returned, this time with Lester Hatch in the lead. "Of course it's Lester," Tom thought, "he's always been Bob's right-hand weasel."

Tom and his crew waited patiently and watched with interest as the security gate opened about a foot. Lester did his best to look Tom in the eyes before speaking. "Anyone wishing to return has five minutes to be at their work station."

A dozen strikers caved in and slipped past Tom and through the gate. None of them would make eye contact with him and most kept their eyes glued firmly on the ground. Boos and catcalls were hurled at them from behind, but stopped quickly when Tom turned and held up his hands. "Remember, people," he shouted, "our issues are with Bob Wright and the company leadership, not the workers here. We all face tough choices and I choose to focus my energy on those who have been at the root of our problems for years." The crowd was silent for a moment, then cheers and applause rang out again. Tom turned to face Lester through the now closed and locked fence. The two men looked at one another with mutual loathing.

"Those people will keep their jobs, the rest of you are fired," Lester said. "Now, you are on Wright company property and must vacate the premises immediately or face the consequences."

Tom looked Lester in the eyes and wordlessly crossed his arms in defiance. While he couldn't actually see the others, he could hear arms being crossed behind him. Simply knowing he wasn't alone gave Tom courage. "So be it," Lester concluded. He turned and led his group away without another word.

Tom remained silent as he watched them leave. When Lester was out of sight, Tom and the strikers resumed their protest with more enthusiasm than ever. Their chants grew louder and louder, rising to the point where they drowned out the other sounds from the area. His first warning of danger was when some of the chanting from the edge of the protest became screams. Tom again jumped up on the bench to get a better view over the strikers and their signs.

At the far edge of the crowd was a large group of rough looking men armed with bats and pipes. Tom looked around to see similar groups attacking from different directions, trapping the protesters between the armed men and the plant's fence. The other group, identifiable by their red armbands, had to be Bob Wright's men; the 'consequences' Lester had warned them about.

Tom's anger took over without thinking. His strong hands clenched in rage around his sign when he realized there wouldn't be a peaceful way out of today's situation. He cupped his hands together and yelled at the top of his lungs, "Fight back! Get 'em! Fight through and get away!"

He ripped the cardboard sign off and held the stake as a weapon. All around him he could see men and women doing the same thing.

Tom waded into the melee, helping other strikers as best he could. A well-placed punch dropped one man and several others he grabbed and threw off his people. All around him punches and kicks were being delivered by both sides. Clubs and pipes met stakes, the loud, violent crashes mixing unevenly with screams of pain and anger. He couldn't tell who was winning the battle. Between the hundreds of his fellow protesters and hundreds of Bob's goons, it was too big for that, so he kept his focus on what was right in front of him.

As he neared the edge of the protest, Tom saw two thugs kicking a woman on the ground. He pushed his way past a pair of struggling men and approached them from behind, swinging his stake at the head of the closer man with all his might. While not a large man himself, Tom had spent his entire life working physical jobs. As a result, the stake made a satisfying 'thunk' as it struck the man over his right ear. The man staggered and fell face first to the ground unconscious.

The second, bigger man looked angrily at Tom and rushed at him with a length of lead pipe held high. Tom held his ground before he jump-stepped to his right. The man's pipe swung down hard, missing him by less than an inch.

Tom could hear the man grunt as the pipe hit the concrete below and vibrated out of his hands. Tom again swung with all his might and broke his stake across the man's broad back, dropping the big man to his knees with a cry of pain. Tom delivered a kick to the man's left ear and watched him go down without another sound.

Tom dropped what was left of his stake and knelt down to help the injured woman to her feet. Her nose looked broken and her lip was bleeding, but she managed to smile at him and say, "Thanks."

Tom dragged her past the two downed men and pushed her towards the empty street beyond. "Run! Get out of here!" he commanded. The woman turned and spit blood on one of her attackers before stumbling off and allowing Tom to return to the fight.

He stood on his tip-toes to try and get a better look. He could see a few people laying on the ground and it looked to him that his crowd was shrinking as they escaped the thugs, but it was still hard to tell for sure. Through the rain, Tom could make out another man approaching, this one carrying a metal baseball bat. Empty handed, Tom turned to face him, crouching as he let the man make his move. The lefty swung hard at Tom's head, but gave Tom plenty of time to duck under the swing and step closer to the man. His heavy work boot connected with the side of the man's knee and he went down screaming, grasping at his shattered limb. Tom ignored the screams and helped himself to the man's bat.

Not far away, Tom spotted Zach and Collin standing together protecting some people behind them with bats they had also captured from Bob's thugs. He waded back into the thinning crowd towards his friends and helped a few more of his people with their fights along the way. As he gave another man a blow to the kidney with his bat, he sensed the thugs were losing steam, which certainly made his job easier.

He reached the pair to find both men bloodied, but still ready to fight until they recognized him. Behind the two men, Jamie sagged under the weight of an injured man she was trying to support. The blood streaming from her forehead had mixed with the rain and covered her face and chest. "Well," she said, "you said there'd be sacrifices."

"Yeah, no shit," he said as he grabbed the injured man and helped carry him away. Together they made their way towards the edge of the crowd, where Tom paused to look back. It was finally clear that the fighting had ceased. The only strikers left in the area were laying on the ground not moving. Most of the attacking thugs were now struggling for breath or holding their wounds, with a few still on the ground.

On the far side of the parking lot, a police car arrived, lights and sirens going strong. Tom recognized Officer Walker when he emerged from his car, but was stunned to see him walk past a knot of thugs and put handcuffs on an unconscious striker. He let his arm slip off the injured man and took a step towards the police before Zach stopped him. "Tom! You can't help them now. There are going to be a lot more cops here in a minute and they're on Wright's payroll, too. We have to get out of here!"

Two more police cars and a van proved him right and Tom could only watch as his fellow strikers were dragged into custody. Zach and Collin led the escape from the plant and they tumbled into Tom's van. With a heavy heart, Tom told the van's auto-drive to get them to Zach and Collin's. They watched silently as more police cars passed them headed to the plant. Round One of the revolution had not ended as planned.

Chapter Sixteen

It didn't take long to reach Zach and Collin's apartment. Once inside, they examined their wounded colleague, a new hire that nobody knew, and were relieved to find his wounds were relatively minor. He was now resting on a sagging couch in the living room as Tom and the others sat in the kitchen, holding ice to some of the bigger bruises. Tom had helped clean up their wounds, but the gash on Jamie's forehead needed stitches, which was far beyond his abilities. He bandaged it as best he could and made plans to go back to his house to let Jenn work on her.

The morning's sprinkles had turned into a summer downpour as they hurried to the car. "I guess the old sailors were right," Tom thought to himself remembering the early morning. It seemed so long ago already.

The car had driven about six blocks when, when Tom's omniphone rang. He looked down in surprise to see Scott's hologram. "What's up, buddy?" he answered.

"Hey man, I need to warn you two!"

"What's going on?"

"You can't go home. The police are already at the house waiting to arrest you and anybody else with you. They know you guys were in charge and know you're probably coming here. Penny called me to pass on the warning."

"Holy shit!" Jamie looked over at Tom, who was looking back at her wide-eyed.

"Yeah," Scott replied. "She says it was crazy there today. She said...oh my God, what happened to you?" He finally noticed that Jamie had blood soaking through a thick bandage on her forehead.

"Sorry, buddy," Tom said, "but we have to go. Jenn will know where. Be safe, we'll call when we can."

He ended the call and looked at Jamie. "If they're waiting at my house, they're probably tracking our phones, too. You need to power your phone off and right now."

Now grasping what Tom was getting at, Jamie said, "Phone, power off."

"Good, thanks," he said. "Vehicle," he commanded, "turn off auto-drive and deactivate GPS systems. Phone, call Zach."

His mind began filling with thoughts about their crazy new life. They were wanted criminals now. The police had been at his house! It was so outrageous he had difficulty staying focused on his driving.

Zach's number rang until it went to his message center. Tom tried Collin's number next. No hologram appeared, but a voice answered, "Mr. Erickson, this is the police. We have your friends in custody and we urge you to turn yourself in immediately."

"Shit!" Tom said. "Phone, power off!" He knew the police were tracking his omniphone's signal. Hell, they were probably already on their way. He needed some time to think and regroup, but time was one thing he didn't have. Inspiration struck and he drove to park a few miles away where he and Jenn had gone a few times when they were dating.

After weaving deep into the park past the Wright Pavilion and stopping in a secluded area. "Shit, this is happening too fast."

"My place is probably being watched, too," Jamie said.

"Yup, I'm sure it is." He closed his eyes, rubbing his hands on his widow's peak. "We're going to Lane's farm. Most people don't know he's reconciled with Jenn. That may buy us some time. We've talked about going there in the event of an emergency, like after a tornado. She'll know."

Jamie looked in the night. She imagined they were the only vehicle in the park, it was impossible to tell. Sheets of rain chased one another across the open spaces revealed only by the flashes from the sky. They stuck out now and that was terrifying.

Tom was thinking the same thing. "We need to get out of here. I don't like being this exposed."

"You're right. Think we can get to Lane's?"

Tom frowned at the thought. There would be police looking for them across the city, cameras, too. He had to think! Of all the things Jenn had taught him over the years, stopping to think was perhaps the most useful.

After a moment that dragged on forever, he got out of the van and walked to the front bumper. Jamie squinted to watch through the rain as he smeared mud on the license plates. She smiled, that would limit any camera's ability to identify and track them. Tom repeated his work on the rear plate before getting back in and wiping his hands on the seat. "I hope the rain don't wash it off too fast," he said as he started back out of the park.

They drove for a while in silence, each alone with their thoughts, until Tom ordered the radio to a local news radio station to break the monotony of the windshield wipers. They were forced to listen to several commercials before the news came on, including an employment ad for their own former employer before a female newscaster began her report. "Across Des Moines, a number of companies were hit with a series of illegal strikes by workers demanding a response to yesterday's riot at Des Moines University. In addition, local schools were closed as students staged a walk-out in support of the strike. Exactly what the protesters were hoping to accomplish is still not clear, however. The strike did shut down multiple local employers and at the Wright Security Systems plant, violence broke out as the strikers refused to leave company grounds and then attacked unarmed bystanders. Order was eventually restored by the police, but not until after many injuries were reported. Police have an undisclosed number of the strikers in custody and are closing in on the other criminals," she concluded.

Tom shook his head and ordered the radio off. "Make a note," he said to Jamie, "we need to fix the media, too."

She snorted and felt her bandage. "Yeah, no shit. I don't know about you, but I didn't see a lot of unarmed bystanders or the police restoring order."

"I'm pretty convinced the news people are allergic to the truth."

Jamie exhaled deeply and shook her own head. "On another note, where did you learn to fight like that? Holy shit."

"I grew up in a pretty tough neighborhood in St. Paul. I got into a lot, and I mean a lot, of fights when I was a kid. My grandpa always said you have to stand up to bullies, so… I got this," Tom paused to point to an inch-long scar above his right eye," in a brawl on St. Patrick's Day."

"Your grandpa? What did your parents say?"

"I barely knew my parents, actually. They were shot and killed when I was three, so my grandparents raised me."

"Oh, I'm so sorry to hear that. And to dredge up those memories for you."

"It's OK. You couldn't have known. Believe it or not, I got hit, too" Tom pulled up his shirt sleeve for enough for her to see a scar and a tattoo above it saying simply "RIP Tom & Stephanie – 12/3/13."

"Oh wow. I'm so sorry. I know how much something like that hurts."

Tom reached over and patted her on the knee. "Yeah. I know you do."

Jamie nodded and drifted back to her own thoughts as she let Tom concentrate on driving through the rain and darkness, doing nothing that would draw extra attention to their vehicle. How he could drive at all was beyond her, she could barely make out the far end of the headlights.

Silently, relief swept over Tom when Jamie dropped the subject. His grandfather had become a sore point in his life. For years Tom had tolerated his grandfather's open racism, even getting into fights based on those beliefs. Tom was never allowed to have friends who weren't white, even going so far as to move when a Hispanic family had moved into their neighborhood. But when he had called Jenn a 'half-breed' and wouldn't welcome her into his home, Tom had severed all ties with him. The last time they'd fought about Jenn, the taut veins on the old man's fists had resembled rivers on a map of the world. Tom had stormed out and not spoken to him since. The old man never got to see his beautiful granddaughters. Tom had gone to his funeral alone, standing alone in the back of the chapel, not shedding a single tear.

The drive to Lane's farm that normally took 45 minutes now took closer to 90. The rain had turned into a severe thunderstorm, which Tom enjoyed even more than he usually did when it helped redirect his attention from his grandfather. He turned the headlights off as they eased into the farm's long driveway and stopped under a massive maple tree, angrily shaking from the wind a hundred yards from the house. The same weather conditions that had been their ally a few minutes ago were now conspiring against them. The jagged slashes of lightning gave them frequent, brief glimpses of the house and other buildings, but it was impossible to be sure of anything. After ten minutes of waiting and peering into the dark, all they were sure of was that there were no lights on inside the house.

Jamie shrugged and threw her hands up. "Man, I got nothin'."

"Yeah, there could be a thousand cops out there and we'd never know. Shit!"

Neither was completely sure, but finally agreed they had no choice but to go forward. Tom kept the headlights off as they approached the old farmhouse. He turned the van around before putting it in park.

"I'll go up to the house," he said to Jamie. "You get into the driver's seat and be ready to get the Hell out of here if it's a trap." Jamie nodded. "We'll know pretty quick either way," he added before taking a deep breath and exiting into the rain. Jamie crawled over into the driver's seat and peered into the darkness as Tom approached the house and began to climb the three steps to the porch.

Tom cringed as the top step creaked under his weight, unsure if the rain masked the sound or not. Another flash of lightning lit up the sky and the house shook under the weight of the thunder as he took the final step up. Before he could take another step, a man stepped out of the shadows. All Tom could see was the silhouette of a man and the shiny barrel of a gun leveled at his chest.

Chapter Seventeen

Tom's heart went from pounding like a snare drum to a complete stop. He silently raised his hands over his head as he looked up at the man.

"Tom? Get in here!" Tom's heart started again when he recognized Lane's deep voice and watched him lower his weapon. He stepped forward under the porch roof and wrapped his arms around Lane in a giant bear hug.

"Oh my God am I glad it's you!" Tom said in Lane's ear. He held onto his brother-in-law for a moment, allowing the fear and anger to leave his body. He could also feel Lane's retrievers, Spark and Smudge, nudging his legs, their tails wagging in excitement.

The men separated and looked at one another. Tom finally broke the silence, "Jamie's in the car. We had to get away from the city after today's fun." He leaned down and scratched each of the dogs behind the ears. "Good to see you guys, too."

"Yeah, I saw that on the news, bunch of crap. We better get your car hidden. There's no telling how long it'll take those dumb bastards to come looking for you out here." He reached back into the house and grabbed a rain coat, which he offered to Tom.

"No," Tom said, "I'm already soaked, you might as well stay dry. Got an umbrella, though?"

Lane laughed and put on the rain coat. He stepped into the house for a moment and returned with a gray umbrella, which he handed to Tom. "Let's move your car into that machine shed over there." He pointed to a building Tom couldn't see behind the house. Tom nodded and the two men headed out into the rain with the dogs close behind. Lane banged on the hood and motioned to Jamie to follow him to the shed.

Once inside, the musty smell of dust, oil, rotting wood and stale grain swirled Tom's thoughts around in his head. He had visited a great uncle's farm so many years ago with his grandparents. The sight of an orange-brown cat stalking something in the corner made the memory come alive. "Wow," he thought, "I had completely forgotten about that place. What was the cat's name?"

Lane got his attention back on the present and together they threw a couple of old tarps over the van before moving some barrels around it. With their work done for the time being, they headed back to the house with Tom and Jamie huddled under the umbrella as Lane led them through the storm.

Inside the house, the smell changed to that of dinner coming from the oven of the large farm kitchen. Strewn across the table were tools, a book, a couple of half-dead plants and more than a few unwashed dishes. "Sorry," Lane said, "I don't have much company out here. Just me and the dogs most of the time." He hung his raincoat on the door knob before continuing. "I'll find you some new clothes, you can change in the bedrooms back there." He gestured down a short hallway past the living room.

Although Jamie swam in the oversized clothes, at least they were dry. She tied the shirt at her waist and held the pants up with both hands as they returned to Lane's cluttered living room. Both were presented steaming cups of coffee and waved to a pair of threadbare recliners. Tom sat down with a grunt in the more abused of the chairs. Spark tried to climb into his lap, but he pushed him off and reluctantly the lab curled at his feet next to Smudge, their tails thumping on the wood floor. Jamie sat down in the other chair. "Thank you. You have a great place here, it beats the Hell out of where I live."

"Thanks," Lane replied. He produced a jar of homemade whiskey and with their ready approval, added it to their cups. The house shook again from the thunder. "It looks like today got a little out of hand."

Jamie took a drink and coughed as the whiskey hit her system. "Smooth." She took another drink with more success before telling their story. "Yeah, it went all to Hell. I wasn't sure what to expect, but pretty sure arrests and bandages were not it." She continued with the details and Lane listened without interrupting. Jamie was rather shocked by that; most of the men she knew couldn't wait to talk over her. "What I want to know," she concluded, "is how the Hell Bob Wright was able to get together that kind of mob with that little time?"

"Maybe he has spies, too?" Lane answered. "With that many employees, it makes sense that somebody would be willing to tell him stuff."

Tom and Jamie looked at him in silence as the realization that he was right hit them. But who would sell them out to a man who openly abused his own employees? "Shit," Jamie said, "as if I'm not mad enough."

"We're going to have to start thinking a little differently," Tom admitted. "I don't think I was fully prepared for this. I wish I was as smart as your sister."

"Yeah," Lane agreed, "she's always been that way. And not only that, she thinks about things in ways I never imagined." He stopped talking as the dogs suddenly leaped to their feet and looked towards the door, the hackles on their necks standing on end. Lane couldn't hear anything, but he trusted their instincts. He looked at Tom and Jamie, "You two better get out of sight." He pointed back down the hallway. "If you hear it going bad out here, get out and get away, don't worry about me."

"The Hell we will! If it goes bad, we'll stay and fight!" Jamie's anger spilled over as she jumped out of her chair, nearly losing her pants in the process.

Lane looked at her with surprise. "What do you think you can do against a bunch of cops?" he asked. "Look at your head!"

Jamie looked him in the eye. "I held my own today. I got this shielding one of our guys from a guy with a pipe!"

Lane looked at her with admiration, a half smile crossing his face. "OK then, if it comes to that we can make a stand, but if it goes too bad, you got to get out of here, understood?"

She continued to glare at him. "OK," she said, "but it had better be pretty bad." With that, she and Tom slipped down the hallway into the darkness by the back door. Lane turned off the lamp and headed back to the porch with the dogs pushing their way past him.

From the shadows, Lane watched a pair of headlights creep down the driveway through the still strengthening storm. All he could do was wait, his mind racing, cradling his shotgun as the headlights grew closer. Finally, a long lightning flash lit up the yard and he smiled as he recognized Tom's old beater pick-up rolling to a stop in front of the house. He returned his shotgun to the corner and donned his raincoat again before walking to the truck. Through the rain streaked window, the relief on Jenn's face was evident as he motioned her to follow him back to the machine shed.

Jenn was forced to laugh as a blur of black fur shook rainwater all over her when she got out. "I can't tell you how happy I am to be here," she said to Lane. He nodded and shooed Smudge out of the way so he could give her a hug.

After the mandatory hugs, the girls helped him hide their truck, too. The women donned their own raincoats and backpacks before following the dogs back to the house. The first thing Jenn saw when the lights came on was Tom and Jamie waiting for them. She threw herself into Tom's arms and they held each other without a word. Jenn was now trembling from a combination of fear and elation at finding her husband safe. Finally, Tom kissed her and pulled slightly away. "Hey, babe," he said softly.

"Hey." She leaned forward and rested her forehead on his. His trembling told her he was every bit as wound up as she was.

They broke apart as Jamie nudged her and offered her a cup of coffee. She nodded when Jamie held out the whiskey. Jamie then turned to Steph, "And you?"

Jenn answered for her daughter, "No!" She didn't care about the circumstances, she was still their mother.

Jamie refilled her own cup and set the coffeepot down. "I get it," she said, "I know how a mother worries."

Jenn looked at her curiously, remembering Jamie's words from the other night until her attention was drawn to the wound on Jamie's head. "Mind if I take a look at that?" she said, pointing to the blood-soaked bandage.

"That would be great, thanks." Jenn pulled out a chair from the counter and gestured for her patient to sit down underneath the ceiling light.

Jenn rummaged through her backpack and produced a first aid kid. Out of habit, she put on a pair of gloves before gently starting her work. "Lane, can you get me some warm water and a washcloth, please? And Tom, can you hand me that garbage can, please?"

The two men did as they were asked and stepped back out of the way. Delicately, she undid the bandage and threw it away before examining the wound through the bifocal part of her glasses. Most of the bleeding had stopped, but a little blood still oozed from the wound. Jenn probed gently with her fingers. Jamie gritted her teeth, sucking in some air in pain. "Sorry, I know that hurts."

"I'll be OK," Jamie said. "I've had worse."

"Still, I'll be gentle." Jenn looked over at Ellen. "Honey, can you dig in my medical bag and get out the bio-glue, please?"

"Sure, Mom." Ellen rummaged through her bag and delivered the requested items. She stayed as close as she could and watched in fascination as her mother went to work on Jamie's head

It took Jenn only a moment to smear the adhesive ointment around and hold it closed while the bio-glue sealed up the wound. After applying a clean bandage, she declared the job done and disposed of her gloves. From her bag she pulled out some pills and offered them to Jamie. "Here are some antibiotics and some pain killers. And that's the last alcohol for tonight," she said nodding towards Jamie's cup.

"Thanks," Jamie replied. She gently felt her new scar and nodded approvingly. "Your husband put on the first bandage this afternoon. He was a lifesaver."

"You're welcome." Jenn stepped over to her husband and kissed him on the cheek. "Nice work."

Tom grinned at her. "And you thought I never listened." Behind their backs, Ellen and Steph exchanged eyerolls and pretended to vomit.

Jenn smiled back before locating her coffee. "Oh, I forgot to tell you! Casey Frost called to see if we would be his spokes-family. I told him no." She had tasted Lane's home brew before and braced herself before taking a drink.

"Mom!" Ellen all but shouted. "You told him he could shove his idea up his-" Jenn's look cut her off. Tom started to giggle as he pictured the conversation.

"In my defense," Jenn said, "I also suggested that since he has health insurance he could get it taken care of." This sent Tom and the rest of the room into gales of laughter.

When they were able to stop laughing, Jenn put her supplies away while Lane brought a small roast and vegetables out for dinner. He hadn't been expecting company, but they made due. The group sat or stood as best they were able and ate while sharing stories of their respective days. As they talked, Tom could see Jenn's mind hard at work as she tried to pull all of the pieces together. "I had some delusions that it would be possible," he said, "but after today I'm pretty sure it's not. Bob Wright and his kind own the police and the media and have the money to make whatever they want happen."

Jenn looked up from the slice of bread she was buttering. "I hear what you're saying, but we can't lose hope, certainly not this early. We need to persevere and be smarter than they are. We need to think of it like a chess game, thinking long term and a few steps ahead. That's how we're going to beat them."

Jamie cocked her head and looked at Jenn. "I've never really heard someone talk about stuff like you do. Are you as smart as these guys say you are?"

Jenn blushed. "I don't know about that. My time in medicine has helped train my brain to think about things in different ways, I guess. Sometimes you have to focus on what's right in front of you and other times you have to see a bigger picture. Right now I'm so frustrated with how I can't help people that I've decided to try and make a change. I can't bear to watch another kid suffer while I'm not allowed to help them."

Tears welled up in Jamie's eyes and her voice began to quaver. "How do you remember that? Remember him?"

"Remember what?"

"About my son, Marshall. You saw him at your clinic. He died earlier this spring. He slipped and cracked his head and there was bleeding in his brain and..." Sobs cut off the rest of her words.

Now Jenn began to tear up. "Oh my God. I'm so sorry." She shot out of her chair and hugged Jamie. The two women cried together, while the others looked at one another awkwardly and did their best to keep their own emotions in check. Lane slid a box of tissues across the table to where the women could both reach them.

Jenn blew her nose before speaking again. "I'm sorry, I guess I never connected that you were his mother. I treated him, well, I saw him, at the clinic the day he got hurt. I spoke to you on the phone, right? I'm so sorry I couldn't help you. I couldn't help him." Again, they broke down into tears. Tom had seen Jenn cry before, many times in fact, but this a side of her that he had never seen in all of their years together.

Eventually, the women cried themselves out of tears. Jamie looked Jenn in the eyes. "Thank you. I'll always remember you from that phone call. You were so kind. I know you did all you could. Those bastards killed my son, not you."

Jenn breathed in deeply and began to collect her thoughts. She stood up and looked around the room. "OK, now what are we going to do about it? I know we talked about this already, but things have changed. We need to adapt faster than they do. It's going to be uncomfortable for all of us, but we need to make them react to us."

The group moved into the living room. Not all of their members were present, but those that were had a new sense of urgency. If Bob Wright wanted a fight, he was going to get one.

Jenn let Lane take the lead in the conversation. "You know, I've been thinking about what I said the other night. About the might of the US Army? If we're going to have a chance, we need to work magic on them." He looked at Steph and Ellen. "And girls, what is magic?"

Steph looked at Ellen for an answer and was not disappointed. "It's sleight of hand or deception," she said. "The magician distracts you with one hand or something and then does the trick with the other while you're not looking."

"That's right. What we need to do is work some magic. Especially with small numbers like we have, we'll have to make them look at one spot when our real target is somewhere else."

Ellen nodded. "I think there's a parallel thought from my theater class. Illusion is a good word for it. With some work, we can make them see what we want them to see and then we can do what we need to do."

"Kiddo, you are exactly right." As he looked at Ellen, he realized that not only did she look like her mother, she was thinking like her, too.

Into the night they developed their plans, with Jenn and Lane bouncing ideas off one another and everyone chipping in when they could. After midnight, exhaustion finally won out and they went to bed with dreams of the coming battle in their heads.

Chapter Eighteen

A cold drizzle made daybreak even bleaker across Des Moines. Armed security patrolled the locked down Wright complex and grounds, paying extra attention to the employees entering the plant. Like the strikers themselves, none of corporate leadership team really knew how to manage such an event, which was the only item on their agenda. Their biggest problem at the moment was that they had fired most of their production workers and while finding people to fill those spots wouldn't be terribly hard, getting them up to speed and meeting their production schedule would be difficult.

Bob and Robert were the last to arrive, looking like they could spit nails. Mollie, Kristen and Lester, along with the Directors of Security and Human Assets, assumed their seats and waited for Bob to begin. Robert got both of them cafe au laits, allowing Bob to call the meeting to order.

"First things first," he began, "thank you all for your extra work yesterday. The hooligans were driven off and taught a lesson. And their terminations were handled with the utmost efficiency. Well done." He paused to taste his coffee before continuing. "However, we now need to look to the future. You have a plan to replace them, correct?" he asked the Human Assets Director, who nodded her assent.

"Good, good. Of more concern to me is that we need to make sure the plant is secure against any sabotage from those people and to make sure nothing like this happens again."

The Security Director took his cue, "We have done several things already, sir. We have extra security personnel patrolling the grounds and have changed the security protocols to both the plant and especially this office complex. Access to the upper floors are restricted to select retina scans only. No one who doesn't need to be up here will be."

Bob sipped his coffee. "I confess, I was pretty shaken by how many people participated yesterday after all the things I've done for them. I hope that they are done with their little tantrum and have left us to continue our good work."

"One more thing," Lester spoke up, "I have a mole inside the remaining workers. One of the night shift employees, Ricky Arroyo. He's the one who tipped us off to the strike yesterday. Without his help, we would never have had time to be prepared like we were. He's the ex-husband of

Tom Erickson's wife, so he has incentive even beyond the extra money he's getting."

Bob nodded thoughtfully. "That is good news, Lester." He paused to take a drink. "Only next time, don't hire a bunch of out of work, out of shape drug addicts to do your dirty work."

Lester felt the heat and flush of embarrassment coming over him. His head sank as he tried to hide from the others. All of his life had been a series of failures and humiliation. Latching onto Bob had been the biggest success of his life. Someday things would have to go his way. They had to! He'd suffered enough for one lifetime.

Across the table, Mollie couldn't contain her laughter, which drew a withering look from Bob. "We are in this together. We must work together to make sure we're back up and running quickly, got it?"

"Yes, sir," Mollie replied.

"OK, what's next?" Bob asked the group. "What else do we need to think about?"

Lester spoke in an effort to redeem himself. "I'm worried about Penny Stevens. I told you there was more dissent in the plant, but she downplayed it. I'm worried that she might secretly be on their side."

Mollie laughed again. "Oh, Lester, you're not serious? Penny's been with us for years and does an adequate job. I don't like her much, but I think we can trust her."

Kristen nodded and added "She's even alerted us to problems in the field. I also think we can trust her."

Robert looked at the Security Director and asked, "What do you know about her?"

The Security Director had seen this coming and was already on his computer. "One second...here we are. She's been employed here for twelve years with no major issues. Quiet, generally liked by the other workers, no known addictions or major vices, married, three kids." He looked up, "Really, she's pretty unremarkable. She does live next door to Tom Erickson, but nothing in her file indicates she's any kind of trouble maker."

"OK," Bob concluded, "we'll trust her for now, but keep a close eye on her. Anything else?" He looked around the table. "Good, now go ahead and find us some new workers."

Out on the farm, Jamie woke with a start. Whether it was the exhaustion or the lump on her head, it her took a moment to remember she was safe in Lane's house. As she gained consciousness, she realized she was in Lane's bed, where he had insisted she sleep the night before. He had slept on a couch in a spare room, while Tom & Jenn had the guest bedroom and the girls had slept in the living room chairs. The dogs had stood guard, but nothing had bothered them during the night.

She yawned and swung her feet out of bed, but had to wait for her head to stop spinning before she could even look around the room. When she could, she spied her clothes, dried and neatly folded on a chair next to the door. Careful not to move too suddenly, she dressed and followed the smell of bacon frying past the half-sleeping girls to the kitchen. Lane was already awake and had breakfast well under way when she arrived, the dogs sitting at his feet. He pointed to the coffee pot with his chin and returned his attention to his griddle full of pancakes. Jamie poured herself a cup and sat at the table, poking at her wound. It still throbbed, but the bleeding was thoroughly stopped. Steph and Ellen trudged groggily into the room and joined her at the table, all of them grateful for the lack of conversation this early.

Finally, Tom and Jenn joined them and the group ate in silence. The thoughts of their day ahead weighed heavily on everyone's minds. Only the dogs had energy, as evidenced by the pounding of their tails as their vigilant eyes searched for fallen food. When Spark nuzzled her hand, Steph broke a piece of bacon in half and dropped the halves on the floor, where they disappeared in a single bite. She looked up at Lane with a wink, "Oops, snackcident."

Ellen giggled and then spoke, reciting the newscast from memory. "The news is saying that nearly thirty protesters were arrested yesterday, some with minor injuries. All are being held without bail, including two of the ringleaders. In addition to criminal trespassing, vandalism and assault charges, the ringleaders have been charged with inciting people to riot, criminal mischief to a business, disturbing the peace and resisting arrest. The other two ringleaders are at large but police are following up on a multitude of credible leads and expect to have them in custody at any moment."

Lane glanced at the door and then back to his niece. "Ellen, is there any way they can track your computer here? Is that one of their leads?"

Ellen looked up at her uncle and grinned. "Give me more credit than that, Uncle Lane. I took the liberty of building my own digipad, so it doesn't have that nonsense. To be on the safe side, the data link-up is originating from Simone LeBlanc in Belgium."

Lane laughed and threw his hands up in surrender. "Just asking. You'd think I'd know more about this stuff by now, but I really can't keep up with it all. Man, I thought it changed fast when I was a kid."

Now it was Jenn's turn to laugh. "You should try keeping up with medicine some days. I was reading about a Japanese team working on making artificial lungs." She sighed and continued, "I suppose it's time to get down to business. I want everyone to be ready to move out in 45 minutes. We have to take advantage of this rain while we can. Any questions?"

Steph's head popped up. "I have one." She pulled a picture frame out from under the counter and set it on the table. "What in the world is this, Pops?" Jenn recognized the picture, of course, astonished that Lane had a copy of it. It was the first picture she and Tom had taken as a couple.

"What's wrong with it?" Tom asked. "See, we were young and fun once."

"Pops! What's with that beard you have going on?"

"Hey, that was very fashionable at the time." Tom felt himself getting defensive. He stroked his chin, fond memories filling his head.

"Oh, Pops, no." She burst into laughter.

"Mom, why is your hair pink?" Ellen said. "And is that a nose ring?"

"Those were called 'highlights,' it wasn't all pink," Jenn answered.

"And hey, she looked really good in those jeans," Tom said. He tried to kiss Jenn but couldn't when they both broke into laughter at how their appearance had changed.

Ellen shook her head and ran her finger over her mother's nose in the picture. "Wow."

"Alright, you've had enough fun, time to get to work," Jenn ordered.

The group split up and went about preparing for the day. Jenn and the girls changed the license plates on their vehicles with some old plates from Lane's shed before loading them with food and the few medical supplies they could gather. Meanwhile Tom and Jamie followed Lane to his personal armory. Both stopped and stared at the array of firearms before them. Neither had ever seen such a collection in a person's home before. Tom looked at his brother-in-law, "I know you said you had some guns, but..."

Lane laughed. "I guess you can never be too prepared."

"OK, then, now why don't you show us how to use these." Lane gave Tom and Jamie a quick lesson on loading and using a couple of the weapons they'd be bringing. Tom hadn't shot anything in years, but he remembered the basics. Despite never having fired a gun before, Jamie caught on quickly as Lane guided her hands into position and demonstrated how to shoot.

When Lane finished his instructions, he looked at his students. "Look, if shit goes really bad, this won't get it done against the army, their body armor is too good, but it should work for today. If you have to fire, aim for their chest and shoot until your target is down. Got it?" Tom and Jamie both nodded. "OK, good, let's get these out to the truck. It took several trips to get all of the weapons and ammunition outside, but when they were done, they had enough to equip their supporters and then some.

Despite their protests, Ellen and Steph were forced to stay at the farm. "This sucks, Mom," Steph complained, her hands pressed into her hips. "We're in this, too, you know?" Ellen stood next to her sister with her arms crossed, unable to mask her frustration with being left behind.

"Girls, look," Jenn said looking back and forth between them. "You'll both have your time to do something, it's just not today. For now, stay here and try not to get on one another's nerves too much. Got it?"

"Fine," Steph said. Inside the truck, Tom flinched at the word. He knew what it meant when Jenn said it to him; it was time to find a better place to be.

Tom and Jenn took their truck, while Lane and Jamie took one of his. Like Tom's, Lane's truck was an old combustion model, but more importantly, it also didn't have the government tracking program attached to it. With one last wave to the unhappy girls, the adults moved out.

They made their way quickly, yet cautiously, into the city and parked a block from Kaplan's Market. Once Jenn and Tom had started walking to the store, Jamie assumed the driver's seat in their vehicle. They were being careful, but was it careful enough?

Tom held Jenn's hand gently as they walked down the sidewalk. He pulled his baseball hat down low and had the collar of his coat turned up. She had wrapped a scarf around her head and held an umbrella up against the rain. They both hoped it was enough to hide their identity from any casual observer. The rain was keeping most people inside, but there were still plenty of police cameras around.

They entered the market, pleased to find it nearly empty. Joseph began to come around the counter, but a subtle shake of Tom's head stopped him and without a word, he returned to the order he was placing. Jenn casually grabbed a cart and headed back to the meat department, where Brett was measuring out packages of hamburger. Jenn looked around and then quickly led Tom through the swinging doors into the back stockroom, Brett followed.

Once out of sight, Brett was the first to speak. "Oh my God, I'm so happy to see you! From what they're saying, I thought you two would be locked up by now."

"We may be at some point, but not yet." Tom said. "Things are moving faster than we thought and we need to get ahead of it."

"I guess it's moving fast. Your picture is all over the place. Jamie's, too."

"She's waiting for us in the truck, but first we need to use your omniphone. I'm sure they're tracking ours and I need to reach some people from the plant."

Brett didn't hesitate. He peeled off his gloves and removed his omniphone from his wrist. "Here." Tom made a few calls to the people he had seen escape the day before. He asked each of those people to bring themselves and two more trustworthy folks to the plant and to be ready for it to turn violent.

While Tom recruited, Jenn brought Brett up to speed and told him their plans for the day. He interrupted numerous times, but eventually she was able to share everything. When she concluded, Brett looked at her with admiration. "Damn, that's great!" he said. "I want to stop talking and get out and actually do something, you know? What can I do to help?"

Jenn thought for a moment. "For now, stay here and be inconspicuous. We may need to hide out or to communicate like today or whatever and having someone to make that happen is going to be important." Brett wasn't thrilled, but he agreed to his new role.

They could hear Tom ending another call and turned their focus to him. "That's the last one for me," he said. "It all goes down in an hour." He looked Brett squarely in the eyes as he returned his omniphone. "Thanks."

Jenn hugged Brett before they left. They slipped out the back door and down the alley. Brett watched until the door clicked shut behind them. "Be careful."

Jenn and Tom made their way back to the trucks, again remembering to keep their heads down. Lane followed Jamie across town through the increasingly empty streets, as deep in his thoughts as Jenn was in hers on the seat next to him. A lot of the traffic in this area came from plant workers, Tom realized, and with them all gone, things were likely to stay quiet. As they neared the plant, Jamie parked close to where Tom had the day before and they waited for the others to arrive.

Fortunately for everyone's frayed nerves, they didn't have to wait long until other vehicles appeared. Soon, twenty men and three women were gathered in front of them, happy the rain had finally stopped.

With a nod from Jenn, Tom spoke to the crowd. "People, you now see what we're up against. Many of you have scars from yesterday and you've seen how far Bob Wright will go. You've seen the news and know how we're being described. Well, it's time we earn the names they're calling us. I've called you here to take over the plant by force. The time is now!"

This time, no one cheered. They nodded and stared at him. Several displayed knives or clubs of their own, while others showed him their guns. Tom's smile was grim. It was exactly the kind of crowd he'd hoped for, angry, but under control. "OK, anybody who needs a gun, see the nice man at the gate of the truck. Then we'll move out." Lane held his hand up over his head and about a dozen people went to see him, where each got one of his guns and ammunition to use in it.

Jenn stood and faced the group. "Listen up," she commanded with a fire in her eyes Tom had never seen before, "here's the plan. First, Tom is in charge of getting into the plant. Anybody have a problem with that?" She paused and waited for dissent but heard none. "OK," she continued, "we'll try and talk our way in. Tom will ask to be allowed to come in and speak with Bob Wright. If they open the gate, you'll head inside and go from there. If they don't open it, we have explosives here in the truck to blow it open if we need to. Once you're inside, you'll proceed to the administration building. Your goal is to take control of the building. I expect you'll face armed resistance from their security personnel, but you're prepared to deal with that. If you have wounded people, bring them back to me. Any questions?" Jenn paused and looked around the group, but nobody spoke up.

"OK," she continued, "along the way, you'll encounter all kinds of people. Some will want to fight you, some will want to join you, and some may make you angry. Our goal is not to hurt anyone we don't need to. By all means, defend yourselves with all the force you need, but we're not psycho killers here, people. Eventually you'll get to the big fish, Bob Wright and his people. We want them alive. I know you're angry with them and trust me, I understand that, but they're worth more to us alive than they are dead, got it?"

She looked out at the determined faces nodding at her. "Then go to it."

Chapter Nineteen

Tom gathered his force and split them into three squads. He would lead one squad and two Marine Corps veterans would lead the others. He knew it was moving too fast and not knowing exactly who or what they'd be facing didn't make matters any easier, but there wasn't time to do more extensive planning.

Lane jumped down and joined Jenn to watch Tom lead his troops off to the main gate. He'd been in too many battles to show how nervous he still got. Fear was contagious and the last thing they needed now. With their departure, the street became deathly quiet, with only the rumble of retreating thunder breaking the silence.

Tom approached the gate with his troops behind him in a semi-circle. While he was unarmed at the moment, it was impossible to hide the long guns many of the others were carrying. They arrived at the gate and pressed the button to speak with the lone guard, whom Tom had known for years. "Liam, it's Tom Erickson. I am unarmed and I want to talk with Bob Wright. My friends are armed to prevent a repeat of yesterday, but I am unarmed. What do you say, can you let me go see him?"

Liam's head was all that was visible through the protective glass in the guard house. Tom watched him lean forward to his microphone until only his straw-colored hair was visible and waited for his response. It took a few agonizing moments before Liam spoke. "I'm sorry, Tom, but Mr. Wright says to remind you that you have been fired and you are to leave the grounds at once."

"Liam, listen to me. What we're doing here is a big deal. I need to get in and talk to him. Please?"

"I know what you're doing and that it's a big deal, but you know I can't let you in." This time, Tom sensed that Liam's heart wasn't into his message.

"Liam, I know you're just a pawn in all of this. You will be safe, I promise. Our issues are with the same people yours are. Last December didn't you tell me how discouraged you were with your kids' school and your own lack of opportunity here? That's what our battle is about."

Tom watched Liam as he hung his head for a moment. He could imagine the whirlwind of thoughts running through his mind. When he picked his head up, Tom could see a strange look on his face. "No, Tom, I can't do it. My job is to make sure this plant is secured," he said. His last words were mostly drowned out by the sound of the gate opening. Tom's eyes locked with Liam's. The two men shared the moment.

Tom led the stream of former workers through the gate to the guardhouse, where Liam was already standing outside waiting. Tom shook his hand and simply said, "Thanks."

"You're welcome. I know they were listening to my talk with you, so I had to say what I did. I'm surprised they don't have a remote control over the gate, actually. In any case, they know you're inside now, they can see you on the camera." Tom glanced up and knew Liam was telling the truth.

Liam continued, "They have about four times as many guards as they usually do and they have guns, too. I'm not sure who's going to do what in there, so you guys be careful."

"OK, thanks," Tom said. He turned away from Liam and looked at one of his soldiers, as he now thought of them. "Jamie, you stay here with him and keep this gate under control. It wouldn't surprise me if Wright really does have some central command over it and I want to keep the odds in our favor." Jamie nodded and stepped up next to Liam. She desperately wanted to do more, but her head just wouldn't let her yet.

Tom turned to his group. "Now it gets serious. Be safe and let's move!" Another man handed him a black backpack and a holster with a 9mm handgun in it, both of which Tom put on before drawing his weapon.

The squads split up and began a three-pronged advance towards the main entrance to the Wright building. Several of his troops had served in the military and remembered their training. They made sure they were spread out and kept checking above and behind them for danger.

As the strikers reached the main entrance, they encountered the first resistance. Crouched down behind the low stone planters in front of the entry were a dozen armed men. Inside the doorway, in the building's reception area, he could see more lurking.

Tom raised his hand and his troops stopped. He cupped his free hand around his mouth and shouted to the guards, "Hold your fire, we want to talk!"

It took only a moment for a reply to come back, "There's nothing to talk about. The police are on their way and we will not let you pass into the building. Put down your weapons and you will not be hurt."

Tom looked at the man next to him and saw the man's black eye, which was five shades of purple. "Yeah, we're not going to do that."

The man grinned at him, "Good plan, boss."

Tom yelled again to the guards, "If you all put down your weapons, you will not be hurt. We are armed and we are going to enter that building if you want us to or not."

He pointed to his squad leaders and motioned for them to move out and flank the guards. He watched with interest as his forces began to work their way around the grounds using the building's plants and décor for cover.

"We are armed, too, and you will not be getting through our lines! We advise you to surrender and you will not be harmed." From the guard's confident tone, Tom knew there would be no talking his way through this one.

Shots rang out off to his left. Tom looked, but the heavy shrubbery blocked his view. He could hear screaming and more shots. He chambered a round, gulped hard and yelled to his troops, "Move in! Stay low and cover one another!"

Rock fragments exploded from the wall above him. The guards had also heard the shots and were opening fire in every direction. More gunfire erupted from the group on the right. He couldn't see them either and he couldn't count the shots, but it sounded like the finale of a 4th of July fireworks show. He dropped to one knee to look around the corner. The guards were currently focused on the squad on the right, who seemed to have gotten close and were attacking with everything they had. Tom took aim at an exposed guard and pulled the trigger. His shot was a clean miss and went into the wall of the building behind the man. "Damn it," he muttered, firing two more misses in rapid succession at the guard already diving out of sight. Tom, too, ducked behind the wall as more rounds hit near where he had been.

He wiped the sweat out of his eyes and tried to catch his breath. His heart was pounding like he had never felt it before. Even when he had proposed to Jenn it had not beat this hard. He took a deep breath and looked around at his troops. He still could not see the other squads, but his own group had advanced to within about thirty yards of the door. One of his men, lying in a heap on the neatly manicured grass, was not moving.

Tom swung around the wall and fired without aiming. Staying low, he made his way towards the doors, crouching behind a water sculpture for cover. He fired several rounds towards the only guards he could see and again hit nothing. Not ten feet away, another one of his troops went down, grasping his side as blood gushed out, coating the man's hand and pants. Two guards fired tear gas out into the plaza, adding to the mayhem.

Tom pulled a water-soaked bandanna from his backpack and tied it on, indebted to Jenn for preparing them for this exact situation. He stuck his masked face around the sculpture and got off one round before his gun locked open, out of ammunition. "God damn it," he said, ducking behind the statue again and inserting a fresh magazine. Now that he was closer to the building, he could hear more screaming and moaning from the wounded. He couldn't see exactly who was screaming, but it didn't matter, the sound was horrifying.

Tom paused to catch his breath and take stock of the situation. Damn it, he was so alone! How could there be this much action all around him and yet he was so alone? In that moment, he learned what soldiers in combat had been learning for centuries.

A deep breath and a shake of the head got him focused again. The first thing he realized, was that the wind was carrying the tear gas away from him and towards the troops to his left. Secondly, the shooting from the building seemed to have diminished, but frankly he wasn't sure of anything anymore. He pulled his bandanna down and watched what was left of his center squad close in on the guards.

His troops in the center and the right had good positions, but what about the squad on his left? Tom took one last deep breath before heading that direction and seeking cover behind another large planter. In front of him, three guards were exchanging heavy fire with his troops. The guards seemed not to know he was there, so Tom lowered himself to the ground and crawled forward a few yards through the sopping wet grass until he had a clear field of fire.

Lane's advice was fresh in his mind and Tom took careful aim at a guard's chest. This time, he remembered to squeeze the trigger and was rewarded by watching his target go down. He swung his gun to the right and fired at another guard, who fell to the ground grabbing his thigh. The last guard turned to run and was shot twice in the back by one of Tom's troops. Tom got to his knees and waved to his squad leader, who indicated that they were moving forward.

Tom turned his attention back to the main door, thrilled to see his other troops occupied the outside of the entrance. Two guards had their faces pressed against the wall and their hands up as his troops guarded them. Most of his other troops were aiming into the building, but were not firing at the moment.

Cautiously, Tom ran to the doorway where he took in the situation with more detail. His other squad leader was kneeling over a downed striker, a long ponytail sticking out the back of her baseball cap. She looked up at him and shook her head, her rust-colored hair flying around her shoulders. Laying on the ground were two guards who looked dead and five with varying injuries. Seven of his troops were also wounded, but only two dead so far. The glass doors that once glistened in the sun had been shattered beyond recognition. Tom stuck his head out to look through the door but jerked it back as a volley of shots came his way. He ducked back around the side and tried to think.

"Well chief, what now?" one of his troops asked. He was kneeling with a shotgun aimed towards the door.

Tom never hesitated. "Get the wounded back to the trucks. I don't care if they're our guys or theirs, if they're wounded, get 'em out of here. Jenn will take care of them. And take the captives with you."

His troops didn't hesitate to carry out his order. Three of the wounded had to be carried away, but the others were able to walk under their own power. When they had left, Tom surveyed his situation and it wasn't good. He hadn't really thought about trying to take over the building with only nine other people.

The wail of countless sirens drew his eyes towards the outside world. He couldn't see the police, but he knew by the sound that they were close to the plant. He was able to see the figures of maybe a dozen workers coming from the production plant, many of them were carrying wrenches or long screwdrivers. As they drew closer, Tom recognized several of them who had quit the protest the day before. "Well," he said to himself, "at least we have a few more bodies to work with."

Tom slipped away from the door and waved his new troops forward, careful to keep them out of the line of fire. When they arrived, Tom surveyed the newcomers. Some stared numbly at the shattered glass and bodies at their feet. Others couldn't make eye contact with him, they stood around looking at each other.

Tom squinted his eyes, recognizing the problem. "Welcome, people," he said, "I'm glad you could join us. I know some of you feel embarrassed by walking out yesterday, but that was then and this is now. We are now one force and together we'll make the changes we all know are needed." He was relieved to see more eyes looking up and he smiled directly at those individuals.

After a nervous glance back at the doorway, Tom returned his attention to his new members. "OK, we are going to be taking over the central building shortly. Look around and grab whatever guns and ammo you can. Theirs, ours, I don't care, just go find 'em. If you can't find a gun, that's OK. We'll have plenty of jobs for everyone, but let's start with that. I'll see you back here in five minutes." The newcomers nodded and scattered around the grounds as ordered.

As Tom waited, two of his people returned from delivering the wounded to Team Jenn. One set a basketball sized box at his feet and took a step back. "This is for you. That Lane guy said you'd know what to do with it."

"Excellent," Tom replied, "right on schedule. Did he and Jamie leave yet?"

"No, sir, not yet. They were staying to help with the more seriously wounded first. Two of our people also stayed behind to help. Where are they going?"

"Sorry, but I can't tell you that. Operational security." Operational security was something Lane had started beating into his head and he was taking it seriously. The man grunted his response.

"What else can you tell me from back at the gate?" Tom asked him.

"Not much. We handcuffed the two guards to a post for the time being. Your wife had her medical stuff all ready to go when we got there. The gate was locked again, which was good because there's a lot of angry cops outside. Our guys at the gate are using old man Wright's own security to keep them bastards out!"

"All good news, thanks," Tom concluded.

The man shocked Tom by saluting and then taking a position near the corner of the building. While Tom now considered them "his" troops, he wasn't quite prepared for a real salute. He shook it off and tugged at the arm of one of his squad leaders. "Emma, this is a bomb my brother-in-law cooked up. He said he made it with 'stuff he found around the farm.' Does that make any sense to you?"

The red-haired woman knelt down and examined the bomb for a moment. "Yes, sir, it makes a lot of sense. Part of my training was in IEDs, improvised explosive devices, and this looks to be a pretty good one." She motioned Tom down closer. "Smell this." Tom stuck his nose out and inhaled deeply, only to cough and pull back at the biting smell.

"You can make a fucking bomb out of ammonia and diesel fuel and that's what we have here. Looks like we hit the ignition button, chuck it in there and we have about 10 seconds to get our asses under cover. Whoever built this knew what he was doing, I'll say that."

"Wow, I may have to give that boy some more credit," Tom thought to himself. "You ready to do this?" he asked.

"Yes, sir," she replied, but at least she didn't salute him, Tom was happy to see. "And sir? I don't know exactly how big this explosion is going to be, so when I start running, try to keep up."

Tom stood upright to issue his orders. "OK, people, get away from the building and find some cover. On my signal, I want a couple of you to open fire in there and give us some cover. Emma will ignite and deliver the bomb on my order. Once it blows, in we goes. Got it?" He watched as the order was passed around and his people pulled back away from the doorway. Shawn, his other squad leader, directed them into defensive positions and posted lookouts to the rear.

Tom and Emma stood outside the shattered doorway. Tom again cupped his hands around his mouth and shouted into the building. "This is Tom Erickson. If you come out with your hands up, you will not be harmed. If you do not, we are prepared to take the building by force. Come out with your hands up!"

"No chance in Hell, Erickson!" a voice shouted back. "We have the position here and there's no way you can get us out! It's not too late to surrender yourselves to the police."

Emma shook her head. "Now?" she mouthed silently.

Tom's upturned hand signaled she should wait and he returned his attention to the guards. "Look, we have the means to take this position by force. You've seen what we can do. We don't want to hurt you, but if that's your choice, we will. You have 'til the count of ten to come out with your hands up!" He began to count in his head.

"Screw you, Erickson! You can't get through here!"

Tom's counting reached eight and he looked at Emma, who nodded she was ready. She had knelt down next to the door frame and had her thumb poised over a silver button on the side of the bomb. Without looking back, Tom raised his arm and quickly brought back down. Shawn and three others opened fire with their rifles through the doorway into the building. Emma pressed the button, heaved the bomb around the corner and jumped to her feet in one motion. "Run!" she yelled as she sprinted away from the building.

The whole sequence was so peculiar to Tom. In part of his brain it was all in slow motion and in another it was happening too fast for him to process. In the real world, he reacted quickly and was right behind Emma as she dove behind one of the planter boxes. Tom hurled himself down next to her, covering his head with his arms.

The force of the explosion caught everyone by surprise. The few remaining panes of glass around the entryway blew out, raining glass down on the plaza as a fireball shot out of the doorway. Tom was still trying to understand what had happened, when he realized Emma was already on her feet. "Let's go!"

She ran into the building with half a dozen other troops. Tom shook his head to clear it and stood up, looking around to see if any of his people had been hurt in the blast. No one he could see was injured, but most were yawning, trying to clear their ears. Acknowledging they were safe, Tom drew his pistol and ran to what was left of the doorway. What he saw inside appalled him.

The bomb had blown away the security desk, leaving the splintered structure no longer recognizable. Toxic smoke rose from the smoldering furniture, now strewn about the lobby, a far cry from its normal, orderly state. Water streamed from the building's sprinkler system, already working to put out the resulting fire. Worst of all, more than a dozen bodies were visible around the room, either dead or severely wounded.

Chapter Twenty

The sound and fury of the explosion caught Jenn off guard, even hundreds of yards away. She was suturing the leg of a wounded guard when the explosion rocked the compound causing her to instinctively cover her patient. He eyes rose from her work towards the Wright Building. "Please be OK. Please be OK," slipped from her lips.

She was alone now, more alone than she'd ever been. At Lane's insistence, he and Jamie had sneaked out the loading dock in a delivery truck for their part of today's mission leaving Jenn to do her best. Their departure had left her with Liam and a few others who were now more focused on the growing number of police outside the gate. Jenn's truck now stood as a barricade, reinforcing the locked gate. They all knew it would only be a matter of time before the police tried to retake the plant.

From the acrid smell to the shouts of the police to the bright red blood on her gloves, it was becoming more real by the minute. Jenn swallowed hard and returned to her patient, who was writhing in pain. "Hang in there. It'll be OK," she said, unsure if she was talking to him or herself.

———

High above the battle, Bob Wright sat with his son in the security office, watching a bank of video monitors showing images from the shattered lobby. He felt physically secure up here in the shelter of his office, but still he was uneasy. His anger was flavored with a something new for him-fear. In all of his life, he'd never been physically threatened. He'd faced down competition and dealt with some shady business partners in his time, but never had he been physically attacked. Robert nudged his arm and pointed to a different camera which showed a stream of police vehicles arriving at the gate. Bob nodded and breathed a sigh of relief.

———

Penny stood next to Mollie, Kristen and Lester, watching the battle below through the conference room window, powerless to do anything about it. Penny could feel Mollie shaking, either from fear or rage, she couldn't tell which. Powerless was not something Mollie or Kristen were used to feeling.

Lester spoke without taking his eyes off the situation. "Well, I told you they were upset. This doesn't surprise me in the least. But I'm sure our internal security measures will keep them at bay until the police can drive them out."

Kristen turned to stare at him. "You'd better be right about that! Who knows what those people would do to us!"

Any further conversation was cut off by a sudden explosion below which shook the building, even this high up. Mollie screamed out loud and clutched at Penny's arm. Penny hoped her smile wasn't visible in the window.

———

Outside the gate, Sergeant Rodney had again been one of the first officers on the scene. He had tried to reason with the man in the guard booth, but the extension of his middle finger had made things abundantly clear that they would not be surrendering to him.

He was pacing around his squad car, waiting until he had sufficient numbers and the right tactical equipment before moving in on the plant. Today would be different than students and unarmed protesters of the last few days. This was an angry, armed mob, which had not only superior numbers, but had him on the wrong side of the fortified gate to the plant.

The explosion from the building reaffirmed his assessment. "Well," he thought to himself, "at least we don't have to hold back this time."

———

In the lobby, Tom took a deep breath to compose himself, then two more. For the time being, he couldn't spare the people to haul the wounded back to Jenn, so his troops were doing their best to treat them where they had fallen. He watched in amazement as some of the veterans treated the wounded in ways even he hadn't imagined.

Finally ready, he grabbed Emma by the arm and they picked their way through the rubble to the elevators. He pressed the button, only to realize the cars were all up on the top floor and couldn't be summoned down. Feet away, Emma tried the door to the stairway but it was electronically locked. Having helped build similar doors, Tom knew that short of another, larger IED, they were not going to breach this one anytime soon. This challenge was going to be conquered by brains, not brawn.

———

Jenn threw her gloves in the overflowing garbage can and let her shoulders slump. She had finished with her patients, but her day was far from over. Most of the wounded were inside the production plant's cafeteria, which had become a makeshift recovery center. The more serious cases had been evacuated out of the shipping bay back to her clinic before the police had sealed it off as well. Jenn couldn't help but wonder if her medical friends were relieved to be doing their work without worrying about insurance.

Her blood boiled as she watched more and more police gather in full riot gear. The last thing she wanted was to see more bloodshed, but at least this time it would a fair fight. Tom had assured her that the gate itself would withstand significant damage, which was a good starting point. Her truck had been replaced with a big red delivery truck to secure the gate even further. Armed workers had taken up defensive positions, ready to fight back if police breached the gate or loading dock. Lookouts had been posted to alert her as well. It wasn't much, but it was all she had.

———

Near the main door, Tom flipped a small couch back on its feet so he could sit and think. Emma plopped down next to him and took a long drink from her canteen before offering it to him. Gratefully, Tom took one drink, then another, emptying the canteen. He hadn't realized how thirsty he was. "Thanks."

"Gotta stay hydrated, sir. What the fuck do we do now?"

"I'm open to ideas. You're more of an expert at this than I am."

Emma screwed her lips together and thought for a minute before speaking. "My guess is that they're locked out from the security office upstairs and only authorized personnel have access. Can any of our people bypass that? Is there a manual control we can get to?"

Tom looked at the few people he had with him in the lobby. They were all from the production side of the plant and he doubted any of them had the ability to do what Emma suggested. He shook his head, drops of water flying off his head.

"OK, then, do we have another big fucking IED? One to punch through the door to the fucking stairwell?"

Another shake of his head turned into a shiver that shook his whole body. Between the wet clothes and helpless feeling, Tom had never felt cold like this. His head sank into his hands as he struggled for a solution.

Abruptly, the sprinklers stopped. The fires were out and their sensors had shut off the system. Emma wiped her face with her sleeve. "A penny for your thoughts, sir?"

Tom's head snapped up so hard Emma pulled back, her sage green eyes wide in surprise. "That's it! I need you to make a call." From his omniphone, he retrieved a number, which he had Emma call. When Brett's hologram appeared, Tom spoke a few hasty words and asked him to relay a message before hanging up. Then came the waiting.

———

The vibration of the omniphone on her wrist startled Penny, but she had enough of her wits left to not answer it in front of her bosses. Under the best of circumstances they frowned on personal calls at work. She had to stifle a laugh as she thought about what their response would be at this moment. She waited for two minutes before making her move. "This," she gestured down towards the grounds below, "this craziness has me feeling a little sick to my stomach. Excuse me." Kristen and Mollie seemed not to even notice as she slipped away, although Lester watched her departure with great interest.

Penny entered the restroom and checked to make sure she was alone. She entered the stall furthest from the door. The message from Brett simply said, "Call me ASAP."

———

Down in the lobby, Tom sat and waited, alone with his thoughts. The wounded had finally been brought out to Jenn and he had ordered the dead removed from the lobby, the bodies weirded him out. All around the first floor, Emma and Shawn led his people in searching for anything useful, but they'd turned up nothing of value yet. Tom looked up as he heard Shawn call his name and then walked across the lobby to where they were standing.

"Sir, do you want us to disconnect these?" Shawn asked, tilting his curly brown hair up at two video cameras. "There are a couple more, too."

Tom looked around and saw the entire lobby area was under surveillance. He looked back at Shawn, "Yeah, but I'll get the last one."

———

With a sinking feeling of his own, Bob watched the lobby cameras turn to static one by one. The last unit, camera L-5 showed the traitorous Tom Erickson stand on a chair and look directly into the lens. Bob and Robert leaned in to see Tom's face filling screen. While there was no sound, Tom's words were clear before it, too, went fuzzy. "We're coming."

———

Grateful to be alone, Penny called Brett back, not surprised he answered on the first ring. "Hey, Brett," she replied, keeping her voice low, "what's the word?"

"Tom needs you to unlock the stairway doors and release the elevator. He wants-"

Brett's words were cut off by the restroom door slamming open. Kristen and Mollie stormed in and quickly checked the stalls for Penny, who had barely enough time to end her call before they banged on her door. "Penny, come out of there!" Mollie demanded.

Penny took a deep breath before exiting her stall. She brushed past Kristen and Mollie and washed her hands in the sink.

"What were you doing in there?" Mollie asked angrily.

"I told you, I wasn't feeling well." Penny rinsed her mouth out for show before drying her hands. "This whole business has me pretty upset."

Kristen glared at her. "Let me see your phone. Lester thinks you're part of this."

With a calmness she didn't know she possessed, Penny handed over her omniphone. Kristen punched a few buttons and retrieved the call history. "Who is Brett Kaplan?" she demanded.

"Brett runs the meat department at Kaplan's Market. I was going to talk to him about an order I made for my daughter's birthday. I called him while I was in here because I knew you'd be upset with me taking a personal call at work. I'm sorry."

Kristen continued to glare. "I thought you were in here sick?"

"I almost threw up, but I didn't, really. Not yet, anyway, maybe a little bit in the back of my throat. So, I sat down and called him, hoping it would pass. Again, I'm sorry, it won't happen again."

Kristen looked at Mollie, who shrugged and gave her standard cop-out answer, "I don't know," right on cue. It was Mollie's way of never giving a wrong answer.

"OK, Penny," Kristen said. "I'll let it go this time, but you're on notice." She handed Penny's omniphone back. "This is not the time for you to be pushing your luck." Without another word, Kristen and Mollie left the restroom. Penny breathed a sigh of relief; now she really did feel sick.

———

Sergeant Rodney continued to pace and evaluate the tactical situation outside the gates. His superiors had pulled officers from all across the city, who were massing around the plant. To counter that, an even larger number of armed citizens were now circling around his forces. And as he had thought earlier, these were not students or unarmed protesters.

An Army veteran himself, he knew his forces were in a dangerous, unwinnable position. The gates would be difficult to penetrate and he'd be fighting in every direction against superior numbers. With a sigh of resignation, he called headquarters on the radio and gave them a situation report, concluding with his recommendation to withdraw and make their move once their tactical situation improved. Within moments, headquarters responded, "Hold your position and wait for Captain Allen to take charge."

On the radio, Sergeant Rodney responded, "Roger that. Rodney, out." Off the radio, he shook his head and thought, "Fuck, this is bad."

———

Tom continued to wait. And wait. And wait, alternating between sitting on his couch and wandering quietly about the lobby. Shawn and a few of the others were dozing in the driest chairs they could find. He returned to his couch and sat back down, envying those who could nap at a time like this. Emma returned and offered him a dry shirt and some pretzels from a vending machine. Tom accepted the shirt, but declined the food. "How could she eat during this?" he wondered. He shivered when he stripped off the wet t-shirt he'd been wearing. The new one was a tight fit around his chest, but it was infinitely better than his still wet pants.

Emma shrugged and sat down next to him, chewing happily while watching him change. She swallowed the last bite and smoothed the bag out in her hands. "Sir?" she asked, "Do you mind if I say something?"

"By all means."

"Sir, I spent nine years in the corps. One of the biggest things I know about command is that it's a bitch sometimes."

Tom laughed. "Tell me something I haven't learned in the last hour."

"Sometimes it's leading by example. Sometimes it's recognizing all of your assets and using them wisely. And sometimes, like right now, literally all you can do is sit and fucking wait. The bitch is knowing what you can and can't do."

Tom blinked and nodded, hoping against hope that he wouldn't have too many more opportunities to use his new knowledge.

———

Jenn slammed her hand against window. "Damn it!" She had done what she could, but there were limits to her skills and supplies. Two of the surviving guards had died in front of her and one other was touch and go. She didn't like losing anything, certainly not patients. If she could get them to a hospital, they'd have a chance, but for now that wasn't an option.

Outside the gate, more and more police officers were gathering, although they had yet to make a move. She had reports that there was a growing group of people gathering around the police, which gave her hope. While she hadn't gone to church since she was nine, she bowed her head and said a prayer requesting that the day end without further bloodshed.

———

After a long moment to compose herself, Penny left the restroom and took stock of who was around the office. Most of the office staff was there, going about their work as if nothing was happening, as were the usual janitorial and maintenance staff. They were all frustrated, but were they to the point where they'd help her in her mission? After all, they had all crossed the picket line.

The biggest problem was that the computers that controlled the doors and elevators were in the security office. That room was protected by armed guards inside the most secure door Wright Security Systems made. Even getting into that room would be difficult if not impossible.

She stole a glance through the glass as she neared the conference room. Kristen and Mollie were having an animated discussion with Lester. She could see him shaking his head as Kristen acted out the scene from the restroom. With no desire to rejoin them and no ideas coming to mind, Penny returned to her cubicle and sat down, absentmindedly thinking about her to-do list. A muted cough behind her got her attention. She turned to find Hugh, Leigh, Nancy, Lori and a few others gathered around her cube.

Leigh led off, "What the Hell is going on around here?!"

Penny decided to gamble. "Well, you know the strikers and the people attacking downstairs? I'm one of them."

Lori exchanged a look with Nancy, "I knew it!"

Leigh smiled and said, "It's OK, we're with you."

Hugh nodded. "We've been talking away from work and agree that things have to change.

Penny looked at each of their faces and knew they were telling the truth. "OK, quick, if anyone asks, we're talking about the shooting and stuff and wondering if we'll be safe. Got it?" Everyone nodded.

"We need to get into the security office and unlock the elevators so Tom and his troops can get up here," she continued. "I don't know what they want to do, but our part is to get them up here. Any ideas?"

No one answered.

———

Sergeant Rodney's distress was mounting. He had a large contingent of armed officers, but he was still vastly outnumbered and in an unwinnable situation. Captain Allen was tied up in traffic and he doubted headquarters would let him withdraw, even if it was the right decision. He was sure they cared more about pleasing Bob Wright than about the safety of line officers.

Finally, he made a decision. He switched to his command channel and spoke to the officers on-scene. "This is Rodney. We are going to withdraw to the 12th precinct. Repeat, we are withdrawing to the 12th precinct. Be alert and know that you are authorized to use deadly force to protect yourself and your fellow officers. Mount up and move out! Rodney, out."

He looked around at his officers, the relief obvious on their faces. His radio crackled, followed by, "Attention all units, this is Captain Allen. I am in command and am ordering you to hold your positions. Sergeant Rodney is not in command, I am. I will be on scene in a few minutes and we will act then. In the meantime, you are ordered to stand your ground. Allen, out."

Sergeant Rodney looked back at his officers to see their reaction to the new order. They could see and hear the growing mob and they understood the situation as well as he did. His answer came as they got into their squad cars to begin their withdrawal. To his relief, the mob parted enough to let their cars through, though he could see guns aimed at them as they passed. Sergeant Rodney spoke into his radio again. "Captain, this is Rodney. The situation is unsafe and we are pulling back as I ordered. The units are already moving. We'll have to make our move from the 12th, sir." Getting no response from his Captain, Sergeant Rodney got into his own car and pulled away, the last one to leave the gate area.

At the loading dock, Officer Walker wasn't happy, but he began the retreat as ordered. The crowd parted for him, too, pounding on his squad car and shouting obscenities at him. Out of frustration, he pressed the accelerator down hard and was thrust back in his seat as the squad car leaped forward. The roar of his engine was enough to get most protesters to jump back, but two were slow on the uptake. He hit them both, one a glancing blow and one squarely, sending the woman catapulting over his roof. "Shit!" he yelled and kept on driving.

Seeing two of their members get run down was the spark that ignited the fire. Despite knowing the car would protect him, Walker flinched as bricks and rocks began to rain down on his car. A strange thud from the passenger window made him look over. Stuck in the bulletproof glass was a bullet meant for him. They were shooting at him! With disregard for common sense, Officer Walker drew his service weapon and ordered the car to take over driving and roll down the window. In an instant, he was able to reach out the window and begin firing indiscriminately at the crowd in his way. In seconds, he had emptied his magazine towards the crowd, though car was accelerating too fast to see if he hit anything. The bulletproof windows caught a dozen more shots before a shotgun blast ripped through the open window and into his unprotected head. The car's computer system didn't need him alive, it continued its escape without any further commands.

All of the other officers were sane enough to keep their windows up and fled without further injuries. Once clear of the mob scene around the plant, the journey back to the safety of their precinct house was made with relative ease, not even realizing Walker was hit.

In the garage of the 12th Precinct, Sergeant Rodney's computer reported a problem with the status of Officer Walker. Rodney shrugged, the car was in its designated spot, probably suffering a technical glitch after the beating the vehicle had taken. He dispatched a probationary officer to check on him while he listened to the reports from a couple of his other units.

Before the first one could finish, Rodney and three other officers heard a scream and went running. The white-faced rookie couldn't speak, but was able to point to the bloody corpse in the car.

"I can't tell if it's Walker. He ain't got a face." one of the officers said.

"Yeah, it's him," Sergeant Rodney said. "Look at the skull tattoo on his left arm." Rodney shook his head in frustration. "God damn it." It was exactly what he had hoped to avoid.

Chapter Twenty-One

Despite the burst of shooting outside the plant, Jenn felt relieved when she saw the police cars depart. She knew they'd be back, but it gave her time to regroup.

Upon closer inspection, Jenn realized that many of civilians now pressed against the gate were fellow strikers. She knew a few of them, but somehow that didn't click in her brain. It even took time to recognize her ex-husband in the sea of faces. With a shake to clear her head, Jenn ordered the gate opened and the reinforcements to flow in.

Jenn pushed her way through the crowd and climbed up the side of the red truck, where she waved her arms to quiet their conversations. She had a bullhorn, which she liked because she hated yelling, but she wanted their full attention, too. When they had quieted down, she started to speak. "Thank you and welcome to the revolution!" The gathered crowd erupted in cheers. It took several moments for Jenn to get them back under control, but inside she was pleased.

She spoke more slowly, careful to pronounce every word. "What we have here is merely the beginning of a movement. A movement that has been a long time in coming. As we speak, a number of other things are happening around the city," she continued. "Not the least of which is that the police are regrouping and planning to return. If you're not willing to fight for your freedom, this is the time to leave." The crowd was quieter, but few left.

"OK, good. Here's how we're going to proceed..." Jenn continued on for a few moments and outlined her plans. She divided the group up into teams, including those with weapons, those with medical training and those with food service experience. She had listened to Lane and knew they'd have to be prepared for all aspects of the siege ahead.

In the security office, Bob was sickened by what he had seen on his monitors. The police had given up and run away, allowing his plant and his grounds to be occupied by these people. He spoke to his security director. "Do you think you can hold them off? Keep them on the ground floors until the police or whoever can get it together and drive them off?"

"Sir, as long as nobody breaks into this room, it should be nearly impossible to get up here. We've been over the plans and you know them as well as I do."

"OK, that's reassuring." Bob turned back to his son, "Robert, I need to speak with you in private back in my office." The two men departed, leaving the security team to watch their monitors.

Robert sat in one of the guest chairs and waited for his father to make himself a drink. Bob ran his fingers through his silky white hair before taking a large swallow. "Robert, we're possibly in a lot of trouble here. Like he said in there, it will be difficult to get up here, but it's not impossible."

"Father, I believe we'll be OK. You know the strength of our products and the security troops are loyal to you. You saw what happened to the ones downstairs. I think that pissed off the rest of the ones up here."

"I hope you're right, but nonetheless, the crew is pre-flighting the helicopter. You can never be too careful in these situations."

"Won't fleeing send the wrong message to everyone? It will only embolden Erickson's people and I think that's the last thing we need."

Bob finished the rest of his drink and pondered another. "You make a valid point, but we're not leaving yet. I want to be prepared to get to safety and fight another day if that's what it comes down to. 'Better safe than sorry,' your grandfather always said."

He decided against another drink. This situation would demand his full faculties.

———

When Kristen and Mollie relayed their story from the restroom, Lester shook his head in disapproval. He looked back and forth between the two women, sweat oozing from his forehead. "I can't believe you two bought her story. I know she's part of the mob. She has been from the beginning."

"Don't talk like that to us." Mollie was baffled by his tone. "We will make the decisions here. You are just Bob's assistant. Remember that fact."

A bright flash of anger crossed his face. "Just his assistant? Bob listens to me maybe more than he listens to you."

Kristen looked up from her computer. "I checked and she does have a daughter with a birthday later this week. I don't like her doing it on company time, but I highly doubt she is planning to murder anyone."

"She's probably plotting on how to kill us right as you two sit here and talk about who's in charge!"

"Lester, if you don't calm down, we're going to have to ask you to leave." Mollie was doing everything she could to keep from raising her voice, but Lester had experienced this tone and stiff body language before. She was approaching her breaking point and that wasn't good for anyone.

"Whatever." Lester turned away and left the two women looking at him with distaste.

Mollie leaned over to Kristen and whispered, "Some people need to learn their place." Kristen nodded her agreement before looking back out the window.

———

Dusk was approaching and still Penny was alone in her cube, frustrated by the fact that nobody could come up with a way to help Tom's team. She had kicked her shoes off long ago and finally put her head down to try to rest.

She dozed off, but the memory of her encounter in the restroom kept her from getting any real sleep. "Damn Kristen and Mollie," she thought, "They still think they're the queens of the world." Her eyes sprang open. A calm enveloped her. A smile spread across her face. She knew how to get into the security office.

Penny stretched and walked to Lori's cube, where she beckoned to her other conspirators. Through the glass wall, she could see Kristen and Mollie seated at the table, with Lester standing off by himself. Still, she spoke quietly to her group and outlined her plan. It was really quite simple: the queens would help her into the security office.

The rest of the group looked at her in astonishment. They had spent their afternoon thinking about blowing up doors and rewriting computer programs. In quick order, though, they all saw that Penny's plan was good and had a real chance of succeeding.

With no further hesitation, Penny led them to the conference room. She was not surprised to find the door unlocked, they trusted their workers. She opened the door and the whole group surged in, surrounding her bosses before they could react. Kristen looked at them curiously over her glasses. "Yes, what is it? What do you need?"

Penny snorted as she looked down at her. "What we need, is for you three to join us in a little game my husband calls 'sit down and shut the Hell up,' got it? We have you and if you have any working brain cells, you'll do exactly as you're told. There's new management here."

"What? That's outrageous!"

"I told you she was in on it!" Lester said. "I've told you this from the very beginning."

Penny glanced at him and smiled. "You're right, we are with the folks downstairs. Always have been."

"Penny, Leigh," Mollie pleaded, "look, we're in this together. We've always treated you like family here. You need us!"

Penny burst out laughing. "Family? See Leigh, she does have a sense of humor."

Kristen tried to get out of her chair, but Hugh shoved her back down with more force than he needed. Penny laughed again at their arrogance. These people still thought they had power. It was one-part amusing, one-part infuriating and one-part dumbfounding.

Penny collected herself before speaking to the two women. "You two stand up."

Mollie glared at her. "We will not, Penny. You will stop this madness and return to your desk."

Almost casually, Penny slapped her across the face, knocking her glasses askew. "It's Penelope, you bitch. Now, in terms simple enough for even you to understand, get up."

Penny looked up at the familiar sound of Bob Wright's helicopter taking off from the roof. Of course he'd sneak away and save his own skin. She looked back down at her former bosses. "Don't you get it? Bob knows when he's been beat. He's left you here to deal with us and he never gave you a second thought. Now stand up and do exactly as you're told." Kristen and Mollie rose from their chairs, acknowledging the hopelessness of their situation. "Hugh," she continued, "can you and Nolan stay here and keep Lester company?"

The two men smiled. "Yeah," Hugh said, "we can do that."

Penny led the group from the conference room with the others close behind. Leigh and Nancy kept close rein on their captives as they entered the main work area. The few remaining workers gawked at the scene before cheering and joining them. Together, the group marched their hostages to the security office, where Penny rang the buzzer. "What do you want?" a voice asked.

She looked into the camera and took a deep breath before speaking. "We are in charge out here and have control of the entire rest of the plant. I need you to lay down your weapons and come out or these two will start getting payback for all of the suffering they've caused us over the years." Kristen tried to voice her objection, but Nancy put a quick end to that.

"No way," the voice responded. "We can't let you in here."

"Sure you can. Put your guns down and open the door. You have my personal guarantee of your safety. We are becoming more and more desperate and we will not hesitate to demonstrate on these two."

"We can't let you in here. We have our orders and we're calling your bluff."

"Bluff? Bluff? If you don't come out in the next thirty seconds, you'll see my bluff." Penny turned and nodded to her friends, who forced both Kristen & Mollie to their knees. She turned back to the camera and looked at her omniphone. "Fifteen seconds. If I can control the situation, Kristen and Mollie will live. If not, don't say I didn't give you a chance." No reply came.

Penny turned to her group and shrugged. The ferocity of the response was all she imagined it would be considering the long festering hatred they felt towards Kristen and Mollie. These two had made all of their lives miserable for years and it was revenge time. Leigh and Nancy were joined by the circle of others in delivering a series of slaps, punches and kicks to both Kristen and Mollie, who fell screaming to the floor. When Lori stomped her heavy shoe on Kristen's left hand and she could hear a bone snap, Penny stopped the assault.

She returned to the camera. "Still think I'm bluffing? You should see what we have planned for Lester, we really don't like him. You heard Bob abandon you. Come out slowly and you will not be harmed." She reached down and grabbed Mollie by the hair, lifting her face up towards the camera. "Anything you'd like to tell them?" she asked.

"Save us!" Mollie sobbed. "Come out and give them what they want!" Penny gave her head a forceful shake to signal she couldn't talk any more.

"Look, we can't let you in here. We don't want any more violence, but we can't let you in here," the voice on the speaker continued.

Penny didn't have to speak this time. While Nancy held Kristen's hand out, Pablo the maintenance man began breaking her fingers one by one with his claw-hammer. Kristen's screams made Penny's skin crawl, but it had to be done.

Penny let Pablo finish the left hand before speaking again. "Still not bluffing. Want us to go for the right hand?"

"Open the door you idiot!" Mollie screamed again. "They're killing us out here!" Kristen curled into a ball and sobbed on the floor.

The voice on the intercom returned. "How do we know you'll keep your word?"

"You're not one of them. You know that. You'll have to trust that we don't want to hurt anyone else and come out."

Penny grew tense when the voice didn't respond. Just as she turned and pointed to Kristen, the voice finally spoke again. "OK, we're coming out."

"Hold on," Penny demanded. "Open the door slowly and make sure we can see your hands." Behind her, her fellow conspirators picked up Kristen and Mollie to use as human shields.

Penny's heart was pounding; she didn't trust the security people at all. As directed, the door slid open, followed by half a dozen men and women walking out with their hands clasped on top of their heads. At the end of the line was their director, his head hanging in shame. Penny pushed past them and into the security office as the officers were secured with their own handcuffs. She could hear Leigh ordering all of them down the hall to the conference room as the door closed.

Penny looked around the control room. She had never been in here before, it was one of the plant's most mysterious departments. There was a wall of video monitors, some of which showed nothing but static. The others showed armed protesters spread out across the complex. "Wow," she thought, "they really did it!"

She sat at one of the work stations and studied her options. The security system was similar to the operating system she used and it wasn't long before she pulled up the building's security control system. After entering the proper commands, Penny held her breath as she displayed her eye to the retinal scanner. A lifetime passed before the computer beeped and her command was accepted. She was finally able to breathe again and entered another command.

———

Fifteen floors below her, Tom was grasping at straws. Maybe he could get another IED from Lane or maybe his welding equipment could cut through the wall? All of their work was about to be for nothing because he couldn't figure out a way through a door. He hung his head, his hands covering his eyes, and tried to think of something that would help. A muted bell rang from the elevator, a sound he knew well. He looked up to see the elevator light indicating it was on its way down.

Tom stared as the numbers crawled downward. 8...7...6... "Let's go!" he called to Emma and Shawn. They, and a hand-picked team, jumped to their feet and aimed their weapons at the door.

The elevator doors opened to display its emptiness. Tom's team leaped inside and without a word, the elevator began to rise, traveling as fast as the slightly overloaded car could go to the top floor. Shawn and Emma exited first, looking around the room over the sights of their rifles, followed by four more armed men. Inside, two others stood in front of Tom and waited for the signal to make sure it was safe before allowing him to get out.

Tom looked around the deserted cubicle park. The only people he could see were along the far wall, standing on either side of an open door. A woman he didn't recognize stuck her head in the door and said something Tom couldn't hear. Tom ordered a couple of troops to stay by the elevator before joining the party.

He entered the conference room into a cloud of heavy smoke. Someone had "liberated" some cigars from Bob's office and they were celebrating their success. He was pleased to see a bunch of guards seated peacefully at the conference table. On a couch by the window, couple of women icing Kristen's hand while they tried to ignore Mollie's whining. He smiled his biggest smile when he saw Lester bound and gagged on the floor. "Nice work, people," he said to them all. "Where's Penny?"

Leigh answered, "She's in the security office. Follow me." She guided Tom down the hall describing how things had transpired. The door to the security office was unlocked and they entered to find Penny sitting in a high-backed chair, watching the wall of monitors. She stood when she saw him, tears flowing as she hugged her friend.

After a moment, she pulled away. "I thought you'd never get here!"

Tom let out a sigh. "Me neither. Good work."

"Thanks. It looks like you did great down there."

"We caught a few breaks. And you helped, you know. I see you were able to take them all alive. That's good."

"Not all of them, Bob and Robert escaped. They snuck out in his helicopter before we even took the security office."

Tom sighed and glanced up at the ceiling. It had all gone so well he couldn't be upset at Bob's escape. Penny and her unprepared group of office people had successfully captured the security office without firing a shot. It was damned impressive he had to admit. He looked fondly at Penny. "We'll get that bastard soon enough." He turned to the monitors, "Have you seen my wife on here?"

"No, I didn't see her, there are too many cameras. On the other hand, there are more and more of our people here with guns and from what I can see, it looks like we're in control out there."

"OK," Tom replied. "Are you comfortable staying in charge up here?"

Penny thought for a moment, her face contorted in discomfort. "No, not really. I did what I had to do, but I'm wiped out. I about threw up when they were breaking Kristen's fingers. They crunched like potato chips! I don't think I'm made for this."

Tom nodded. "I get it, I really do. It's one thing to talk about this stuff, but suddenly the 'doing' is not nearly as cool as it's made out to be. I'll have some of my troops take over this office and get you out of here."

"OK. Home sounds really good." She hugged him again before relinquishing command.

Chapter Twenty-Two

A look of confusion crossed Casey Frost's face as he ended the call on his omniphone. How in the Hell could this be happening? And in his district, no less! Initial reports about the attack on Bob Wright's plant were coming in and indicated a situation that was rapidly going to Hell. He slipped into his suit coat and headed out the door. "Tell the Speaker I'm coming down and it's an emergency," he ordered his secretary over his shoulder.

Since Casey didn't hold much power as he thought, his office was not close to the Speaker's and it took a six-minute walk to reach his destination. When he arrived, the secretary jerked her head towards the door to the Speaker's private office. Inside, the Speaker was seated at his desk focused on his computer monitor. "Hello, Casey," he said, not looking up, "it looks like some real trouble back in Des Moines."

"Wow," Casey thought to himself, "bad news really does travel fast." He then spoke out loud, "Yes, sir, I spoke with my people back there a minute ago."

The Speaker looked up, his thin face giving away none of his feelings. "And what did they say? I saw the overview, but maybe you have more."

"It seems that a long-term plant employee, Tom Erickson, we tried to recruit his wife, you'll remember, anyway, Tom led the strike yesterday and escaped the police. We interrogated the other strikers, but none of them had any information on their whereabouts." He paused as he remembered how rudely Jenn had treated him when he called her the last time. What was wrong with people?

"Then, evidently, he orchestrated an armed takeover of the plant earlier today. It looks like he had some people on the inside who helped him gain access and a number of people with small arms to make his stunt work. Several people are dead, we're not sure how many, including one police officer. And three of Bob Wright's top aides plus some security personnel have been taken hostage by the strikers. I am pleased to report that Bob and his son escaped unharmed. The Mayor and the Governor are working on an appropriate response. They will retake the plant by force tonight or tomorrow."

The Speaker's face grew taut with his displeasure. Protests and even strikes were one thing, but this! This was the brink of disaster. Slowly, he rose from his desk and leaned over it towards Casey. "I hadn't heard about the hostage part, that's good information to have. I have to go brief the

President. It seems that the seriousness of the civil unrest is growing and we as a nation are going to have to put an end to it. We can't let these people undo all of the good work we've done."

Casey nodded. He knew the Speaker and the President went back to when they roomed together at Exeter. Their response would be decisive and make a statement to other subversives. He also knew there would be a good photo-op for himself at some point.

———

Back in Des Moines, Tom was trying to manage a situation that was growing crazier by the minute. From the scattered reports he had heard, the strike was on all around Des Moines and armed citizens were in the streets. Another rumor said that the Governor had been killed. To temper that news, though, came reports that the police or the National Guard were rallying to take back the plant by force. The lack of reliable information was maddening.

What he did know was that once word of the revolt had spread through the lower 14 floors, they had gained countless new recruits who were looking for roles around the plant. There were too many people to try and manage at once and he barely knew where to start.

He had left Shawn in charge of the security office with orders to treat the captives humanely. Problem was, he had been so focused on the actual attack, he hadn't really planned on having long-term prisoners. He needed Jenn's brains for that one. He knew his wife had some plans that she hadn't shared with him, but mostly he needed to see his wife and know she was alive and well.

Emma and two others guided him to the medical ward. Once inside, Tom paused to watch her fussing over a patient until Jenn sensed she was being watched and looked over. She smiled with relief when she saw him, gesturing for him to join her in a nearby supply room. "I'd like to get your report in private," she said. Emma and the other soldiers exchanged knowing glances before leaving to find something to eat.

The door had barely clicked shut, when Jenn turned and fairly jumped into his arms. She kissed him ferociously and they held one another in blissful relief from the chaos outside. Once they were able, they pulled slightly apart, still holding hands. Tom spoke first, "I'm glad you're OK, babe."

"I'm glad you're in one piece! When I heard Lane's bomb go off, I didn't know what to think. I kept getting little bits of information and didn't want to ask too many questions about you, cause, well, you know."

"Yeah, I know. I don't want people to think I got this job because I'm sleeping with the boss." Tom grinned at her as she shook her head.

"Really? The world is blowing up around us and you're making jokes? How did I get so lucky?" She kissed him again. "I was really scared."

"So was I. For me, for you, for the girls. How are they doing?"

Jenn shrugged. "I don't know. We don't dare use our omniphones, so we'll have to get back to the farm and see. I'm really nervous not knowing how they are. I'm not sure I'm ready for this."

Tom hugged her again. "Yeah, but you got it done when it mattered. And from what I've heard, you did a great job."

"Thanks. I had some great people helping me. Now we've got to get out of here."

Tom blinked and pulled away. "What?"

Jenn nodded her head as she spoke. "The police pulled back because they were surrounded and outnumbered, but they'll be back in bigger numbers and maybe with the National Guard. That's going to turn this into a bit of siege warfare and our job is to get out where we can lead the bigger picture."

"But, we..."

Jenn cut him off. "No buts, our people here have jobs to do and so do we. We are of more use to the rebellion if we are able to focus on other things."

Tom looked at his wife unhappily. He didn't want to leave the troops he had become so fond of, but she was his commander. After a long moment, he nodded and replied, "Alright."

"OK, tell me about your day, dear."

———

Casey Frost was pacing the floor of his private office waiting for news from back home. The Speaker was still off with the President, leaving Casey to worry about what was happening in Des Moines. He jumped when his omniphone buzzed and the hologram of his assistant, Lance, popped up. "What is it?" he said as a greeting.

"Sir, you're not going to believe it," Lance answered without hesitation. He was used to his boss' brusqueness. "Shortly after the attack at the fence plant, a group of people, they must have been from the same group, well, they stormed the central jail and released all of the detainees from yesterday's strike."

"What?!" Casey said so loud his secretary looked up from her desk outside. "How the Hell could they overwhelm a jail?"

"Most of the police had been pulled away to help at the plant. The, the, sir, I don't know what to call them...raiders? They had guns and bombs and there was a sufficient number of them to take over the jail."

Again, Casey could only stare in disbelief. "Was anyone hurt?" he asked, more to buy time than out of real concern.

"Yes, sir, there were minor injuries to nine of the jail guards. They're being treated at the hospital."

"Great, so we have all kinds of criminals running around the city in addition to the attack."

"Um, sir, no we don't, actually. The raiders only released their people from yesterday. They left the other criminals locked up. They left the guards behind, unharmed. The only things they took were all of the weapons they could find. It's very strange, sir."

"I'll say it is. Any other good news?"

"Not at this time, sir, no."

"OK, thanks. Keep me posted." Casey ended the call before Lance could reply.

———

As dusk fell, Jenn and Tom gathered some of their key people in the break room and were laying out their plans. Most of the prisoners had been condensed into one group in the training center and were being guarded under Hugh and Leigh's supervision. Shawn was in charge of the special prisoners on the 15th floor as well as being Tom's aide, while Emma was in charge of perimeter security. All in all, Jenn thought, things were shaping up nicely.

She had even arranged for the injured guards to be evacuated to the local hospital. The authorities had been willing to take them, so a deal had been reached. As she wrapped up her talk, an aide signaled that the ambulances had reached the main gate. While all eyes were on the transfer, she, along with Penny and Tom would slip away and head back to the farm.

Tom chased Emma into the hall to speak privately before they left. "You were awesome today. Thanks for helping me through it."

"No problem, sir. You didn't suck yourself. Next time, though, don't get so focused on the target right in front of you that you forget the rest of the world."

"Duly noted." He stuck out his hand. "Good luck."

Emma shook his hand. "You, too, sir." She watched quietly as Tom, Jenn and Penny made their exit.

———

Casey rolled onto his side and tried a new position to nap on the couch in his office. The stress of the day and the wild thoughts prevented sleep, but he had to try. He was bewildered by the series of events back home. It made no sense. His head jerked up at the sound of a commotion in the outer office. Casey blinked his eyes several times and got to his feet. The Speaker had arrived with his usual bluster. "Come in, sir," Casey offered.

Once the Speaker was inside, Casey closed the door and the two men sat. "Casey, after meeting with the President and the Senate Majority Leader, we're ordering some military units to a higher alert status. We spoke with the Governor, as well, and we approve of her plans to institute a curfew and establish checkpoints around the city. She's also activating units of the National Guard to help the local law enforcement officials. We are going to put an end to this disaster."

"That's excellent, sir. Are we going to mobilize any of our army units?"

"We hope we don't have to, but the President is prepared to issue those orders if we can't get control of this. We're even discussing some plans to discredit the local dissidents if it gets that far. In fact-" A sharp knock at the door cut him off and a split second later, the door swung open.

It was Casey's secretary, who was looking at them wide-eyed. "Gentlemen, you need to come see this."

The two men rose together and went to the outer office, where the Speaker's aides were gathered around a television. On it was a disheveled looking woman at a news desk. The Speaker pushed their way to the front for a better view.

Casey looked at the screen, stunned to recognize the broadcast news center of one of the Des Moines stations. He had been a guest on that set numerous times and often watched the local news, too, so he knew it well. But why was he seeing it now? And how was he seeing it here in DC?

The woman on the screen was talking without a script. "My son, Marshall, was killed by our government last spring." The camera zoomed in on the photo of a young boy smiling for his school picture, which she held up. "For all of you who are terrified about the future for your children, I'm speaking to you. The time has come for us to give our children a chance at a real future, not what is being dictated to us by those who don't care about anyone but themselves.

The wealthy elite in our country control our government and the laws they passed no longer do anything to protect or help its citizens. The government has betrayed a sacred trust to the people. 'Promote the general welfare' is something we've forgotten about and because of their actions there is blood on the hands of President Joshua

Little and every member of our government." Casey and the Speaker exchanged wary glances.

The camera panned back to the woman. "I represent the American Liberation Movement, and I am declaring that we, the citizens of America, are at war with the government. To our fellow citizens around the country who are as sick of this tyranny and oppression as we are, we say the time has come to take up arms and take our country back. Whether you join the conflict or perform acts of sabotage or participate in the general strike, your time to be on the right side of history is now. It's not too late to give our children the future they deserve.

To our government, we have only two demands. First, we demand the immediate arrest of every police officer and soldier involved in the Des Moines University shooting, the Chicago massacre and every other time in recent months that the government has shot and killed unarmed demonstrators.

Second, we are giving you, both Federal and State elected officials, the opportunity to resign your office. Those who leave peacefully will not be harmed. Those who do not resign within 48 hours will be considered traitors to America and dealt with accordingly.

Our actions speak for themselves. Prisoners and the wounded will be treated fairly. When we freed our comrades from jail earlier today, we left the real criminals behind with their usual guards in place. Our goal is to fix our society, not create anarchy." The woman looked away from the camera at someone and nodded.

"The police are closing in, so we've got to be going. But remember, America, true freedom is earned. You have to want it. You have to be willing to go take it. You have to be willing to fight and die for it. As Patrick Henry once said, 'Give me liberty or give me death' and we are at that point. From Des Moines, this is Jamie Page with the first step towards a new America." The woman unclipped her microphone and abruptly walked off the set. The camera followed her as far as it could and then returned to the regular news anchor, who had reclaimed his seat.

"Well, folks, normally we just report the news, but tonight we appear to have been part of it. To recap..." The Speaker spun on his heel and returned to Casey's office with the Congressman.

The Speaker turned and faced Casey, who barely had time to shut the door. "Damn it! This is an affront to everything we've worked for! I have to go back and meet with the President." Casey watched, still stunned, as the Speaker left with his aides hurrying to catch up.

———

Jenn, Tom and Penny had cleared out of the city before the checkpoints went up. It had taken some time for the government to get organized and they had to give people time to get home before the curfew took effect. That was good news for now, but it would change fast enough.

Tom led the way through freed strikers turned freedom fighters spread out around the farm sharing tearful stories. While individual members of this group knew parts of the plan, hearing all of the stories come together was eye-opening. Tom felt a swell of pride for his wife as he listened to how her plans had worked out. So far, she had managed to do everything in a nearly bloodless fashion, saved lives and spread their message well.

When they reached the house, the other Book Club members were chatting in kitchen, happy to be safe for the moment. The only ones not happy were Steph and Ellen and that was only because they had been left behind. As expected, the girls didn't say much to her until pressed.

"Don't worry, we pretty much did exactly what you told us to do, mom," Ellen said.

"Yeah, mom," Steph cut her off, "we're both still alive. I spent my day making Molotov cocktails out of old beer bottles. We are definitely not going to get our deposits back. We must have like, fifteen cases outside the barn."

Ellen glared, she didn't like being cut off by her older sister. She faced Jenn and Tom again. "Did you know the Molotov cocktail is named after the Russian Foreign Minister during World War II? The Finnish people improvised firebombs out of wine bottles and gas or kerosene and named them after him. They were really good at it and..." She stopped talking when she saw her parents starting to laugh and laughed herself when she realized she was rambling.

"Anyway, I did some research and gave Steph some tips and she did the rest. I didn't really make any, but I have been keeping an eye on the news from around the country and our message got out. And I mean, it GOT OUT. I thought we were going to be limited to the local station, but somehow it went national and even international." She turned and looked at her uncle, "How'd you do that?" she asked.

Lane laughed. "Thanks for the vote of confidence, but I didn't really do it. Turns out one of the guys we got out of jail, Alex Schultz, got fired from that station about a year ago. Once we were inside the station, he used their own technology to send the message via satellite to their network feed and it sounds like it worked pretty well."

"Alex Schultz, huh?" Ellen asked, tilting her head to the side. When Lane nodded, she continued, "I go to school with his son Blake, he's a good kid. He's in my computer club. Anyway, 'well' is an understatement. It got picked up and was on the BBC, Sky News, Telemundo and Al-Jazeera and pretty much everywhere."

"And it was on locally," a familiar deep voice said from around the doorway. Scott and the girls had finally arrived and were crowding into the kitchen. Penny all but knocked Tom over on her way to hug Anne and Abigail.

She looked over their heads at her husband. "I'm glad you're all safe!" she said through her tears.

"Yeah, me too" Scott said. "Abigail was getting some things at the market when your call came in," he nodded to Tom, "and then Brett told her what was happening. She told me and we packed up and came here. Once they figured out it was Penny, I was sure they'd come after us next."

Tom looked at his friend. "I'm sorry. I should have warned you sooner. I couldn't think about that many things."

"Hey, it was close, but we got out OK."

Tom hung his head as he thought about the danger he'd put his best friend in. Scott reached over and punched him gently in the shoulder. "Don't beat yourself up, man. We're OK." Tom lifted his head and hugged his friend.

"There is bad news, though," Scott said, pulling away. "The Kaplans all got arrested. We seen it as we were driving."

"What?!" Jenn asked, startled.

Abigail answered, "Yeah, the police must have figured out that he was our middle man. They must have some program that tracks calls and then put two and two together. We saw Brett and his parents being put into police cars."

"We've got to get them out," Jenn said. She looked around desperately, stopping when she reached Lane, who was shaking his head. "What?" she asked.

"I don't think that that's gonna be possible. We were able to free our guys once because the police weren't expecting it. After that, and with the high value of these targets, I'm sure they are locked down tight. I can't imagine how we can get them out."

"We can't leave them there!"

Lane thought for a moment. "What do you think of a prisoner exchange? Our three for the three VIPs Penny captured today?"

Jenn nodded. "I can live with that. She turned to Ellen, "can you find a secure way to get that offer to the police tonight?"

"Sure mom, no problem." She turned to head to the living room.

"And honey," Jenn stopped her, "however careful you think you're being, be more careful. I know you're really good at this, but the government clearly has the resources and abilities to track people, including you. Be extra careful."

Ellen pursed her lips and nodded before leaving the room, her shoulders slumped at the realization that her mom was right.

Jenn turned back to her brother. "We need to get out of here and find a new place to hide, too. I'm surprised they haven't raided us here yet and we can't guarantee that nobody will talk. I'm sure they'll use any means necessary to get the information from him."

"Yeah, I had that thought, too," Lane said. "I hate to leave this place, but you're right. Let's hope they don't have something up there watching us already. With their infrared cameras, their powers are even greater at night."

Jenn cast a furtive glance at the ceiling. "You really can't worry too much," Lane continued, "cause there's really nothing you can do about it. If they want to kill us, it'll be over before we even know they're there."

"Wow, that's reassuring." Jenn couldn't stop the tremble in her voice.

"The only defense we have right now is to find a new place to hide."

"I'm glad you understand. But where are we going to go?" In the chaos of the day's events, Jenn hadn't quite thought about this particular situation.

Lane closed his eyes and tilted his head back. No one spoke as they struggled with ideas for a new hideout. Only Spark and Smudge failed to realize the gravity of the situation as they nudged Lane's leg to remind him that they were hungry. He bent down and looked at them with a smile on his face. "All right, I'll feed you two." He scratched each one behind the ears for a moment before he stood straight up.

"I've got a solution. I have this friend who lives a couple of miles west of here. He's a subsistence farmer, grows and raises and makes most of his own stuff. He's got plenty of space and stays off the government's radar. He gave me the dogs a few years ago when he quit breeding them."

Jenn nodded. "And he'll be OK with you and forty of your closest friends coming over unannounced to lead a rebellion against the government?"

Lane's smile got even broader before he stood up. "Hell, he may try and take over if you're not careful.

"Sounds like a plan," Jenn said, nodding again. "OK, girls, please go and tell everyone outside that we are abandoning this farm and will be moving out in one hour. Have them grab whatever personal gear they have and then come here so we can load up the vehicles with supplies. One hour, got it?" Steph, Anne and Abigail all nodded and headed out the door.

Jenn turned to Lane. "That's the strategic plan, you get to implement the tactical plan."

Lane winked at his sister. "You know, you're picking up the language pretty fast if nothing else." He raised his voice and directed everyone on what to gather and where it could be found.

The hour flew by with the frantic activity. Tom and Jamie brought all of the weapons out, while Scott and Penny gathered as much food as they could. Ellen came back and joined Jenn in rounding up miscellaneous essentials. As each vehicle came to the house, it was loaded with as much as it could hold.

Lane took one last look at his home before opening the truck door to let the dogs jump inside. Without looking back, he led the procession of vehicles into the night.

Chapter Twenty-Three

Once he got past the surprise of a large group of strangers pulling up to his farmhouse, Austin Fox welcomed his new guests with open arms. Even his bushy eyebrows couldn't hide the excitement in his clear, blue eyes. He was one of the tallest men Jenn had ever met. Even bent with age, he was at least 6'7" tall. A white beard covered the bottom half of his face, but behind it Jenn could see deep lines that had quite a story to tell, she was sure.

Austin shook hands with each of the rebels, introducing himself as he went. As he greeted Steph and Ellen, Jenn sidled over to her brother. "I gotta hand it to you, he seems like a heck of a guy."

"Yeah," Lane agreed. "He holds no love for the government and hasn't for...forty...fifty years? He doesn't talk about it much, but it sounds like the government screwed him pretty good around the turn of the century."

"I see. Well, it sounds like we're in the right place." With that, Jenn set about helping her people get settled. It took some time, but eventually everyone had a place to bed down and relax. What surprised her most was how much special attention they needed. From allergies to anxiety to high blood pressure and more serious conditions, nearly everyone needed some kind of medication. Jenn had samples for a few people, but she couldn't help them all.

Of greater concern were the injuries people had received during the initial strike at the plant and at the hands of the police, who had then given them little in the way of medical treatment. Jenn treated a concussion, administered stitches and began treatment for two nasty looking infections. Two days into the battle and their medical supplies were already beginning to run perilously low.

Around midnight, Jenn's weary team met in Austin's living room. The old widower didn't have any family, but he did have plenty of furniture from a time long passed. Much to Tom and Scott's delight, Austin brewed his own beer, which he was more than happy to share.

Austin sat in his comfy armchair and stroked his beard as Jenn let Ellen lead off. "The bad news," she reported, "is that the Indigo social platform is dead to us. Somebody figured out how we were using it and shut it down. I also talked to the police and they were not interested in a prisoner exchange." She paused to let people talk, but her mother motioned for her to continue.

"The most exciting news is that Jamie's newscast was a massive hit nationwide. I've been in contact with my friends around the country and we have supporters pretty much everywhere. It sounds like the strike is going to spread tomorrow and people willing to take up the fight in their towns, too."

Her mother was shocked, nearly dropping her beer. She hadn't really thought things would move like this. Maybe, she had thought, things would grow slowly starting in Des Moines, but this was more than she'd ever imagined.

Tom's calloused hand grabbed Jenn's. His gentle smile reassured her more than his words. "You've got us off to a great start, babe. What's next?"

She glanced down at their hands and then up into Tom's eyes. Tom got the message and relaxed his grip to a gentler level. All these years and he sometimes still forgot how strong his hands were, especially when he was excited. Jenn smiled back. "Thanks. Everyone on our side had done so well. I can't really take credit for much. I had some ideas and you all went out and did the dirty work. I'm pretty sure I couldn't shoot someone or take over a police station."

Austin's sudden burst of laughter startled them all. "You don't know much about how the army works, do you? It takes a lot of planning and brains to make it work well. If the plans aren't good, lots of people will die who don't need to. You have a team here to take over some of the day to day stuff so you can focus on getting rid of those bastards." He paused as a fit of coughing took over his body. When that passed, his voice was even more gravely than before. "I'm in no shape to go out there and do the fighting, but I can help here at the farm with pretty much anything else."

Penny and Abigail followed Austin's lead and volunteered to take over base operations. She was a little puzzled when Scott offered to help his wife, but she accepted his offer without question.

"Thank you," Jenn said, "I appreciate that. Now we have to work out our next few steps." She looked at her brother, "Lane, what are their next moves likely to be?"

"They're going to have to retake the plant. It serves as a symbol of the revolution and if they can take that back, it's a big, bad sign for our side." Jenn listened intently as he spoke. Ellen's fingers flashed around the keyboard as she took notes on her computer.

Lane continued, "And we're going to need better weapons and more of them. We're off to a good start, but if the army comes for real, we're going to be in trouble. Our guns and firebombs will be OK against the local cops and maybe the National Guard for a while, but in a day or two, the army is going to be here and we'll need better weapons then. My guess is that they'll try to do it with minimal physical damage to the plant at first. Old Man Wright ain't gonna want his plant blown up if it doesn't have to be. But if push comes to shove, they're going to bring in tanks and maybe aircraft and then we're in real trouble."

When Lane paused, Tom spoke up. "I need to be back at the plant. Jenn, I know you think we can do more good here, and maybe you're right, but I got those people into this and I need to be with them."

Jenn didn't reply. She stared at him as silence engulfed the room.

"Pops," Steph said, "I think you're safer out here. I don't want you back there." The computer screen reflected off Ellen's glasses as she looked up and nodded her agreement.

"Girls, look," Tom sighed before continuing. "I know it's safer out here, but I have a duty to those people."

"Pops, you have a duty to us, too!" Steph's voice was trembling with fear.

"This revolution is not going to just be fought by other people. How can I convince those people to put their lives at risk when I won't do the same thing? I wouldn't be able to sleep and I sure couldn't live with that example for you two."

Neither of the girls could respond. Ellen looked about to cry and Steph sat back with her arms crossed and her lips drawn together tightly. Finally, Jenn spoke, "I don't like it much either, but you're right."

Steph half jumped out of her chair "Mom! I-"

Jenn cut her daughter off with a raised hand. "One of the problems we've had for the last hundred years has been leaders who have been quite willing to sacrifice other people's kids and haven't actually gotten involved. That lack of leadership has got to stop. If we want to inspire people to change things, we have to lead the way, whether I like it or not."

Steph sat back down and turned away from her parents in silent protest. Ellen returned to her typing, muttering under her breath, "She should so run for president."

Penny spoke up from the corner for the first time. "Are we going to try and get Bob again? I said that a long time ago it seems, but, I mean, if we truly see him as the enemy, we have to try and get to him." She looked around and saw a lot of nodding heads.

Jenn finally spoke again. "OK, what do you all think about this?" She laid out her plans for the next 48 hours and accepted some minor tweaking from the rest of the group. They had made great progress by the time they were all too tired to think and retired for the night.

———

Dawn came too soon for Jenn's liking. Her inclination was to roll over and go back to sleep, but her brain took over and she grudgingly swung her feet to the floor. She rubbed her eyes and looked around, slowly remembering where she was. She had dragged herself up the stairs and promptly fallen into a deep sleep without bothering to examine her new surroundings. As she looked around, it became clear that Austin didn't use this room much. Dust blanketed everything and it had a stale smell from being closed up all the time.

Tom was already up and gone, so she turned her attention to the window overlooking the farm. Her first move was to pull back the curtains, unleashing a cloud of dust that made her sneeze twice. With no other options, Jenn wiped her nose on sleeve and finally pried the window open to let in some fresh air. Around the farm, the rising sun was shimmering off the dewy grass like diamonds. She closed her eyes for a moment and sampled a breath of the farm air. It was radically different than the air at her own house in the city. It was like perfume.

It all looked so peaceful, so idyllic, she thought. It was unreal that the world could go from this to guns and bombs. And at her command, no less. A handful of people emerged from an outbuilding, talking and stretching. At first, Jenn wondered what they were talking about. Then she wondered if they'd make it back alive. She turned away, unable to think about their fate. Behind her, she discovered her husband watching her silently. He stayed quiet and handed her a cup of coffee, which she allowed to warm her hands for a moment before drinking.

"You look to be thinking some awfully deep thoughts for this hour," he said. He had always been pretty good at reading her mind.

"I guess I'm more worried about what's going to happen to our people than I'd anticipated. I'm used to having some control over life and death at work, but this is different. I wonder if Washington or Eisenhower ever felt like this?"

Tom smiled before he spoke. "I think they got plenty worried about their people getting killed. If they hadn't cared so deeply, I don't think people would have followed them like they did. And if memory serves, they were able to do their jobs and stay human. You will, too."

She nodded. "Thanks. You're ready for your part today?"

"Yes, ma'am." He drew himself to attention and saluted for as long as he could before they both broke into laughter.

With smiles still on their faces, the couple made their bed before going downstairs to the kitchen. Judging by the exaggerated hand gestures, Lane and Austin's conversation at the table had to be about the day's mission. Austin's hands paused in mid-air and he simply said, "Dig in," as he nodded towards the counter before continuing on with Lane.

Tom did a double take when he saw the spread and tried not to show his excitement. Biscuits and gravy were among his favorite vices and exactly the kind of thing Jenn hated. "Doesn't anyone believe in fruit around here?" Jenn kept her thought to herself, but the twinkle in Tom's eyes made her think he was still inside her head. He joined Lane and Austin before he said something he'd regret, leaving Jenn's thoughts to drift to the next moves on the chess board.

She hadn't gotten far, when the girls all came down from their room looking like they had the weight of the world on their shoulders. Jenn greeted them all more cheerily than she felt, while the three men barely looked up from their discussion. Ellen shared the few overnight developments she had read on-line as the other two girls sampled the unfamiliar food.

Penny and Scott startled Jenn when they entered the kitchen singing "Happy Birthday" at the top of their lungs. She looked over to see Anne trying to hide, but being blocked by Steph's hug. Mortified that she had forgotten Anne's birthday, Jenn began singing along and soon everyone joined in.

"Be it known, that it was on this day in 2038 at 9:17 PM that Anne Louise Stevens was born. Let us remember this momentous day with much rejoicing." Scott's voice filled the room. Anne's cheeks darkened with embarrassment and she tried to hide once more. Her father had made this ritual announcement since she was born no matter where they were. "Happy birthday, honey," he concluded. He gave his daughter a hug and a kiss on the forehead.

Penny hugged her from behind and added her own, "Happy birthday. I'm sorry, but we couldn't find red velvet cupcakes this year."

"I understand. Thanks, Mom and Dad." Scott and Penny released their daughter and found a place to sit, their duty as parents satisfied for the moment. Breakfast was consumed over more birthday wishes and a few stories before they got to work.

The forces formed up into two groups before leaving the farm on separate missions. The girls got their wish and jumped inside Jenn's mini-van, with Anne claiming the front seat as the birthday girl. Lane pulled his truck in close behind with four more troops crammed inside and more in the open box. With his own truck still at the plant, Tom was using one of Austin's, with Jamie next to him. He looked past her at the girls and waved. As the two groups moved out in different directions, he silently wondered if he'd see his family again.

———

Tom and Jamie guided their team into the city, avoiding checkpoints along the way. In the backseat, Alex Schultz was at the controls of a small UAV scouting their route for Jamie who had grown up here. The government's computers would track them if they used the auto-drive programs, so they relied on her knowledge of the back ways around town.

As they approached the fence plant, they were startled to see armed men on every street corner and not a police car in sight. Out of curiosity, Tom pulled over and asked one group of men what was happening.

"We're here to support the strike at the plant!" was the response he got.

Tom looked at Jamie wide-eyed, while she mouthed the word "Wow." Neither one was quite prepared for this.

Tom reached out the window and shook the man's hand. Once he explained who he was, they were rewarded with cheers and raised fists. The man reported that they had seen a few police cars drive by, but that was it. "Really?" Tom asked, stunned by the man's words. He was sure he'd have to fight his way into the plant.

"Yeah, no shit," the man answered. "The damn police are still trying to figure out how to deal with what you started. There's a city-wide uprising and they can't handle it all at once." Alex confirmed that the UAV showed no massive police build-up and that their way was clear.

"I'll be damned," Tom said and shook the man's hand again. "Go ahead and grab a couple of cases out of the bed of the truck and we'll be on our way then." Tom drove off to more cheers and men banging on the side of his truck. Inside, he could only shake his head in amazement.

They arrived at the gate to find it still closed and blocked, but that problem was easily remedied with a call to Liam at the gate house. Tom returned to his former workplace with a rush of emotions. Last week it had been a prison; now it was the center of the battle for freedom.

Jamie took charge of distributing supplies, while Tom proceeded up to the 15th floor to meet with his people. The guards there welcomed him back and led him to the conference room, where Shawn, Emma and a man he hadn't met yet were in a deep discussion around a hologram of the plant.

"I'm impressed, "Emma said. "Kind of in shock, actually. I never expected you to come back."

Shawn echoed her sentiment. "Yeah, I haven't seen a civilian leader ever do anything like that."

Tom was a little embarrassed by it all. "Shit," he said, "I couldn't look at myself in the mirror if I knew I'd left you here."

"Well," Shawn added, "in any case, it's good to have you back, sir."

Tom offered his hand to the new guy as a way out of the conversation. "I'm Tom Erickson. And you are?"

"Peter Kim, sir. I'm pretty new to the company, I started as a delivery driver about a month ago after ten years in the Army. It's good to finally meet you."

Tom joined them at the table and they brought him up to speed. Overnight, they had secured all of the entry points and had worked up plans for how to handle different attack scenarios. They had enough food in the cafeteria to last for a month and even their casualties were recovering as well as could be expected. All good news, Tom thought, but it's way too early to get excited.

Shawn took him to a small meeting room to where their star prisoners were being held, watched over by some office workers Tom didn't know. Kristen, Mollie and Lester were sitting together at the far end of the room looking miserable. He was pleased to see food and beverage containers in the trash can and that the prisoners were being treated right.

Tom left the prisoners without saying a word to any of them. He really didn't have anything to say and rather enjoyed having control over his interaction with them. It was such a nice change from a week before.

─────

Lane and Jenn's trip to Bob Wright's mansion on the outskirts of town had been equally uneventful. They hadn't even seen a checkpoint until they got within a mile of his neighborhood. The flashing lights of the squad cars could be seen at quite some distance and they turned onto a nearby side street before they were spotted. "OK, girls, it's time to go to work," Jenn said without turning around.

Jenn got out of the van with the girls and watched Steph and Anne stretch their legs, fear sucking the life from her. "It's OK, Mom, we got this," Steph tried to reassure her. "We're just like, going to run by and take a little look to see what we're getting into. It was your plan, remember? You said a UAV circling their heads would raise their suspicions?" She hugged her mom tightly.

"Yeah," Anne agreed, "they probably won't even look at us and we need to get in some miles anyway." Jenn hugged her, too.

"Alright," Ellen spoke up, "look here." She was holding her computer out for them to see. It showed a map of the neighborhood they were in with a couple of spots highlighted on it. "We're here," she pointed to one spot, "and the cops are here, 1.1 miles up this street," she pointed to another. "If you go up to Bush Drive and go left, you can run through that intersection a block in front of them. Then you make another left and come back on Eagle. Got it?"

Steph and Anne nodded. Ellen closed her computer and set it on Lane's tailgate before speaking to the other girls. "Come back safe, you're the only sisters I have." The older girls hugged her before starting off up a slight rise towards their objective.

———

Tom stared out the same window Kristen and Mollie had the day before, his stomach churning with the same uneasiness. He hated not knowing what was going on and the constant waiting. Yesterday had been bad, but this was killing him. He turned his head at the sound of snoring to find Shawn sound asleep, his head tilted back on his chair. His radio and rifle were resting on the table within arm's length. Maybe that was why all his troops looked better rested than he did? Out of politeness, he let the man rest while he returned to looking out the window.

His gaze shifted from the courtyard below to the main gate to the factory building and the streets beyond. After what seemed to be a million repeats of that sequence, Tom was ready to go lay his head down, too, when Shawn's radio crackled to life. "East lookout to Alpha-Two. Over."

Shawn sprang to life, fully awake, and grabbed the radio. "Alpha-Two, go ahead. Over." He got out of the chair and joined Tom at the window, where he gestured to the far corner of the plant.

"They are starting to gather their troops. I can see two armored vehicles, a couple of transport trucks, a couple of squad cars and about a shitload of ground troops. I don't think these are cops, they're dressed like real soldiers, which probably makes them the National Guard. Over."

"South lookout reporting. I can see about twice that many of those fuckers on our end of the building. Over"

Shawn pointed again. "Anybody else see anything in their sector? Over." All of the other lookouts reported their areas clear.

"Bravo-Two here," Emma joined the conversation. "It's the two-pronged pincer attack. It looks like they're going to hit the two gates simultaneously and try to overwhelm us with numbers. I am deploying additional troops to those locations. Over."

Tom took the radio from Shawn. "This is Tom. Did Jamie get you the supplies?"

The radio was silent for a moment before Emma replied. "Yes, sir, she did. I think the Guard troops are in for an unpleasant surprise. Over."

Shawn took the radio back. "Affirmative. You have command out there, Gunny. Over."

"Roger that. Out."

———

It took Steph and Anne seven minutes to reach their turn, hardly a personal record for either. Despite their bravado, the girls' legs were wobbly and their breathing faster than normal when they arrived at Bush Drive and paused to peek around the corner. The street was deserted, so they continued with their run. Exactly as Ellen had told them, they came to an intersection a block from the checkpoint. Both girls tried hard not to be too obvious, but they were looking at the police often enough for one of the officers to make eye contact with Anne. Whether it was out of fear or genius, she didn't know, but Anne raised her hand and waved to the police officer, whom she could see smile and wave back. The two girls didn't speak until they had turned the next corner, where they stopped and grabbed a sign post. "Oh my God!" Steph blurted out.

"I know! I didn't know what else to do!"

"Let's keep going. I haven't heard a siren, so I think we should like just keep going." Anne agreed and the two resumed running until they had reached the trucks. They arrived to Jenn's relief and even a hug from Lane.

The troops from the other vehicles gathered around as the girls made their report. Anne spoke first, "There were two cars and four officers. They had the cars parked nose to nose blocking the road up into their neighborhood."

Lane nodded. "Did they recognize you? Or do anything out of the ordinary?"

"No," Steph answered, "one of them even waved! It looks like they saw exactly what they were supposed to see, a couple of girls out running."

Lane spoke to Ellen. "You were right about that, kiddo. Good work." Ellen smiled while Lane continued. "Let's hope they see what else we want them to."

————

An evil smile crossed Emma's face as peered through her binoculars. From her position overlooking the main gate, she could at last see the police and National Guard troops for herself.

She lowered the binoculars, putting them in their case while she calculated her chances. First, she knew the enemy would have to pass through the armed mob before they arrived at the plant. On one hand, she guessed that the mob possessed no weapons that could penetrate the armor plating on the vehicles. On the other hand, the damage to the soldier's morale would be significant. The people they were "protecting" from the big, bad strikers would be shooting at them and that would demoralize them. More importantly, when they got to the plant, her troops would hold them off. What tomorrow would bring, she didn't know, but for today she felt supremely confident.

Finally, the enemy began to advance. The armored cars took the lead, flanked by infantry troops. The police cars and officers in riot gear brought up the rear. She spoke into her radio, "Stand ready. Charge your weapons. Hold your fire until you have clear targets."

————

Officer Cruz watched a beat up pick-up truck approach her checkpoint with bored eyes. They had been here since dawn and only a handful of cars had come through, most of them residents of the community behind her or their workers. To make matters worse, those assholes had been offended that they had been stopped. "I'm protecting you, and you're offended. Screw you!" she thought. She could see two men in the bed of the truck holding rakes and shovels and two more in the cab. She snorted and shared a knowing look with Officer Hiatt. It made perfect sense that the gardeners would have to come to work in the midst of this madness. When the truck was closer, she held up her hand and signaled for them to stop.

She approached the driver, while Hiatt took the passenger side. The other two officers were leaning against their vehicles watching. When the two officers reached the truck, they were taken aback to see the occupants of the cab pointing guns at them. The men in the back dropped their tools and leveled rifles across the roof at the other two officers. "Down on the ground! Now!" one of the men commanded.

It only took a nanosecond for Officer Cruz and the other officers to know they'd been had. The others followed her lead and reluctantly complied with their orders. From her spot on the ground, she could see another vehicle pull up and a bunch of people get out of it. With more efficiency than she'd expected, Officer Cruz and the officers were disarmed and hauled back up to their feet, where they stood handcuffed, facing their captors.

Jenn looked at her new prisoners and finally spoke. "Officers," she nodded politely to Cruz, "thank you for not resisting. We have no desire to hurt anyone we don't have to. As long as you cooperate with us, you'll be safe, fair enough?" The officers nodded. "Good," Jenn continued as she turned back to her troops, "Put them in the back of their cars." She watched silently as the four officers were carefully confined and the cars were backed up to allow her vehicles to pass and drive half a block up the street.

She looked at Lane, "Are you ready?" He nodded, but the look on his face caught Jenn's attention. "What's your question?" she asked.

"These guys are the enemy. Why are you so nice to them? If it were me, I would have fucking wasted them all right here so they can't come back and bite us in the ass later. You're the boss, so we'll do it your way, but what's the deal?"

As usual, Jenn thought before answering. Lane knew how she hated being interrupted and waited patiently. "I don't see these four as the enemy, necessarily, they're pawns in the same game we are. The politicians and the Bob Wrights are the enemy. If they'd started shooting, I'd be fine with shooting back, but once we win this war, we're going to want them on our side and I guess treating them kindly is a good start. Well, that and I'm not big on shooting people if there's a better option...too much work for me." She winked at her brother.

Lane laughed and nodded. Trust his sister to be thinking that far ahead. Without another word, he grabbed a duffel bag out of his truck and carried it to the gate. To his surprise, Ellen came along with him.

He set the bag on the ground and looked at his niece, his face again showing that he had a question. "I want to see how you do this." she said before he could actually ask it. "Explosives are chemistry and physics and I can count this as educational."

Lane smiled and shook his head at her. "You are so much like you mother."

"I'll take that as a compliment."

From the duffel bag, Lane removed a small, cone shaped device. "This is a shape charge. It focuses the force of the explosion on a smaller point to maximize the damage. This is a relatively small one, but it still packs a wallop."

As Lane explained the details, Ellen nodded appreciatively. She knew her chemistry and that combination would certainly work. She stayed quiet and let him focus on his work as he stuck the device to the fence's lock. He looked around and checked to see that all of the vehicles had pulled back to a safe distance, which they had. "See this switch," he pointed, once you flip it, we have 15 seconds to get to safety. It's a simple circuit with a timer, so there's no going back after it's activated." Ellen gave him a slight nod.

"Here's what we're gonna do," he continued. "You get to flip the switch and then you and I are gonna run like Hell and get behind the truck." This time Ellen's head bobbed with excitement. Lane grinned, "Ready when you are."

Without hesitation, Ellen reached out and flipped the switch. As directed, she ran behind her uncle's truck, where she ducked down behind the front wheel. Lane was right on her heels and shielded her body with his, covering his head with his hands.

Even though she knew it was coming, Ellen still flinched when the shape charge exploded. When she stuck her head up and looked over the truck, the mangled gate was now open several feet and threatening to fall off completely. Beyond the fence were some perfectly sculpted shrubs and a long, manicured lawn leading up a gentle rise to Bob and Marsha Wright's striking white house.

———

Exactly as Emma had anticipated, the attackers' approach was slow moving. They had to push cars out of their way and exchanged fire with people in what seemed like every other building they passed. Molotov cocktails rained down, creating a smokescreen her binoculars struggled to penetrate.

Nonetheless, as Emma expected, the caravan made their way up the wide street essentially unscathed, leaving behind it bodies strewn in the street and hanging out of windows. She didn't have many weapons that could stop the armored vehicles either, so she couldn't fault them too much.

The police cars, trucks and the remaining ground troops stopped short of the plant and formed a defensive perimeter. Emma could only listen and watch helplessly as the lead cars' diesel engine began to howl and accelerate towards the plant. The car aimed itself at the center of the parking lot gate and hit it at its top speed of 40 miles per hour. The gate itself got knocked off its foundation, but only as far as the delivery truck behind it. As an added obstacle, Emma had had the starter removed from the truck once the assault had started.

Behind her, she could hear shots coming from the loading area, but she didn't turn to look. Peter had established a similar defensive position and while she didn't know him well, he seemed OK for an Army puke. She had to trust that he'd get the job done.

The dust had not yet cleared from the gate, when four of her troops lobbed flaming Molotov cocktails. They landed right on target in the small openings between the truck and the fence, filling the air with the choking smell of burning gasoline. At least she could deny them this entrance for a while.

———

Lane and Jenn led their group inside the gate. They had half of their crew with them, while the other half had stayed behind at the checkpoint. The police cars had been parked in their original spot to give the appearance of normalcy to anyone who didn't look too closely.

Once inside, Jenn had to pause. She had been to the homes of some wealthy doctors before, but this was beyond her wildest imagination. The "community" contained only four homes, but what homes they were. Each home had its own gate and fence system for added security. Beyond them, she could see swimming pools surrounded by ornate fountains and neatly trimmed greenery. Not a house had less than a six-car garage. From what she'd read, Jenn knew the streets were all heated so they would never be covered with snow or ice, nor would any chemicals damage the residents' cars. In front of the house stood uniformed servants looking at them and pointing.

They approached the Wright's gate first, where Lane parked the truck and stepped out to the ornate gate with Jenn. She pressed the intercom button and looked at the camera, while Lane's eyes wandered up to the house. He watched as the servants debated their decision, their arms waving wildly at one point. Jenn waited a moment and when there was no answer, pressed it again. Finally, a man's face appeared and he asked, "How may we help you?"

"Open the gate, please," she responded. "If you don't, we obviously have the means to come in anyway. We promise you won't be hurt."

Jenn was pleased when the gate opened without another word. They climbed back in the truck and drove up the gently winding driveway to the house. The girls in the van behind had their faces pressed against the windows, mesmerized by the grandeur of the grounds. They were used to their homes with small yards and big trees, not massive expanses of grass without a tree in sight.

Lane drove up the winding driveway and parked in front of the house with Steph stopping the van behind them. They were met by the group of servants, who shuffled their feet and whispered among themselves. Having their routine interrupted by a group of armed strangers was clearly not an everyday occurrence. Even Lane could read their fear and left his rifle in the truck as he and Jenn approached the group.

"Now what?" a man in a dark uniform finally asked.

"We are not here to harm any of you," Jenn answered. We are looking for the Wright family. Bob, Robert...the whole family. Are they here?"

"No, they're not. They skipped out on us last night. They took the kids and the dogs in his helicopter to the airport and then headed to their place in Lake Forest."

"That sounds about right. And left you here to deal with us, right?"

"That's right. They left and said you'd probably kill us all because we worked for them. I was the head butler, by the way. But I heard how you let the police live at the jail and knew he was lying. He lied to us all the time." The man spit on the ground.

"You don't mind if we take a look through the house, do you?" Lane asked.

"Go ahead. They're not here."

Lane and two others entered the house and did a room by room search. Still others did a walk around the grounds and outbuildings. As reported, the Wright family was gone. Lane rejoined Jenn and the girls outside, shaking his head as he approached. "Wow, if you thought it was excessive out here, you should see the inside. Who the Hell needs all this?"

The butler had taken off his jacket and tie and was sitting in the shade. "Satisfied?"

"Yeah. Sorry, but we had to look." Lane offered his hand to the man, who stood and shook it.

"Not a problem. I would have checked, too." He switched his gaze to Jenn and asked, "So, how do we help?"

Jenn smiled at him. "Thanks. If some of you can help us gather up food and other supplies that would be helpful. Anybody here know anything about their place in Lake Forest?" She looked around at the servants, all of whom shook their heads.

"OK," she continued as she turned to face the Wright's former staff, "you all can do a couple of more things. First, stay here and keep this place secure. We may need it for a while. And, if you want to go out and cause some problems for the powers that be, that's fine by me. Remember the lesson from here, though; regular working people are not the enemy. Treat them well and with respect. You know who the real enemy is." She looked deep into the eyes of the new recruits as she spoke. They all nodded before leading the girls inside and some of the others to the garage.

Once Jenn was alone with Lane, she brought up the obvious. "Looks like we're going to have to go to Chicago."

"Yeah. We can't let him get away again."

"Nope. I'll take charge here with the girls and the new people. You go to the other houses and see what kind of supplies you can find. I'm guessing you'll find the workers there as helpful as the ones here. And hurry, there's bound to be some kind of response by the police."

"You got it. What about the owners? They're going to be Wright clones."

"Take 'em alive if you can. Then we can hold them here."

"Got it." He stuck his fingers to his mouth and whistled to get the attention of his troops, who he directed to the vehicles. Jenn watched them depart before entering the Wright mansion through the heavy double doors.

Within ten feet, Jenn stopped at a marble fountain with cherubs spitting water and stared at the space around her. She thought she was prepared for the excess, but this was beyond even what she'd seen on TV. She walked in closer to a painting on the wall and gaped open-mouthed when she realized it was an original Marc Chagall.

"Stunning, isn't it?" a voice from behind asked.

Jenn turned and nodded to one of the servants. "I'm Jade, one of the maids. Mrs. Wright often complained about the burden of properly furnishing their three homes. They took some of the pieces they liked better when they left."

Jenn was dumbstruck. It was an exquisite masterpiece and it wasn't good enough? If anything symbolized the disconnect between the Wrights and the rest of the country, here it was. Finally, Jenn was able to speak. "That's crazy. I really don't even know how to respond to that."

"I know," Jade said, "You can imagine the rest of the house is the same way. Upstairs he had a Honus Wagner baseball card and an original Spider-Man comic book that he took with him. And I live in a crappy two-bedroom apartment with my husband and two kids struggling to have enough to eat. Whenever I could, I'd sneak home leftovers from the kitchen."

Jenn reached out and held her hand. "I'm sorry you have to go through that. We're going to try and change things if we can."

"I know. It's exciting, but it's frightening, too. What if you fail? Then what happens?"

Jenn pursed her lips. "I don't know that answer. All I know is that we have to try. You have kids, you know why."

Jade pulled her hand away. "Good luck. I have to get back to work." With that, she left Jenn and headed back down the hallway.

With one last look at the painting, Jenn continued in the search for supplies. She grew increasingly annoyed as she wandered up the winding staircase and through the many rooms of the Wright mansion. It was hard to find a use for the animal heads on the walls or the medieval suits of armor and Jenn was left shaking her head in frustration and amazement.

On the third floor, she followed the sounds of the girls to the master bedroom. Inside, the girls stood on a thick Persian rug, afraid to touch anything. "Well, girls, what do you think?" Jenn asked.

"Mom," Steph said, "the closet is bigger than my bedroom. I think she has a different outfit for every day of the year."

"Mama Jenn, this is crazy. Nobody needs this much stuff," Anne answered as she stared around the room.

"You're right, sweetie. I don't really know what to tell you. It's madness." She walked past the canopied bed to one of the dressing tables and poked at a silver-plated hairbrush. Against the mirror, a carved jewelry box caught Jenn's eye and she had to look. The collection inside took her breath away. Diamonds, rubies, sapphires, emeralds, something flawless in every imaginable color. Unconsciously, Jenn played with her own wedding ring. The nicest thing she owned wouldn't be good enough for this collection.

Ever so softly, Jenn pushed the jewelry around the satin interior, her mind now off on a new thought. After a moment, she closed the lid and tucked the box under her arm.

"Mom?" Ellen asked, "What are you doing?"

Jenn turned to face the girls again. "At some point we are probably going to need some serious cash and that's one thing none of us really has to offer."

Ellen's head tilted again as she thought. "You're right, Mom, I hadn't thought of that. It's a tool, like guns or my computer."

Jenn was about to respond when gunfire erupted from the police checkpoint. The shooting was over in under two furious minutes, followed by several more of agony as they waited for a report. She and the girls couldn't see anything through the window, but looked out anyway. At last, Jenn received a report that one police officer was dead and one was wounded, while one of her people had a bullet wound to his arm.

As with the raid on the police station, the majority of the police force was engaged elsewhere, allowing Jenn to minimize the number of wounded. How long this strategy would last, she didn't know, but for the time being she was meeting her objectives with limited bloodshed. "OK, girls, we still have work to do."

Within an hour, the old Wright mansion had 19 new residents, including the police officers, being guarded by an array of their former employees. It took that long to load, but Jenn and company left with their vehicles weighted down with food, bedding and more than a few bottles of wine. The staff had shown them Bob's gun collection, which Lane assured them was of the highest quality as he loaded them into his truck.

————

From their vantage point, Tom and Shawn watched the battle below and so far, things were going well. Their attackers had been denied entrance to the plant and had finally pulled back a couple of blocks where they had created a defensive perimeter. Sporadically, civilians took shots at them from the city, which only caused the police to hunker down even more.

Shawn set down his binoculars and blinked his eyes. "Sir, if I read this right, they are setting up those positions to wait for reinforcements. It's simple, we can deny them the plant, they can deny us everything else. It's only a matter of time until they bring in real armor. Then they'll be able to either blow up our barricades or push them out of the way."

Tom could only nod in agreement, he knew it was a reasonable assumption. The police and guard troops weren't going to risk too many lives trying to storm the plant; not when they could call for help and wait him out. His troops had held off the bully to this point, now he had to put his faith in Shawn and Emma's plan and hope it would be enough when his big brother arrived.

Finally, he spoke. "You're right. You've laid in the IEDs? And created some cover for our guys down there? Shawn nodded. "OK, I guess we wait. I'm going to try to sack out in Bob's office for a bit. Wake me when the situation changes."

"Yes, sir."

Chapter Twenty-Four

Jenn was doing her best to be paranoid enough and insisted that her team split up and take different routes back to their new headquarters. Lane fully approved, but his natural curiosity made him choose a route that took him by his farm. He had to look.

Pillars of black smoke billowing up over the horizon was their first clue, visible for miles across the flat plains. As they drew closer to the farm, it took all of Lane's self-control to even stay on the road. The remainder of the drive took place in dark silence, with each of them deep in their own thoughts.

At the farm, Penny ran to greet them before the truck had even stopped. Only after she hugged them all could she speak. "Oh my God, have you been following the news? They launched a drone strike on Lane's farm! From the footage they showed on the news, the whole place is pretty much gone!"

Lane squinted his eyes at her. "We drove past it and saw the smoke." He turned to Jenn, "Looks like you were right to get us out of there when you did."

Jenn hugged her brother, too. "Oh, Lane, I'm so sorry. I know that farm meant the world to you." Lane hugged her back and said nothing. That didn't surprise Jenn, he'd always been the stoic one in the family. Sometimes she wondered if that had kept him single all this time.

Jenn finally released her brother and wiped the last tear from her eye. A small crowd had gathered around them and those that didn't already know were quickly told the story. Even with people dead, this was still the most jarring moment she'd experienced in her new role.

Lane cleared his throat before spitting on the driveway. "Time to get back to work, then." He pushed his way through the crowd and went into the house without another word, allowing Jenn to supervise the unloading of their captured supplies.

While dinner looked like a summer picnic, it felt more like a funeral supper. The talk was hushed and while Jenn tried not to discuss the attack on their former base, it was a hot topic among everyone else. The might of the US military had been used and that was a precursor of what could easily be in store for all of them. Once the dishes had been cleared, most of the people left to sample their new wine selection.

Lane and Austin slipped off to a back room to lay out their plans, while Ellen brought her mother to the living room. Ellen had pushed the furniture together and arranged several computers on the cushions facing a hard-backed chair. Jenn sat and watched patiently as Ellen pushed a few buttons. When she was ready, she nodded to her mother. "Are you sure we're safe?" Jenn asked?

"As safe as Xantha Mbutu from Nairobi can make it, Mom. I know it's a risk, but we've got to try. And like you said, we have to trust some people."

Ellen took Jenn's sigh as her sign to push the final button. She had worked her magic to make contact with rebel groups from around the country and Jenn found herself looking at video links to a number of people who looked as apprehensive as she felt. On each of their screens was their first name and the city they were in. A black man with a patch over his left eye from Chicago spoke first. "Well, here we are. I guess we all know why we're here. I'm Tim Brown from Chicago, everybody calls me T-Bone. I lost my eye and my wife and kids in the Chicago massacre last month. I'm ready to go kill 'em all with my bare hands."

It was hard to watch all of the screens at once, but Jenn could see a lot of heads nodding their understanding. She let the rest of the group introduce themselves as they saw fit before she spoke. Surprisingly, they were all respectful of one another and did their best not to shout or speak over one another. "I'm Jenn from Des Moines. I'm not sure, but the revolution may have boiled over here. Rumor is you've all seen the newscast from here and heard about our takeover of the security fence plant." Again she could see nodding, so she continued.

"Like Mr. Brown said, we're all here for the same reason. My daughter tells me that you're ready to commit to full-fledged revolution and fixing our country." More nodding. "Here's what I propose: we all know the government has amazing tools to track us down and kill us, so we're not going to be too united at first, just a loose alliance. If they capture Mr. Brown, I don't want him to be able to divulge too much information about any of the other cells around the country. So, for now, I don't want to share too much about what we're doing. Anybody disagree?" She paused to let the others consider her words. No one spoke up, which Jenn took as a good sign.

"I know we all may have different visions of what America should be, but it sounds like we're united behind the idea that what we have isn't working. Let me suggest that we all work independently in our own states or cites to get rid of the existing government. If we go at it all piecemeal, they'll kill us all, but if we all act at the same time, it will spread out the military and give us a fighting chance. You heard our ultimatum to the government, they have about 20 hours to leave the country or it's open season on them."

A bald man named Koby from Washington DC interrupted her. "That sounds easy enough in Des Moines, but I'm pretty sure the Army is going to defend them tooth and nail here."

"He's right," said T-Bone, "the battles for big cities are going to be much harder than for places like yours."

Jenn nodded her head before speaking. "I understand what you're saying. On the upside, you also have more human resources, more angry citizens who will want to help in one way or another. From my experience here over the last couple days, pretty much everyone is on board with us."

"I've seen that, too," said Hazel from a reservation in Arizona. "I haven't talked to anyone who wants to keep our current government. Of course, I haven't talked to a lot of millionaires, either." That drew laughs from the others.

"Ain't that the truth," Jenn agreed. "The millionaires and billionaires are as much to blame as any politician. They have to go, too. But I'm a physician assistant and I swore an oath to try and help people, so I urge you to take them prisoner and we can sort things out later rather than killing people outright."

Justin from Memphis broke in, his drawl evident, "I ain't opposed to killing people who need killing. The only way we're going to be rid of them folks is to kill 'em all." T-Bone and about half the others agreed, much to Jenn's dismay.

"Look, I can't make any of you do anything, but if we go and kill them all, we are no better than they are. All I can do is urge you to take them alive and, after a proper trial, we can do what needs to be done." Grudgingly, the others acknowledged she had a point.

Lucas from Denver asked the next question. "Out here, the only thing we really want is to have the government off our backs and to be left alone to live how we want to live. Is that your goal?"

Jenn was ready for that one. "If I remember my history books correctly, each of the 13 colonies had different ideas back in the day, but put them aside at first and joined together to get rid of the British. We need to take that lesson and apply it here. Wipe the slate clean and start over. That's my only goal right now."

Lucas took off his wire-rimmed glasses to rub his eyes and nodded, "That's fair, I guess. I didn't think anybody else remembered about that."

"My dad was a history and US government teacher. I guess I learned more than he thought."

"They also thought black people should be slaves," T-Bone broke in. His voice was close to a shout, his face flared with anger.

"Hold on, now," said Norah from San Antonio, holding up her hands. "Nobody is talking about bringing back slavery or sending women back to being property. Everyone will get a fair shake at the table."

Koby was back. "Don't you see that this is what they want? They want to exploit our differences so we won't fight together. Well I say the Hell with them! We need to put aside those differences, take over and when it's all over we can sort out the details."

"Yeah, I guess you're right," T-Bone said with a more conciliatory tone. "But know that that's an issue."

Jenn took control of the conversation again. "When we get the chance to sit down and listen to each other, we'll find a lot of common ground and we can rebuild our county on those shared ideas." Since she had the floor, she began to wrap things up. "Any other questions or concerns we need to deal with at the moment?" No one spoke, so Jenn brought up her final thought.

"There is one thing my group needs and that's get better weapons. I can't speak for all of you, but our weapons won't be adequate to win this war. So, tonight at 0100 central time, we are going to raid the National Guard armory here. I would guess that starting bright and early tomorrow, every armory in the country is going to be on high alert, so even though it's short notice, tonight may be your last chance."

T-Bone stared at her through the monitor. "How are we supposed to pull that shit off with this kind of notice? We need time to plan!" Jenn could see the same thoughts going through the faces of the others.

"Perhaps the biggest thing I've learned recently is that the element of surprise is extremely helpful. It allowed us to pull off everything we've done to date. By striking boldly, you can make it happen, trust me. If you are all the leaders I've been told, you can make it happen in your own way tonight." Jenn stopped speaking and let the silence take charge.

After what seemed an eternity of no one speaking, she continued. "OK, you all have the plan this far. I don't see this group talking too often for security reasons, but we'll try to set it up again if it's needed. In the meantime, good luck out there. Be safe!" The others all expressed similar thoughts before Ellen killed the feed when it began to get awkward. Once the screen went black, Jenn let out a huge sigh of relief.

"You were great, Mom! When this is over and we've won, you should be the new president!" Ellen's words jumbled together as she began to pack up her equipment.

"Oh honey, not in a million years. My longest-term goal is to go back to practicing medicine and being a mom."

Ellen stopped her work. "But Mom, your words are inspiring. I've listened to some historical speeches and they inspired people to do things and..." She quit speaking when she saw Jenn still shaking her head. "Fine, but just know that I think you're doing a great job."

"Thanks, sweetie, that means a lot."

Jenn helped her daughter carry equipment back to her room, listening carefully as Ellen gave her analysis of the video conference and her take on the participants. As usual, Ellen's insight was on point and confirmed what Jenn herself thought.

———

The clock struck midnight as Lane led his unit down the driveway. He didn't like the moonlight and the clear sky, but that was the least of his worries. Behind him were a dozen cars and trucks with about 30 rebels. Once they cleared the farm, they split up and took separate routes to the armory. Lane and Austin had spent two hours planning and then another hour sharing the plan with their troops. It was too damn fast, Lane knew, but he didn't have much choice. The sooner they could have proper arms, the better.

He had changed into an old set of army camouflage gear, as had Lamar, the young man next to him. He was, as Lane's father would have said, "a little slow" and was a challenge to converse with, but he was willing and able to fight, so here he was. They drove through the night listening to the all-news station. Lane turned it up when he heard the President's distinct baritone voice.

"My fellow Americans, as you have heard, there is a small faction of society that wants to bring ruin to our country. From what we know of the rebels, they are anarchists who want to destroy the American way of life. They want to destroy everything you and your forebears have worked for since this great country was founded. We cannot let this happen! We must stick together and put down this so-called 'American Liberation Movement' as quickly as possible! To quote President Andrew Jackson, 'Disunion by armed force is treason,' which makes these people traitors to our country.

As you know, we have installed identity checkpoints in many areas and will be establishing a curfew as well. I do not take these actions lightly, but it is my duty to help protect each and every citizen from the dangers these rebels represent. We hope to round up the rebels quickly and return to our normal state of peace and prosperity. In the meantime, if you suspect people of being anti-American, notify your local police immediately. I will do everything in my power to help keep you safe, but you must help with that as well, it's your duty to your family and your country. Good night and God Bless America."

"Turn that shit off!" Lane ordered the truck. What else could the President say? The TV broadcast had worked once, but he was sure the television stations were under heavy protection. And now the President was trying to turn neighbor against neighbor, which was a big problem. How the Hell could he counter someone who had that kind of platform at his disposal?

He stayed so deep in thought that Lamar had to hit him in the arm when he nearly missed his turn. Minutes later, they arrived at their rendezvous point, a grocery store parking lot, and were soon joined by the rest of their unit. Lane gave a few last minutes instructions and the group split up again, this time to surround the armory.

Lane and Lamar drove the speed limit to the armory, where they were stopped by the wire gate and two soldiers staffing the shack outside. Lane rolled down the window and waited for the sentry to approach. He watched as one soldier typed something, probably his license plate number, into his computer and the other came to the window, one hand resting on the butt of his pistol. "What is your business here at this hour?" he demanded.

"We were ordered to report here by the Governor's office. Something to do with the fence plant thing, I guess." Lane tried to stay nonchalant.

"I haven't heard anything about that. This is a restricted area and you are going to have to leave."

"What the Hell is wrong with you, soldier? I get my ass dragged out of bed and told to report here ASAP and you're trying to tell me you don't know anything? I'm getting too old for this shit!"

"It must be some kind of snafu, but we don't have those orders. You're going to have to leave." The young man looked up as two more pick-up trucks pulled up behind Lane.

Lane glanced back over his shoulder and then spoke again. "Look, there's more guys who must have gotten the same order we did."

"Oh, what the Hell is this," the sentry muttered under his breath. "You two, wait here," he ordered before he walked back to the second truck. Lamar casually raised his arm out the window and rested his hand on the roof.

The sentry approached the newly arrived truck much as he had the first, but before he could say a word, he saw the shotgun pointed at his head and froze. Behind him, he could hear angry words and turned his head to see armed men dragging his partner out into of the guard shack. He was quickly disarmed, gagged, bound with duct tape and tossed into the bed of the last pick-up, with his partner being thrown in next to him. His partner winked as they heard the gate open and the trucks proceed inside.

Mere seconds later, the young man understood the wink. The familiar chatter of an M-36 entered his ears, the rounds hitting the truck's window and covering them both with shattered glass.

Lane turned his truck to the side and slammed it into park as Lamar jumped out his door and began shooting back into the night from the cover of the truck bed. Lane crawled across the seat and was soon firing his rifle as well as he tried to take in the whole situation. The second truck had stopped ten yards away and they were also shooting back. The truck with the prisoners stayed in the relative safety of the gate area covering their escape route. He couldn't identify specific targets, but he could see muzzle flashes from at least a dozen weapons surrounding the armory's main entrance. His truck shook as the high velocity rifle rounds struck, but none of the rounds could penetrate the engine area.

Lane flinched as a Molotov cocktail exploded without warning, its flames lighting up the night. His other troops had finally managed to breach the armory's fence and were at last able to engage. He lowered his rifle and watched in horror as a soldier ran screaming into the open, his body covered in flames. Lane recovered quickly, took aim and mercifully shot the man dead.

The soldiers realized they were being flanked and began to pull back to a more defensible position near the building's main doors. Lamar reloaded and ran around the end of the truck towards the building. "Get down! Stay low!" Lane yelled, but it was too late. Lamar staggered and fell to the ground as the soldiers continued firing to cover their retreat.

Through the smoke and fumes from the burning gasoline, Lane could see several of the soldiers were down. With the exception of Lamar, he couldn't see any of his troops, alive or dead, but that was no surprise with the mayhem around him. He ducked low, fed some more ammunition into his rifle and took a deep breath.

Lane eased his head back up over the hood. What remained of the armory's guard force had reached the shelter of their building and were taking cover there. His troops were in a rough semi-circle and were closing in as best they could under heavy fire. Surprise had gotten him inside, but the training and superior weapons of the armory's soldiers was starting to pay off. An unmistakable sound from his right forced him down again. "Great," he muttered, "now they've got grenades."

Staying low and zig-zagging along the way, Lane fell back to the third pick-up truck. With the help of his reserve troops, he pulled the sentries out of the bed and dumped them on the ground.

He turned back to his two men. "You two follow me close. I'm going to drive this right through their front door. When we're through, you two shoot anything that moves. Got it?" The two men nodded and ducked behind the truck as ordered. In the driver's seat, Lane's sweaty fingers slipped off the keys as he tried to start the truck. He rubbed them on his pants and tried again, rewarded when the truck started up with a roar.

Keeping his head down as low as possible, Lane steered the truck towards the building, dodging the first two trucks and Lamar's body as he went. Two hundred feet from the doors, bullets shattered his windshield, spraying his face with glass fragments. With all his might, he drove the accelerator down and tried to hold his course towards the door. The last thing Lane remembered was the momentum and weight of the truck jumping over the curb towards the building. He had no recollection of crashing into the glass on the right side of the doors, the abrupt halt or the airbag deployment that saved his life.

With his head swimming, Lane fought to free himself from the wreckage of the truck. He could hear shots booming around him from every direction, but all he cared about was getting out of the crumpled truck. With a mighty kick, he forced open the passenger door and was able to crawl out of the truck. Outside, he stumbled a few steps before tripping on some debris and falling to the ground. His eyes struggled to focus on two shadows coming through the dust towards him.

"Damn, boss, you're alive!" one of the shadows shouted.

"Hell yes, he is!" shouted the other. The shadows turned out to be the two men who had followed the truck into the building, now the only ones standing upright. One of the men retrieved a chair while the other helped him sit in it. Lane's hands shook as he accepted a bottle of water, from which he took a long drink and proceeded to pour the rest over his face and eyes.

As the cobwebs cleared a little, Lane tried to make sense of the chaos around him. He could see dead or wounded soldiers lying on the ground. More shadows that had to be his troops were entering the building every second. He shook his head and managed to heave himself back onto his feet. "Back to work. Start loading stuff on their trucks and make it quick. There's no telling how much time we have before they send more troops."

"Yes, sir!" the men responded before they went deeper into the building. Lane staggered outside and almost tripped again, this time over the body of one of his own men. Another rebel caught him before he fell.

"Lane, we have to get you out of here. You're in no shape to do us any good!"

"Shut up, I'll be OK in a..." Lane's knees buckled before he could finish his argument.

The soldier propping him up continued. "Look, we know the mission. We got this. We'll get you out of here and get it done."

"OK," Lane grudgingly agreed. "Make sure you... Make sure you..."

"Make sure we only use our trucks." His voice changed to a softer tone. "You got us this far, but you've got to let us handle it from here." He summoned another man over, who wrapped his arm around Lane's shoulder to guide him to a waiting truck with the other wounded. The last thing Lane saw as he departed was the white-eyed disbelief of the two sentries laying on the ground.

———

Casey Frost was not used to being woken up in the middle of the night. The shrill ringing of his omniphone jarred him from his sleep and it took him a moment to figure out what it was. "Hello?" he answered angrily.

The hologram of a uniformed man appeared. "Sir, this is Captain Graham, watch officer with the Iowa National Guard command. The Governor wanted me to alert you about a situation here."

Casey was suddenly fully awake and swung his feet over the side of his bed. "Go ahead, Captain."

"Sir, at approximately 0100 local time, an armed group attacked the Des Moines armory facility. A dozen of our troops were killed and nine were wounded. The attackers made off with five trucks full of equipment, including rifles, pistols, grenades, mortars, explosives, communications gear and medical supplies."

"Holy Hell, Captain! How could you let this happen?"

"Sir, we did not 'let it happen' at all. From the surveillance footage, our men were initially caught off guard, but then put up a valiant fight until they were simply overwhelmed by superior numbers. From the way the attackers moved and fought, they have a good number of military veterans among them. Also, our computers identified one of them as the ALM rebel leader, Lane Santana."

"Is there any other good news?" His voice dripped with sarcasm.

"Yes, sir. Similar raids were carried out at a number of other installations across the country. A couple others were successful, Chicago, San Antonio and Phoenix, while the local security forces beat them back in Denver, and DC. While their methods were different in each attack, it's clear that this was a coordinated attack by rebel groups. We have placed all armories and military installations on high alert."

"My God… My God." Casey's words were taut with emotion. "Captain, does the President know this information?"

"Yes, sir. He was the first official to be briefed. You are number four, sir."

Casey felt his face tighten. He knew the other two without their names being spoken. "Were you able to track them back to their base? I always hear about how amazing your satellites and computer programs are."

"No, sir, we were not. They were prepared for that and were able to evade our network. There are simply too many roads in and out of the city and we don't have the manpower to lock them all down yet."

"Anything else I need to know, Captain?"

"Not at this time, sir. I'm sure the President will have some orders shortly, but nothing else is relevant at this time."

"OK, thank you for letting me know." Casey hung up before Captain Graham could reply. He closed his eyes and tilted his head back as he breathed a deep sigh. It was going to be a long night.

Chapter Twenty-Five

For a change, Jenn hadn't slept well. First, she had stayed awake until the raiding party had returned and had helped treat the wounded. Then, not having Tom in the bed next to her was so foreign that she had tossed and turned all night. It had taken some effort for her to force her eyes open and to finally drag herself out of bed and into some semi-clean clothes.

Her first official act was to make her way down the dark hallway to Lane's room to check on her favorite patient. She knocked gently on his door and counted to three before entering.

Lane's room had the requisite dust as well, which probably didn't help anything, but considering that most of their troops were in sleeping bags in the outbuildings, his private room was a luxury. Lane was propped up, squinting his blackened eyes at her, the lump on his head visible from the foot of the bed. She picked up his makeshift chart and read it by the light cast off by a dim bulb in the lamp at his bedside. Gently, she felt his head, "How are you feeling this morning?"

Lane closed his eyes. "Like I got hit by a truck."

"Well, that's fair, although technically you hit the truck." She withdrew her hand and made some notes on his chart.

"Yeah, well you should see how it looks. I have a splitting headache and I'm having a hard time focusing my eyes. And I feel like I might throw up at any minute."

Jenn frowned. He had all of the classic concussion symptoms, but there wasn't much more she could do for him here. She set the chart down and poured him a glass of water from a plastic pitcher on the nightstand. "Here," she handed him the glass, "and take these." She shook two aspirin out of a bottle from her pocket and placed them in his other hand. "If we can't fix you, at least we can make you more comfortable."

Lane swallowed the pills and leaned back on the pillows. "How did we do last night? I'm a little fuzzy on the ending."

Jenn sat down on a chair they had brought in and held his hand. "You did great, I think. You brought back a couple of truckloads of guns and stuff. I don't know enough to really tell, but at least we'll have a fighting chance."

"How many of our guys were hurt?"

"We had five killed and a dozen wounded, plus you. There are a couple of the wounded I'm not so sure about, they might not have made it through the night."

"Damn. I knew we'd take casualties, but it still sucks."

Jenn didn't know how to respond. Her head knew there would be deaths, but her heart still ached for the dead and their families. She let go of his hand and stood up. "It does suck, I know. But the reports I got told me that you saved lives last night and those weapons will save lives from here on out, so..." Her voice trailed off as she suddenly realized that she had nearly lost another sibling. "I have to check on my other patients. You get some rest and I'll check back when I can."

Jenn made her way to the downstairs family room again, which was currently being used to treat the most seriously wounded soldiers. She was hailed by a serious looking woman who was serving as a nurse. "Two of them didn't make it." Jenn looked around at the empty beds. She bit her lip and took a deep breath to keep her emotions in check. She knew this outcome was a possibility, but it still stung.

"OK, how are the others doing?"

"Two of them were already able to be released to the barn. Seven of them look like they'll make it, but the one is still touch and go." She led Jenn down a row of cots to a patient she had personally treated the night before. She had removed grenade fragments from his abdomen and while she wasn't a surgeon, she'd had no choice but to try. Every medical practitioner was familiar with treating gunshot wounds, they were nearly as common as the cold these days. From what she could tell, she'd done a fair job, but there was so much more the poor guy needed.

Jenn studied his chart before turning around. "Keep treating him as you have been. Let me know if anything changes, please."

———

Tom was also awake and looking out over the plant grounds. Normally on a day like this, there would be people about, making the standard sights and sounds of plant operations, but not today. Today was unnaturally quiet. Outside the plant was a swarm of activity as the National Guard forces readied for their next attack, while inside the only movement he could see was a few of his troops sneaking looks through the fence.

With a yawn, he headed to the conference room to find Shawn and together they wandered over to the cafeteria, where Emma was finishing breakfast with Peter. Between bites of synthetic eggs and toast, Emma updated them on how the National Guard had sealed off all of the routes in and out of the plant overnight. It had been one of the scenarios they had discussed and perhaps the one they liked the least. Peter volunteered his expertise for the first time, "Sir, it's not ideal, but we've had time to work on an 'anti-access strategy' and they'll pay a price to get us out of here."

"That's why you three got this job," Tom said with a wry smile. "I trust you all to get it done."

"Thank you, sir," Emma replied, "but I have one other concern." Tom nodded, so she continued. "Remember how you said you were sure they had spies on the initial strike day?" Tom nodded again and blew on his coffee. "What if they have spies in here? Somebody telling them our plans would be really fucking bad for our well-being, if you know what I mean."

Tom set his cup down hard enough that coffee splashed out onto the table. "Shit, I'd forgotten about that. You're right, that would be bad." He mopped up the coffee with a napkin, visions of an impending disaster racing through his head. He knew there were spies, but it still blew his mind that anyone would sell out to Bob Wright like that.

Tom pushed his cap back and rubbed his forehead before speaking. "I think I have a plan to help us root out that information. Shawn, bring Lester Hatch down to the welding shop in 30 minutes. Peter, find Jamie Page and get her there ASAP. Emma, you're with me." He stood up with his tray and headed to the dish area.

"Yes, sir," the three replied as they raced to keep up.

———

Bob Wright looked up from his desktop monitor, took off his reading glasses and rubbed his eyes. Watching his corgis sleeping on a nearby couch brought a smile to his face that had been lacking for some time. The last 48 hours had been the longest of his life and had no end in sight. Reading financial reports for the Metropolitan Ballet board he sat on gave him some welcome relief, but even that would end.

His gut instinct, which had served him well for years, had told him that Des Moines was falling and Chicago was a much safer location for his family. His private jet had spirited them all away and none too soon from the reports he'd gotten. He could only imagine what was happening to his home, his plant facilities and the people he'd been forced to leave behind. There was no telling what was happening to Kristen, Mollie and Lester. He cared less about his security personnel. They had given up to Tom Erickson and his people, which was inexcusable.

He heard the door open and he watched his son's shadow cross the floor. "Father, I spoke with Casey's aide and you made the right call in getting us out of there. The whole city of Des Moines sounds like it's gone crazy! There are a number of people shooting at the police and city leaders and a whole lot more are not going to work or school. The Army is deploying active duty units in addition to the National Guard. They're expected in Des Moines tonight and they'll retake the plant. He also shared that there's been plenty of similar violence here as well as in dozens of cities around the country. If there's a bright side, there are better forces to protect us here and keep the violence on the south side of the city. Hell, blowing up that public housing will be the best thing to happen to this city in years."

Bob reached into his desk drawer and set ornate wooden case on his desk. From the case, he removed a small, silver handgun, which he handed to Robert, followed by two clips of ammunition.

Robert accepted his gift, fumbling to put the clip in properly. "Is this really necessary? I mean, we have people to help protect us."

Another gun followed, which Bob loaded before slipping it into his coat pocket. Again he looked at his son, "If you take away only one thing from this fiasco, I hope it's this. Fortune always favors those who control their destiny. In the end, you must count on yourself and your own ability to make your own future."

"I know, you've said that for years, but I can't imagine it will come to that. The Army will stop these people and we'll probably see a boost in business as people try to protect themselves even further."

"Son, listen to me. There's no guarantee we'll be safe, even here. I want you to personally make sure that the boat and the jet are fueled and ready to get us out of here at a moment's notice. If we have to… My God, I can't believe I'm saying this… If we have to abandon this house, we may need to head to the Caymans in a hurry and sort things out from there."

Robert left without another word, leaving Bob alone with the dogs. While he believed in the Army, he believed in his father's instincts even more.

———

Tom suppressed a laugh as his troops led a blindfolded Lester Hatch through the steel shop doors. Shawn guided Lester to a chair and forced him to sit. He nodded to Tom, then joined Peter and Emma outside the doorway to watch.

Underneath his blindfold, Lester heard someone dragging something heavy close to him before stopping. Tom took a deep breath and carefully removed the blindfold, causing Lester to squeeze his eyes closed and duck his head at the light.

Tom waited until Lester was able to focus his eyes. They revealed that the hatred and contempt Lester always felt had grown during his captivity, but Tom was well past caring about that. He stepped behind Lester and looked down at the thinning hair of his longtime nemesis. "Les," he knew that would irk his captive, "we know you have spies within our group. Who are they?"

"I don't know what you're talking about."

"Oh Les, don't lie to me." Tom reached down and squeezed the back of Lester's neck. Jenn had taught him about neck muscles and Lester tried to wriggle free from the agony.

"Go fuck yourself." Lester's words came out as a gasp.

Inside, Tom's emotions were a jumbled mess. He found no joy in hurting anyone, but if anybody ever deserved some pain, it was Lester. He released his hold and stepped around the chair so Lester could see him. "Oh, Les, I was hoping we could keep this civil. As you were always so fond of saying, 'it's just business,' right?"

"Go fuck yourself!"

"Les, I'm going to ask you one more time and one more time only. Who do you have spying on us?" Tom began to play with a torch on the cart.

"Go. Fuck. Yourself!"

"You know I can make you tell me anything. Don't make me take it that far." With the flip of a couple of switches the torch sprang to life in Tom's hands, the long familiar smell filling the room.

Lester was silent, tiny beads of sweat popping out beneath his thinning hair.

"Les, in a moment I'm going to show you how good of a welder I really am. Do you have any idea how hot one of these burns? No? This model tops out at 3,542 degrees. Do you know what that will do to human flesh?" Tom stood up.

"Tom, don't do it!" Jamie's voice drew both of their heads to the doorway, where she was struggling to get past Shawn.

"Let her in," Tom ordered, which Shawn did. "What do you want?" he asked crossly.

Jamie looked at him wide-eyed. "What are you doing? You're better than this."

"After all the Hell this fucking little toady has put us through, I'm looking forward to it. And he'll tell me who the snitch is, which is a bonus.

"You don't have to do this. It takes you down to his level."

"You mind your own business." He turned his back on Jamie and adjusted the flame on his torch to a fine point.

"Tom, I came down here to tell you we have your wife on a satellite link-up in the next room. Why don't you go talk to her first?

Tom glared at her. "Please?" Jamie pleaded.

"I'll talk to her," he said glaring at Lester. Tom turned off his torch and put it back on the cart. He left the room cursing under his breath.

Jamie turned her attention to Lester, still trying to look defiant in his chair, despite the dark, wet stain spreading across his pants. "Lester," she said, her voice scarcely above a whisper, "you're welcome."

"What do you mean 'I'm welcome?' He wasn't going to do it."

"Oh Lester, you have no idea how much he hates you. Remember what they did to Kristen and Mollie to get in the security office?" Lester nodded. "And remember how many people got hurt on that first day of the strike?" He nodded again. "And how many times you had run-ins with Tom over the years?" "You're a smart guy, Lester, you can imagine what he wants to do to you. You're welcome for my stopping him. For now, at least."

At last Lester comprehended his situation. Everything she had described could drive a man like Erickson to do terrible things if he felt desperate enough. "If I tell you, will you keep him away from me?"

Jamie leaned back on Tom's cart for an instant before jerking away. "Wow, that's hot!" She returned her attention to Lester, "If you answer my questions honestly, I'll do everything in my power to keep him from the blowtorch. You have my word on it."

The defeated man hung his head in shame before he blurted out, "Ricky Arroyo. Ricky told us about who was a malcontent and about the strike."

"Is that it? Just Ricky?" Lester gave a small nod, his eyes still glued to the floor. "And did Ricky warn you about our attack?" Another small nod.

"Did he call you or Bob or anyone about what we're doing in here? Give you any kind of updates?" This was the million-dollar question.

Lester picked his head up at last, his eyes wide with fear. "He didn't call me. I can't tell you if he tried to call anyone since you took over the plant. I don't know, I swear!"

Jamie looked down at him, her eyes void of emotion. "Lester, if you're lying to me, there's no way I'll be able to keep Tom off of you."

"I was up in the tower the whole time! I don't know if he called anyone! Please..." his voice turned to sobs as his head fell again.

"OK, Lester, I'll keep him away from the blowtorch, but God help you if we find you were lying to me." Jamie turned away from her captive and looked at Shawn. "Can you take him back up to the office, please? And see if you can find him some clean clothes?"

Shawn's face stayed remarkably serious. "Yes, ma'am," he said. The two guards lifted Lester out of the chair and guided him out of the room.

The outside door clicked shut behind the trio, when Tom reappeared. He had a smile on his face that masked his anger. "Well played," he said. "I'm not sure I really could have gone through with it and I'm glad I didn't have to find out."

Jamie smiled back. "He would have spilled his guts to you sooner or later, but I'm glad we were able to find another way. Your wife would be happy, too."

"Yeah, I know. The whole thing was based on what she would have done. If she'd been here, she would have played your role. In any case, Peter and a squad are on their way to arrest Ricky. We'll keep him separate from the others for his own safety."

"Your wife would approve of that, too. What are you going to do with him?"

"He'd better hope my wife makes that decision."

———

For a rare moment, Jenn was out of her element. She had left the familiarity of the recovery ward to learn the fundamentals of using some of their new weapons. Tables and hay bales formed a classroom in one of Austin's barns where some of their Army veterans demonstrated how to properly aim and fire.

Deep in her heart, Jenn hoped she'd never have to actually fire her weapon. Guns had always run contrary to her instinct and she had treated so many gunshot victims she had long since stopped trying to count. Simply holding the rifle gave her butterflies in her stomach. Watching her girls was infinitely worse. However, as a leader, she knew she had to be out there with her new group of soldiers, so here she sat with an M-36 in her lap.

Their instructor's sharp voice snapped her back to the moment, "OK, people, that's the fundamentals. Make sure your weapon is unloaded and we'll move outside for some live fire practice."

Jenn's training buddy, a short, small man with graying hair named Ramirez, gave her a curt nod before heading for the door. Jenn checked her rifle for the fifth time, confirmed it was not loaded and followed the group through the door to a shooting range consisting of hay bales with targets at different distances from their shooting area.

Over the next hour, Jenn discovered a new level of futility in her life, despite one-on-one help from Ramirez and their instructors. Practice rounds were limited for obvious reasons, but she was convinced that no amount of training would make her good at it. She couldn't find the proper motivation. Shooting things, people in particular, went against her core beliefs. While she waited for Ramirez to finish, she observed the rest of the class. She found solace as the older girls proved to be quite natural with their weapons and the rest of the class did well enough that the instructors stopped them early.

Finally, blessedly, the session was over and Jenn left with a dull throbbing behind her eyes. The girls caught up to her half way to the house as she tried to figure out what why this particular skill eluded her.

"Don't worry, Mama Jenn," Anne said, "we can do this even if you can't."

"Yeah, Mom," Steph added, "And you weren't nearly as bad as Smellen!"

———

Casey tapped his foot as he waited for President Little to address the joint session of Congress, the Italian leather sparkling even in the darkened hall. While everyone knew the general topic of the session, they were all wondering about the details. The ALM's threat was out there, but since he, along with most elected officials, got threatened on a regular basis, he wasn't alarmed. To his left, a representative from Minnesota, one of the few from the opposing party was dozing, while to his right a representative from west Texas, looked at him and said, "Better your district than mine."

At last, the Sergeant at Arms announced, "Ladies and gentlemen, the President of the United States!" As one, the assembled guests rose and applauded as the President made his way to the podium and shook hands with Speaker and Vice-President Rockwell. The President stepped up to the microphone and surprised Casey by uncharacteristically raising his hands for silence. From his years of experience, Casey knew he basked in the applause of this group and often let them cheer until their hands hurt.

"Senators and members of the House, as you know, we are under attack. I am sure you heard my remarks to the public earlier, but I wanted to update you and get you involved as part of the process of returning our great nation to normalcy.

Overnight, the American Liberation Movement as they call themselves, attacked several of our military's armories around the country, seizing all manner of military grade weapons. These attacks were coordinated and indicate a much broader conspiracy than we had first believed. These rebels killed some of our soldiers and are arming themselves for war with the United States.

In response, as your commander-in-chief, I am taking measures to protect ourselves and our citizens. I have directed active duty army units to some of the hot spots, including Des Moines, Chicago, Phoenix, San Antonio and Memphis, as well as here in the District. They will assist the local authorities in quelling this uprising and bringing the rebels to justice. In addition, for the time being, a number of travel restrictions will be in place. We want to stop these rebels from resupplying and keep the public safe. Lastly, we have established military tribunals in key cities and will be holding speedy trials for those caught in the act of treason. Their punishments will match the severity of their crimes and will serve as an example to others of what happens to those who betray our country."

President Little paused to gauge the reaction of the assembled crowd. He could hear some murmuring and even some small applause, but mostly, however, he heard silence. The media had let out some of the details of the attacks overnight, but not many. The depth and success of the attacks came as a clear surprise to many members of Congress.

"Let me continue. As you are also aware, the ALM issued an ultimatum to me and to all of you. They insisted that we resign our positions by this evening or face the consequences. I can tell you that the ramifications of resigning would be grave. We have been elected by the people to manage this great country and if we allow a group of angry, armed dissenters, no matter how large, to undercut our democracy, then we are doing a disservice to our constituents and to our forebears. I for one am going absolutely nowhere and urge you to do the same. Our military is on alert and our federal agencies are redoubling their efforts to root out these terrorists. We will come down hard and fast with the full might of our military. We will show no mercy to these traitors. We expect this threat to be neutralized shortly. However, if you choose to resign your position, it will spell the end of your political career and possibly an end to our Republic. Thank you. God bless you and God bless the United States of America."

The crowd stood and applauded again as the President made his way out of the chamber, shaking hands along the way. As he watched the chamber doors close behind the President, Casey pondered his words. No one Casey knew was resigning, but he didn't know all of the members from the other party. Maybe they would do something to pacify the rebels? What an opportunity that would present.

———

In Fort Benjamin Davis, Georgia, First Lieutenant Andrew Stevens gave his M-1A2D tank a parting pat on the tread before the semi-trailer's brakes hissed and began its journey. He watched until the behemoth was out of sight, deep in thought about his impending mission. He and the other members of the 84th Regimental Combat Brigade would be following shortly to answer the call of duty.

The past 48 hours had been a blur. His unit had been in final preparations for deployment to the Middle East when their orders had been changed. One wake-up call and onto the airliners was all that was left when the call came in that they were needed to meet the growing threat of insurgency. Their gear was already packed into shipping containers. Hell, they didn't even have the right uniforms! They were going to look strange in their digitally designed chocolate chip style gear on the streets of the Midwest. Still, when the orders had come down, he and his troops made it happen.

He had hardly slept in those 48 hours, just a cat nap here and there. Dizzy and stumbling slightly from lack of sleep, Andrew returned to the office he shared with the other lieutenants, proud of how his troops had adjusted to the last second change.

Another part of him was deeply conflicted. The rebellion had blown up in his own hometown, possibly with people he knew well. From the official reports he'd heard, it had started with his neighbor, but there was no way Tom could be involved. Not the man who had taught him to drive a stick shift when most of his friends didn't even learn to drive. Not the man who had occasionally slipped him some money when he needed it. Not the man who had taught him about girls. Not the man who had been a second father to him. No, it had to be something and someone else.

Andrew let out a deep breath and sank into his chair. Mixed thoughts were probably not the best way to head into a situation like this, but it was his reality for the time being.

Chapter Twenty-Six

With her two main strategists unavailable, Jenn had her troops stand down for the rest of the day and evening. The fast pace of the last few days had become her new normal and the downtime struck her as odd, but she knew they all needed it.

After looking in on the patients in the house, she took the opportunity to walk around the farm to meet some of the people she hadn't yet. Mostly, she listened to their personal stories and thanked them for their commitment. Twice she saw military jets roaring overhead and a pair of helicopters that flew far too close to the farm for her comfort. Most of their people and all of their equipment were indoors, but it was still unsettling.

Dinnertime for Jenn came as a relief, a chance to focus on something besides death and destruction, if only for a brief time. Zach waved her over to a picnic table, where he and Collin were eating and relaxing as much as they could. Collin's concussion had been minor and he was anxious to get back into the fight.

"You know," Collin said, "your daughters are something else. I spent some time with Steph making more Molotov cocktails and talking with Ellen. They give me hope for the future."

Jenn smiled at him. "Yeah, they do that to me sometimes. It's usually followed by something that makes me want to strangle them."

Zach laughed. "You sound like my mom. I bet most moms have had those thoughts."

Jenn laughed, too. "You're probably right. Not my mom, of course, but..."

"Of course not, mine either," said Collin with a playful look at Zach. All three enjoyed the break in the tension. It had been a long couple of days and the stress had worn on all of them.

Jenn scooped some beans and rice into a tortilla. "So, what does the future hold?" she asked before taking a bite and closing her eyes.

"She and I had a few differing ideas," Collin began, "but we agreed that people have to start needing each other again. And to learn how to talk and listen again. Man, I love my computer, too, but it's become so crazy that I know people in other states, but not the family down the street."

"Yeah," Zach added, "and I think people need to get over themselves. We all have to live together and to do that we're going to have to find some common ground and let some things go in life. Your husband talked about how we have to put our differences behind us and move forward if the country is going to survive."

Jenn opened her eyes and looked back and forth between the two men. "It all sounds good to me. Things have to get better. They cured cancer, but nobody can afford the treatment, so what good is it? I need my girls to have a future." She closed her eyes again, this time to hide her pain. Her mother had committed suicide once she had been diagnosed with cancer. She hadn't wanted to become bankrupt from treatment and leave nothing to her children. Mainly, Jenn and Lane had agreed on one thing, she'd left them a lifetime of agony that would never go away.

"We talked about kids," Zach said, "but in the end we decided that we didn't want to try to raise them in the crazy world we have." Collin nodded and slid his hand over into Zach's as he blinked back a tear.

Jenn forced her eyes open. "I hear what you're saying, Tom and I had that exact discussion. But in the end, we decided that some part of us has to live on and kids are the best way to do it. And maybe, just maybe, they'll be part of righting some of the wrongs and be part of the solution to the mess we're in."

"Well, you're braver than we are, I guess."

"Yeah," Collin added, "and your kids might be the ones to pull that off."

"Thanks." Jenn smiled again as she swallowed her last bite. "If you two will excuse me, I have to go see how my angels are doing."

———

Inside the house, Ellen had at long last realized a way to get into the fight. The monitor on her computer showed a real-time view from her own unoccupied aerial vehicle now hovering over the plant. After a long morning of research, she had spent the afternoon modifying her UAV to carry a small shape charge of its own and was scanning the skies over the plant for her prey. While there was plenty of light coming from the plant and the city around it, the military's UCAV was camouflaged to blend into the sky and the setting sun wasn't making her job any easier. Her nose wrinkled and she admitted temporary defeat by plotting a course back to the farm. "Well," she thought out loud, "there's always tomorrow...I hope."

———

Jenn's search for the girls had been a short one. Ellen had been engrossed with something on her computer, while Steph and Anne had gone out for a run, taking Spark and Smudge with them, leaving Jenn looking for something to occupy her time. Lane had been sleeping when she poked her head in, so she didn't disturb him. Penny, Scott and Abigail were overseeing a clean-up crew after dinner and Penny had shooed her away from the kitchen. After another check on the wounded, Jenn walked out onto the back porch and found Austin sitting in a rocking chair enjoying an early evening breeze. He looked up and nodded towards another faded chair.

Jenn sat and said, "Thanks, and if I haven't said it enough, thank you for all you're doing."

"You're welcome on the first count, but on the second count, we all have to contribute what we can. I'm not risking any more than you are. I'm happy to have some company and to be able to give something to the cause."

Jenn didn't know what to say, so she kept her mouth shut and admired the view. The buildings and the surrounding farms looked eerily like some old pictures she had seen of her great-grandparents' farm. That was long since sold off to some corporate giant, but she understood them a little better. Despite the chaos she had helped create in the rest of the world, at this moment in time, Austin's porch was the most tranquil place on Earth. Beyond the main barn, the breeze rippled through a winter wheat field on the hillside, mesmerizing her. Inside her body, it felt like her blood pressure was dropping even as she watched the stalks sway in a gentle rhythm. She heard Austin say something but was so lost in her thoughts she didn't catch it. "I'm sorry?" she said, turning her attention back to him.

Austin laughed. "I said, it's pretty relaxing, isn't it? I guess I know the answer to that. I've tried to take pictures, but I've never quite been able to capture it right."

"I understand that. Sometimes you just have to take those pictures with your heart."

Austin began to laugh again, but a coughing spasm took over. "You're always welcome to come visit," he said when he was able. "I used to live out in Wyoming, but eventually the fires and the drought made it impossible to live out there. Too bad, the view is even prettier. Fewer people out, too."

"Hm, I had never thought about that. I guess everyone has a place and it's simply a matter of finding it. My parents-"

The door slammed open, with Penny bursting through behind it, stopping her mid-sentence. "You two have to come see the news!" They hurried inside to where Scott, Abigail and Ellen were huddled around a video monitor with the local newscast on. The scene behind the reporter looked familiar, but Jenn couldn't quite place it.

"As we shared at the top of our broadcast," the reporter said, "after days of searching the homes of Tom Erickson and Penelope Stevens in West Des Moines, the police have burned those homes with the help of the fire department. A source close to the President said that rebels across Iowa and across the country could expect similar treatment for their treason. Meanwhile, a neighbor to the Ericksons, Dylan Spencer, was shot and killed as he attacked the police and tried to prevent them from doing their work. He leaves behind a wife and two children. Back to you, Brendan." Scott turned off the monitor while the others stood in stunned silence.

Fat tears rolled down Jenn's cheek as she held the sobbing Ellen. Scott, Penny and Abigail hugged one another as they came to grips with the fact that their home was gone as well. The only homes the girls had ever known were smoldering piles of ruin. And a neighbor they barely knew had died trying to protect them. It was another insane moment in the midst of their new lives.

Jenn's head swam with memories of her home. She and Tom's first night there. The days they brought their daughters home. Birthdays, anniversaries, Christmases and so many other special days. All the time they had spent with Penny and Scott and their kids. Now that houses they had made their homes were gone.

For how long she held her daughter, Jenn had no idea, but eventually their tears ran dry. They split apart and both wiped their eyes with their sleeves.

Scott was the first to speak. "Those bastards...those rotten bastards."

"I can't believe our house is gone," Abigail said, trying, and failing, to choke back her tears.

Jenn blew her nose. "I guess we got their attention. I'm not sure where we go from here, but things are suddenly very real."

"I can't believe they killed him," Scott continued. Those bastards are going to have to pay." His sorrow was turning to anger.

———

High above the fence plant, a JS-8 Hammerhead unoccupied combat aerial vehicle (UCAV) circled, transmitting real-time pictures back to a truck parked half a mile from the gate. Inside the truck, technicians analyzed the information and fed target data to mortar teams surrounding the plant. Moments later, the first rounds were launched into the air.

Tom was with his squad leaders mapping out troop deployments when those rounds impacted around the plant. The explosions drew Tom towards the windows, but

Emma grabbed his arm and pulled him back towards the center of the room. Together they ducked under a table as more shells exploded outside.

The shelling ended as quickly as it had started, allowing Tom and his crew to assess the situation. Much to their surprise, there were no casualties and limited damage to minor things like the guard shack and the truck blocking the gate. Shawn and Peter headed off to deal with the damage before the fires became unmanageable.

Tom sat on a planter, resting his hands on his knees. "Well," he said as Emma sat facing him, mimicking his pose, "looks like we got lucky. That's always good."

"Well, normally getting lucky is a good thing," Emma said with a wink, "but in this case, it's not good. Those bastards could have hit anything they wanted, but they chose not to. They sent those rounds as a message to us. I'm not sure what the message is, but sure as Hell it's not good."

Tom removed his hat to wipe the sweat off his head. "I hate it when you teach me stuff like that."

Emma laughed and set her helmet on the side of the planter so she could adjust her ponytail. "Always glad to show you something, sir."

A voice came over Emma's radio. "Attention! This is Lieutenant Colonel Reuben Casillas of the Iowa National

Guard. I wish to speak with whoever is in charge inside the plant. Over"

Emma handed her radio Tom. "I guess we're going to find out their message, huh?"

Tom nodded before speaking. "This is Tom Erickson. I'm in command here."

"Mr. Erickson, as you know, we can destroy the plant and your forces. We do not wish to do that. This is your opportunity to surrender your forces without any further casualties. Come out of the plant peacefully and your forces will be treated in accordance with military protocols. Over."

"Colonel, we're not going to do that. You may be able to overrun the plant, that's true, but your forces will pay a price. Do what you need to do, but we are not surrendering."

"Mr. Erickson, you do not understand. The shots we fired were simply to demonstrate that we can hit or not hit anything within your complex. We do not want to kill you and your comrades, but if that's the choice you make, we will. I urge you to surrender. You have one hour to comply. Over."

Tom glanced at his watch. "Colonel, I don't need an hour, we are not surrendering."

"Mr. Erickson, I will give you an hour to reconsider your answer. In the meantime, you should also know that earlier today, your home and your neighbor's home were burned to the ground. You are welcome to confirm this with outside sources, but it's the truth. That's what happens to traitors. Over."

Tom was speechless. How could they do something like that?

Colonel Casillas guessed he wasn't going to get a response, "Mr. Erickson, you have one hour. Out."

Emma's shoulders slumped and for the first time since they'd met, she looked afraid. Tom gave her a one-armed hug, unsure of who needed it more.

———

By the time Steph and Anne got home from their run, Jenn and the other adults had gained control of their feelings for the time being. Ellen was still shaken to the point she couldn't talk to anyone and was sitting on the couch clutching her knees to her chest. When Jenn broke the news to the older girls, a whole new round of bawling broke out among the two families.

Still sniffling, the girls headed off with Abigail and the dogs in tow. Jenn watched them depart, her heart aching as she tried to absorb their pain. She knew that being alone together was how they'd deal with their feelings, but she longed to do more for them.

With a deep sigh, she led the other adults to the kitchen tables where Austin had poured them each a glass of his latest beer. Jenn took a tentative sip, then a long drink of the deep brown concoction before she could talk. "Watching the girls suffer is even harder than my own feelings."

"Yeah," Penny replied, "I really wasn't prepared for this, much less having to help them."

"They'll be fine," Scott muttered under his breath.

"I'm not sure I'm fine," his wife shot back, "much less the girls."

"What I mean is, they'll get over it. They're nearly adults." He turned away, knowing he was only making the situation worse. Penny's glare was a laser through his heart as he finished his beer and returned to the counter for a refill.

Jenn knew she had to head off a confrontation between them; this wasn't the time. "OK," she said looking at the clock on the wall, "it's time to get working on inflicting some real harm. We've had a day off and while it's been good for our troops, it let the Army regroup as well. Let's see if we can't put our new weapons to work for us."

———

Bob Wright sat back on a midnight-black leather couch with the dogs between him and his wife. The girls each had their own couch, complete with a buffet of snacks to choose from. It was 'family night' and they were watching a movie his daughters had selected in their home theater.

While he had work to do, Marsha had insisted, as she always did, that they spend time together as a family unit. Bob savored the piney aroma of his drink before he downed a third of it and tried to make sense of what his daughters thought was great comedy.

Robert padded into the theater, grabbing Bob's attention. He bobbed his head slightly towards the door and after a quick look at the screen, slipped back through the door. Despite Marsha's frown, he heaved himself up from the chair and joined his son in the hallway. He envied his oldest son's exemption from family nights. "Father, I'm sorry to disturb you."

Bob's smile was surprisingly genuine. "Don't worry about it. What's on your mind?"

"I got word that they've started shelling the plant. They are trying to force the strikers to surrender first, but then they'll start blowing things up."

Bob's eyes became slits as his face tightened. He had been afraid this would happen. Damn that Tom Erickson! He had started this whole strike nonsense and it was going to be costly if the Army had their way about it. Bob started walking towards the office without saying a word.

Once in the office, Bob finished his drink before sitting at his desk. "Call Casey Frost," he ordered his omniphone. Robert took his father's glass to the bar to make him a fresh drink. There was no need to ask, his father always wanted one more.

Casey's hologram appeared on the second ring. "Bob, my friend, good evening."

"Casey, what the Hell is going on back in Des Moines! They're going to wreck my plant to rid it of a few rats and that's not acceptable to me."

"Bob, we have to let them do their work. And at this point, it's the National Guard, which makes it a state matter, not a federal one. I'm not sure I can really influence how they do their thing. I mean, it's their own world over there and I can't tell them what to do."

"Listen here, you do everything you can to get them to hold off on destroying my plant. I know they want to show how tough they are, but that could cost me a fortune. I know these people and if they can wait for a couple of days, those traitors will lose interest and surrender without blowing up my plant."

"OK, I'll talk to some people and do what I can."

"Casey, if you think it will help, I'm sure certain arrangements can be made from my end."

"I really don't think-" Bob ended their call before Casey could finish his sentence.

———

Tom's hour passed in no time at all. As usual, his lieutenants had reacted better and had taken control of the actual operations. It had taken some time for him to put the news of his home's destruction behind him and get down to business of preparing for the attack. As he went around the plant, Tom had spoken with a number of his troops and offered them the chance to surrender on their own. Much to his amazement, not a single one had chosen that option.

Tom returned the 15th floor conference room with moments to spare when the radio call came with perfect military precision. "Mr. Erickson, it's Colonel Casillas, are you there? Over."

"I'm here, Colonel. Our answer is still no."

"Mr. Erickson...Tom, you've seen what our smallest weapons can do. This doesn't have to end with bloodshed. You have acted honorably to this point. Put down your weapons and come out peacefully. Over."

"Colonel, I appreciate your concern, but we appear to have reached an impasse."

Colonel Casillas grimaced as he spoke his final words into the radio. "Message received. Out."

Tom let out a deep breath. He didn't have a death wish, but the decision had been made. He switched his radio to a secure channel. "Attention all units, this is Alpha-One in the tower. The hour is up. Stand ready. Over."

Across the fence plant, radios crackled with the announcement. Rebel soldiers exchanged nervous glances and checked their weapons one more time.

———

Casey was on his omniphone with Iowa's Governor, Lindsay Parks. It had taken some bluster and half an hour of waiting to get five minutes of her time. "Lindsay, I need you to dial back the attack on the Wright plant. You know full well that the loss of that plant would be of significant economic loss and would greatly harm my constituents."

"Casey, they're my constituents, too, you know," she snapped. "But there's more to it than that. I'm getting a lot of pressure from President Little to make an example of this situation. In any case, they've got federal Army troops on their way and it won't be up to me in a day or two."

"Lindsay, can you not blow the place up? Even a day or two might well be enough time for them to grow discouraged. And you know, Bob Wright would be extremely appreciative if you did him this favor."

Governor Parks understood his words. Bob had preferred her opponent in the last election and had only been a minor supporter of her campaign. His money would be a welcome addition to her war chest. "OK, Casey, I'll have them tone it down. I can't call them completely off, but they'll leave the plant standing."

Casey breathed a sigh of relief. "Thank you. I owe you one."

Governor Parks ended the call. "Yes, yes you do," she said to herself.

———

Tom no longer reacted as yet another mortar round exploded below. Since sunset, shells had landed in the compound every fifteen minutes or so, that was it. They were startling when they hit, but did no real damage to his positions, nor was anyone injured, which left him puzzled. Even more difficult to fathom was that the big attack failed to materialize. Tom knew they were being watched from above, were surrounded with an imminent attack and were powerless to do anything but wait, and yet the attack never came. Lacking a good explanation, his squad leaders had shrugged their shoulders and were keeping their guard up.

Tom took one last look out the window before he headed to the office to try and sleep. He had no news of the outside world, nor had he spoken to his wife. Of the two, not talking to Jenn was far more unsettling to him. She had always been one to help keep him grounded and focused.

He was three steps down the hallway when a rebel he didn't know stopped him. The man sensed his confusion and shook his hand. "I'm Lopez, sir. I have a Matilda Williams from Perth, Australia for you on a back channel, computer link-up. She insisted you'd take the call. If you'll come with me." He ushered Tom to the security office, where Jenn's face filled one of the monitors. Lopez again read Tom's reaction and quietly shut the door behind himself.

He glanced at the other monitors from around the plant and saw nothing happening, so he sat down. "Hey, babe. I'm sorry about the house."

"Hey. Me, too. The girls are pretty shook up."

"We had a lot of history in that house. Those bastards."

"We'll have to make a new history, I guess." As they proceeded to exchange stories of their days, the sight of Tom's face allowed Jenn to smile for the first time since she'd gotten the news. Neither talked too much about the details of their current plans, but Tom knew her emotions well enough to know that she was worried. Usually, they talked long enough for her to open up. He just had to give her the time and space.

Jenn crushed his hope of knowing. "Ellen is telling me that we need to end our call just in case." Her tiny hand opened wide as she reached towards the camera. Tom's hand filled the screen, doing his best to meet hers. "Be safe. Love you."

"Love you, too, babe. And you, Matilda!" The screen went blank, leaving Tom to stare at his own reflection in the darkness.

Chapter Twenty-Seven

Ellen had skipped breakfast and was sitting on the floor, still in her pajamas, Spark and Smudge curled up on either side of her. Her computer was on her lap as it so often was, her eyes barely blinking as she focused on the monitor. She had launched her UAV at the first hint of sunlight and sent it spinning towards the plant.

She looked up only when Abigail came and set a tray with some toast and steaming hot coffee down in front of her. Abigail glanced at her screen long enough to realize what it was showing. "Do you really think this will work?" The doubt in her voice was unmistakable.

"I'm not sure," Ellen answered, pressing the key that engaged the autopilot. She ignored the toast, but blew on her coffee before trying a sip. "Hot, hot, hot," she muttered, setting the cup down to cool. "Thanks. I know this is a long shot, but I have to do something to try and help my Pops. Uncle Lane is sure they have their own surveillance vehicle up there over the plant, which narrows my search parameters. They're most likely using what's called 'Hammerhead,' which can fly as fast as 400 miles an hour and as high as 75,000 feet, but for what they're using it for over the plant it will be lower and slower, which gives me a fighting chance if I can find it."

Abigail laughed and sat on the edge of the bed. "Well, if anybody can do it, it's you."

"Thanks. I've turned my school project into, well, I guess it's a kamikaze bird. I can go up to 200 miles an hour and as high as 8,000 feet. If this works, I'll get to build a newer, better model." Her attention turned back to her monitor. "I'm closing in on the plant now."

Abigail silently watched until boredom overcame her. Ellen was circling the plant at different altitudes looking for the UCAV and when she didn't find it, she chose a new area to search. She became so engrossed with her search, she didn't notice when Abigail stood up and gave the cold toast to the dogs before leaving.

An hour passed and still Ellen had located absolutely nothing. Her back and eyes ached and she was about to head to the bathroom, when a burst of sunlight flashed across the screen before disappearing. She squeezed her eyes tight, all other thoughts gone from her head. With the patience and finesse of a leopard stalking much larger prey, she maneuvered towards the flash and began to pursue her victim.

As she got closer, her target came into focus, circling the plant at low speed and altitude, as she had suspected. Even at its slowest speed, the UCAV was darting in and out of her sight. Ever so delicately, she increased her altitude to the point where she could count the number of photoelectric cells which allowed it to stay airborne almost indefinitely. It was a good guess that her craft was too small for the Hammerhead or any of its handlers to detect.

"Just another minute," Ellen thought to herself, "just another minute..." As she got closer, her breathing became so shallow it all but disappeared.

Colonel Casillas watched the live feed from his UCAV over the shoulder of the young technician as they waited for something to happen. With the coming of a new day, he had issued orders for it to go from strictly surveillance to targeting anyone who was out in the open at the plant. The Hammerhead carried eight guided missiles, among its weapons options, and this technique had worked well in countless other situations. He was confident it would inflict real damage to the rebels as well as demoralizing them. With any luck, it would be enough to force the rebels to give up hope and surrender without further ground combat.

The technician spoke without looking up. "Sir, we have enemy combatants coming out of the building. Four, no, five targets. I will have a clean shot when I loop around and get lined up. What are your orders, sir?"

"Fire when ready."

———

Jamie had joined Tom and his squad leaders as they began to inspect the damage from the overnight shelling. Shawn, Emma and Peter pointed to a number of newly formed gaps around the perimeter and talked among themselves, mostly ignoring Tom and Jamie.

Tom listened from the rear, letting them do their work uninterrupted. His role was mostly to provide moral support and guidance. In these few short days he had now come to trust his life to their abilities.

Tom glanced at his omniphone, wondering what Jenn was doing. Probably eating breakfast. Or maybe directing their next mission? In his mind, he pictured her intently focused on her listening, her hands wrapped around a cup of coffee. He did miss her so.

The sound of an explosion overhead brought his daydreaming to an abrupt halt. Subconsciously, his brain told him that this explosion wasn't a mortar round, but something new. It also seemed a good idea to grab Jamie and pull her into a nearby impact crater next to the others.

Shawn stuck his head up first, when a blue-gray blur fell from the sky, crashing into the ground about ten yards on the other side of the former gate. "Holy shit!" he exclaimed and pointed to the rising fireball. The others joined him in gawking at it. "I'm not sure how, but I think that was one of their Hammerheads."

Emma laughed as she slapped Tom gently, letting her hand rest on his arm. "Either that's the luckiest fucking break in the history of the universe or somebody on the outside figured out how to help us."

Tom couldn't help but smile. "Now let's hope they find a way to drop us some more weapons."

———

"What the Hell just happened?" Colonel Casillas asked as the screen turned to static.

"I don't know, sir. We lost the feed from the Hammerhead. I'll run a diagnostic and see-" The roar of a nearby explosion rolled over the two men.

"Son, I think you can skip the diagnostic."

———

Ellen's triumphant cry startled Jenn. She hadn't made a sound like that since she caught her first fish at age five. Jenn leaped from her seat and raced down the hall, barely beating Steph and Anne to the room. Ellen was still seated on the floor, her head tilted back on the side of the bed with her eyes closed, the corners of her mouth turned upwards in the slightest of smiles. The dogs were sitting next to her, their tails twitching at her excitement. "Honey? What's going on?" Jenn asked.

Ellen opened her eyes, her smile growing even bigger. "I'm pretty sure I killed one of their UCAVs, Mom! Over the plant! I was able to sneak up on it with mine and blow it up. Or at least, I think I did, my camera went out with the explosion, but I know my dive got me within feet of theirs and it was a big explosion."

Jenn looked at her daughter with a combination of immense pride and utter confusion. "That's great, but-"

Ellen had anticipated the question and in a rare move, cut her mother off. "Uncle Lane taught me a little about explosives and I took it from there. It really isn't that hard, you-"

Jenn held her hands up to stop her daughter. She didn't have time for the lecture on the how-tos of bomb making she knew was coming. "Ellen, honey, I'm proud of you."

"Thanks, mom. I was looking for a way to really get involved and since we all know that I can't really shoot a rifle, I thought I'd try this." She positively beamed behind her glasses.

Steph and Anne stared, their eyes wide with amazement. She'd been flying her UAV a lot over the past few days and secretly they thought it was a waste of time. "Wow, nice job, Smellen," Steph said. The two older girls left shaking their heads.

Jenn made her way down to the floor to sit next to her daughter, arriving with a grunt. Ellen set her computer on the floor to her side and leaned against her mother, who could see the screen filled with nothing but static. "I hope I was able to help Pops."

"I'm sure you did, sweetie. According to Lane, what you killed would have given the army eyes into their camp 24/7 and could have rained down bombs and missiles, so yeah, I'm sure you did." She squeezed her daughter as tight as she could from the side. "Now, after you take a shower, I want to talk with you about taking the battle to them. OK?"

Ellen nodded again and popped up to her feet, where she offered her hand. "Do I get to blow something else up? That was pretty cool."

Jenn smiled to hide her pain and gave her head a small shake. "Go take your shower." She left Ellen and headed back to the kitchen to find Lane. They had to make some move to change the status quo with the government. They were still on the defensive and that was a bad choice for all of them, especially Tom and those trapped in the plant.

For a rare moment, Penny had stopped making food and was watching a video monitor with Lane, Anne and Steph. Penny's hands covered her mouth, telling Jenn all she needed. Over the last few days she had seen that look enough times to know it was not good.

On the monitor was a stern looking woman identified as, "FBI Director Maggie Webster." She was in the White House briefing room with two aides at her side. Jenn leaned in to hear her words. "As I was saying, Jennifer Erickson is now at the top of our Most Wanted List. Her crimes are a threat to our very democracy. We know where her husband is, but we are offering a ten million dollar reward for information leading to her location and capture. Smaller rewards are also offered for her fellow rebel leaders."

The camera panned back to reveal life size holograms of Jenn, the girls and pretty much everyone gathered around the monitor with her. Jenn didn't wait to hear her continue. Without a word she pushed herself away from the counter and headed outside.

Chapter Twenty-Eight

Jenn stepped out to the porch alone and stumbled to the chair she now loved. Even rocking slowly in her new favorite place failed to bring her the peace she sought. Everything she knew, or thought she knew, was now a complete shambles. She had passed the current head terrorist leader and the serial killer stalking New England to sit atop the FBI's Most Wanted List. And in just one short week, no less.

She buried her face in her hands and waited for the tears to come. They didn't. The absurdity of what she was dong had drained them all out of her already. She focused on her breathing. One breath at a time. A tractor started and went to the field. Jets flew overhead. Squirrels chased each other around the porch. Time marched on everywhere but in Jenn's head.

A lone cloud made a leisurely journey from one horizon to the other without Jenn looking up. She was buried deep in her thoughts. The events of the last month or so flooded her thoughts. Some of the memories were so vivid she could describe the most minute details, others so vague she could scarcely remember why they had seemed so important.

"Mom? Are you OK?" She hadn't heard Steph come out onto the porch.

Jenn looked up and put her glasses back on. "I'm not sure, sweetie. I'm really not sure."

Steph read Jenn's face, unsure of what to think. It was a look she had never seen before. She blinked several time trying to make sense of the situation or how she could help. She knelt down and hugged Jenn. "There's always hope, Mom. You've taught us that. There's always hope."

The screen door behind them slammed shut. Before she could turn, Ellen was standing at her side. "Hey, Mom. You wanted to talk to me about something? I'm excited to finally be able to do something to help."

Jenn gazed into Steph's face. Looking into her eyes was like looking into Tom's. She looked up into Ellen's eyes and saw herself. So full of optimism and desire to change the world. Where had her own dreams gone?

She stood up. "Ellen, I need you to get a very short message to your father as soon as possible, please. And remember, the government is focused on him, so you're going to need to be extra careful, got it?"

Ellen nodded somberly without breaking eye contact with her mother. "I think I have one last trick up my sleeve. What's the message?"

Jenn leaned in between her daughters and hugged them both. Wet hair pressed against one side of her face, longer hair tickled her nose from the other side. She whispered something Steph couldn't hear into Ellen's ear.

Ellen broke away. "Is there anything else? You made it sound like it was a much bigger deal."

"Sorry, honey, but the bigger deal will have to wait until tomorrow. My brain is just about shot for today."

"OK, I've got one last trick up my sleeve to get that to Dad."

Steph finally let go of Jenn's other side. "Yeah, don't worry, Mom. We got this."

Epilogue

Just after noon, Colonel Casillas made his report to General Walters with all of the enthusiasm of a man on the way to his own funeral. He knew the UCAV had been operating per protocol, but that hadn't saved him from an ass-chewing from his commanding officer. He also learned that while he would be getting another surveillance UAV shortly, there were no Hammerheads available to him. His troops would have to retake the plant the old fashioned way. Deep in his gut, he knew that was going to be an ugly proposition. The folks inside the plant seemed quite capable of making his life miserable.

He had one foot out the door of the command post, when a private called him back to the communications station and handed him a headset. "This is Casillas, go ahead, over."

"Colonel, this is Tom Erickson. I spoke with my commanding officer and she asked me to relay a message to you to send up the chain to your Commander-in-Chief. Over."

"And that message would be what? Over."

"Please tell the President that his 48 hours are up." The radio went dead.

Book Club Discussion Points

- Which characters in the book did you like best and why? Who did you relate to the most/least?

- What do you think the author's purpose was in writing this book? What ideas was he or she trying to get across?

- If you were making a movie of this book, who would you cast?

- What did you think of the book's length? If it's too long, what would you cut? If too short, what would you add?

- If one (or more) of the characters made a choice that had moral implications, would you have made the same decision? Why? Why not?

- What questions do you still have? If you got the chance to ask the author of this book one question, what would it be

Made in the USA
Monee, IL
14 November 2020

47642533R00216